"I'm the g   
Nathan Ha...,
families are enemies,
you know."

Stephen lifted the snifter of brandy. "I know who you are. In light of that knowledge, I must ask why you are here. You realize that we will never be friends."

"Oh, but I don't want to be friends," Josie said. "In fact, I could not be more pleased that our families are enemies. It serves my purpose."

"And might one inquire as to your purpose, Miss Hale?"

"Of course. I've been trying to tell you."

She lifted her glass and took another drink. With a thwack, she set the snifter on the desk, rose, and put both hands between them.

"Lord Westman, I have come to be your mistress."

Other **AVON ROMANCES**

Shana Galen

Good Groom Hunting

AVON BOOKS
An Imprint of HarperCollinsPublishers

AVON BOOKS
An Imprint of HarperCollins*Publishers*
10 East 53rd Street
New York, New York 10022-5299

Copyright © 2007 by Shane Bolks
ISBN: 978-0-06-112496-9
ISBN-10: 0-06-112496-6
www.avonromance.com

First Avon Books paperback printing: February 2007

Avon Trademark Reg. U.S. Pat. Off. and in Other Countries, Marca Registrada, Hecho en U.S.A.
HarperCollins® is a registered trademark of HarperCollins Publishers.

Printed in the U.S.A.

10 9 8 7 6 5 4 3 2 1

For Laura Faulkenberry,
who's had enough adventures to fill three books.
Here's to the many adventures to come.

Acknowledgments

Evan Fogelman, my friend and my guide through this difficult business. Thank you for believing in me and encouraging me. Most of all, thanks for always telling me my hair looks good.

May Chen, thank you for being there when I need you and not interfering when I don't. I'm so fortunate to have you as an editor. You make me a better writer.

Courtney Burkholder, thank you for sharing your work with me and for gifting me with your insights and suggestions about mine. Thanks for boosting me up, even when it's a big job.

Christina Hergenrader, thank you for your

enthusiasm and your brilliant ideas, for commiserating and celebrating with me, and for the pleasure of reading your work.

And to my husband—for turning the TV down, making dinner, listening to my plot problems, and mostly, for understanding how hard writing is and how much I need to do it. I love you.

The FULLBRIGHTs

NO MAN'S BRIDE
Edmund and Cordelia (nee Brittany)
Catherine (20), Elizabeth (17)

GOOD GROOM HUNTING
Mavis (nee Fullbright) and Joseph Hale
Joseph Jr. (22), John (20), Josephine (18)

BOOK III
William, Earl of Castleigh and Ellen (nee Todd)
Madeleine (18)

The BRITTANYs

BOOK IV
Sir Gareth and Imogen (nee Stafford)
Thomas (23), Charles (21), William (20),
Ashley (18), George (15), Devlin (17)

Good Groom Hunting

Chapter 1

London 1801

Eight-year-old Josephine Hale let out a whoosh of air, then stuck her head and shoulders back out the window she'd just climbed through. As usual, looking down made her feel dizzy. She had the sensation that she was falling: tumbling head over toe, rushing at the hard earth below.

She closed her eyes and dug her fingers into the window casement. *Don't be a ninny,* she chided herself, remembering what her grandfather always told her. *Be brave.*

When she opened her eyes again, the night air bit her skinny arms and slapped at her thin face. She ignored the swipes and held out a hand to her

1

cousin Madeleine Fullbright. Madeleine's blue eyes were wide and fearful, and her waist-length chestnut brown hair whipped in the breeze.

"Come on, Maddie. Grab my hand."

Madeleine looked at Josie, then at the ground three stories below. "If I let go, I'll fall."

Josie checked Madeleine's position. She had a firm foothold on one of the town house's outcroppings, and her hands were wound securely about the bed sheets the girls had tied together and lowered to the ground earlier that night. "You won't fall, Maddie," Josie said with a reassuring smile. "I won't let you."

"That's what you always say," Madeleine grumbled.

"And you haven't fallen yet," Josie countered.

"Maddie, hurry up!" Ashley Brittany whisper-hissed from below. She and her cousin Catherine Fullbright were holding the other end of the sheet. Standing beside one another, they looked like night and day.

Ashley was pale and blond with sea green eyes. She stood straight and tall, and she was always laughing. Catherine was dark in looks and mood. She didn't like to look grown-ups in the eye, and she rarely smiled.

Madeleine and Catherine resembled each other, but Josie and Ashley stood out—Ashley for her blond hair and porcelain skin and Josie for her bright red hair and dark green eyes. She was also taller and skinnier than the other girls.

"Hurry, Maddie. I'm cold," Catie called too loudly through chattering teeth. Josie hissed at her and turned to glance over her shoulder. The girls had been sneaking out of this window for two years now, but they were not generally known for their stealth. In particular, Ashley and Maddie found it difficult to grasp the concept of whispering.

Josie listened intently for the sound of grown-up voices or footfalls, then she turned back to Maddie. Once again, she offered her hand, and this time, with tightly closed eyes, Maddie took it. Josie helped Maddie and the other girls climb the sheet and clamber inside.

As soon as the window was closed, Josie yanked off her pirate's eye patch and flopped on Maddie's bed. "I'm exhausted."

Ashley joined her. "Me too."

"It's a good exhaustion." Josie leaned on an elbow and looked at Catie. "I can't wait to grow up. Pirates do this sort of thing all the time."

Catie frowned, two little lines forming between her eyebrows. "No, they don't. Pirates steal from His Majesty's ships and from law-abiding citizens. They start drunken brawls and that's why they lose their eyes and have to wear eye patches." She gestured to Josie's makeshift eye patch, now laying on the bed.

"Ha! Shows what you know," Josie countered. "My grandfather was the best pirate ever to sail the seas, and he never—"

Ashley groaned. "Not another story about your grandfather."

"You're jealous. My grandfather taught me to sword fight and to tie all kinds of knots. He says girls have just as much right to adventure as boys."

"Josie, you think if you want something bad enough, you can make it true," Catie said. "But the truth is that once we grow up and marry, we won't be able to have adventures. If we did, our husbands would beat us."

Josie didn't know if this was correct or not, but the sudden and familiar need to make everything that was wrong right again filled her like a huge bubble. If held inside, the bubble would pop. She had to let it out. "When I become a pirate," Josie interrupted, "I won't need a husband. I'll have loads of treasure all for myself." She looked at Catie. "And I won't steal it either."

She wouldn't need to, not when she found the map.

"And I'm going to have lots of adventures," Ashley said. "I won't have time for a husband, especially a mean one."

"Well, I don't care how poor I am. I'm not going to ever marry," Catie said.

Josie nodded, agreeing with the statement. Her grandfather was always telling her to live life to the fullest and rely on no man. Josie figured that included husbands.

"I propose that we make a pledge," Catie was saying. "We should promise never to marry. I'm the oldest, so I go first." She held up her hand. "I, Catherine Anne Fullbright, swear never, ever, ever to marry so long as I live."

Josie opened her mouth, filled with excitement at making her own pledge, but Catie said, "Now your turn Maddie."

Josie frowned and bit her lip impatiently.

"I, Madeleine Richael Fullbright, swear never, ever to marry so long as I live. Now your turn, Josie," Maddie said.

Finally! "I, Josephine Linet Hale, swear never, ever, ever, *ever* to marry so long as I live." She jumped up and put a hand on her heart. "I promise to be a pirate!"

Catie shook her head. "Now you, Ashley," she said before Josie could say more about her plans.

"I, Ashley Gweneira Brittany, swear not to marry for as long as I live. But you know what this means, don't you?" She didn't wait for an answer. "We're going to be spinsters."

Josie hadn't considered that. *Spinster* was such an ugly word, but then some people thought *pirate* was an ugly word, too.

Catie said, "I'd rather be a spinster than beaten and locked in a closet."

"It won't be bad to be unmarried if we're all unmarried," Josie said. "Nothing is bad as long as you're not in it alone."

"So we'll make it fun," Catie said. "We'll be the Spinster's Club!"

Josie wanted to cheer. "That's right! We'll stick together. No men or mean girls allowed."

Catie was the first to stick out her hand and Josie was the first to take it.

Ten years later

Josephine Hale stuck her head out her bedroom window and waved to her cousin Ashley Brittany. Ashley waved back, giving her a carefree smile.

Josie retreated and tried to quiet her beating heart. Really, she had to settle down. Her mother was always telling her that.

Her mother told her a lot of things.

But now Ashley was here, and this was it. How could Josie possibly settle down?

She stuck her head out the window again, annoyed to see Ashley had stopped to exchange a word with the gardener. Why couldn't her cousin hurry? Of course, Ashley didn't know what she was hurrying for. She didn't know that Josie had finally found the map.

Oh, Ashley was going to be green when she saw it! Josie was finally going to be a pirate—or at least live off pirate treasure.

That was if Ashley ever made it into the house.

Josie peered out the window once more, searching for Ashley, but then the door opened behind her and Ashley strolled in. She wore a morning dress of light green cambric, the long, loose sleeves tied with ivory ribbons. She was dressed in the height of fashion, as always. And as always, one could tell she couldn't care less. There was a splattering of mud on her hem, her skirt was wrinkled, and two of her sleeves' ribbons had come undone.

But Ashley could have been dressed in a sack, and she would still be the most beautiful girl in any room. With her golden hair, her porcelain skin, and her eyes of pale, sea green, she put Josie to shame without even trying.

Not that Josie had tried very hard today, as she was wearing trousers and a man's work shirt and coat. And anyway, Josie didn't care about being beautiful. She wanted to be independent.

Ashley took in Josie's appearance in one encompassing glance and sighed. "What have I stepped into now?"

"Welcome aboard, matey," Josie said in her best pirate brogue.

Ashley raised her eyebrows, and Josie spoke quickly, before Ashley could jump to her own conclusions. "I found my grandfather's pirate treasure map," she blurted out.

"Really?" Ashley began to pull her gloves off, but Josie grabbed her hand and dragged her downstairs. Josie's mother was somewhere in the house, and if she saw Josie dressed like this, she'd have her daughter's head.

"I haven't seen it for years," Josie said, pulling Ashley in her wake. "I thought my father threw it out when my grandfather died." She pulled Ashley to the side of the stairs so they wouldn't collide with a maid dusting the banister. "But he just hid it," she whispered, so the maid wouldn't hear.

"That's very exciting, Josie, but where are we—"

Josie skidded to a stop in front of the library door. "So do you want to see it?"

Ashley raised a golden brow. "Will we get in trouble?"

"Probably."

"Oh, good. Then absolutely."

With a smile, Josie slid the oak-paneled library door open and poked her head inside. "All clear." She slipped through the doorway, closing it after Ashley followed. "It's over here." Josie gestured to the wall of bookcases. Standing guard before the imposing bastion of knowledge was an oak desk. It was a showpiece as were most of the books. No one ever came into the library except Josie.

The girls crept across the room, Ashley's slippers shushing on the thick carpets. A grandfather clock ticked away the hour in the corner. There was a small stepladder at one side of the bookcase, below the volumes of Shakespeare, and Josie slid it along the wall until it stood under the collection of biblical sermons and writings. She stepped onto the stool and reached as high as she could, her fingers grazing a worn copy of *Fordyce's Sermons to Young Women*. She handed the volume down to Ashley.

"Tell me this isn't what we came for." She scowled at the book and set it on the desk.

Josie winked at her and reached through the gap, pulling a large, ragged volume out. It was heavy, and she was glad when Ashley reached up and took it from her.

Unfortunately, her cousin wasn't expecting the book's weight. The volume slammed on the desk with a loud thump. Both girls froze, staring at the paneled door.

The clock ticked on, oblivious, and after sixty tocks, Josie stepped down. They were not caught yet. She indicated the desk chair, and Ashley took it, while Josie perched on the top of the desk. Josie flipped the book open, turning the pages slowly until she reached the center. There, folded and yellowed with age, was the parchment. With two fingers, she lifted it out.

"Is this it?" Ashley whispered.

Josie closed the book, shoved it out of her way, and spread the parchment flat on the desk. The map was familiar to her: the wavy lines to indicate water, the jagged coastline, the three islands. At the bottom was a compass whose ink had been smeared so north was unclear, and at the top—what should have been the middle—was a clean rip. The map had been torn neatly in half.

Ashley leaned back in the chair. "So your grandfather really was a pirate."

Josie nodded. "Of course he was. I told you."

"But your parents always say that story is nothing but rubbish."

"Well, look for yourself." Josie pointed to the map. "Does that look like rubbish?"

Her grandfather had first shown her the map when she was only five. She'd been sworn to secrecy because Nathan Hale said the treasure was bad luck. Even talking of the treasure was bad luck. So for thirteen years she had kept the secret.

Until now.

Ashley frowned at the parchment. "But if this is a treasure map, where's the X? I thought X always marked the spot."

Josie inclined her head in admiration. Obviously she had revealed her secret to the right person. "That, Miss Brittany, is a good question."

Ashley bowed from the waist, and said in an imperious tone, "Thank you, Miss Hale. I thought so."

Josie lifted the document and pointed to the edge. Minuscule fragments of the paper had frayed out from where the map had been folded over and over and then torn in half. "The X is on this portion of the map."

"The portion you don't have." Ashley's eyes gleamed with excitement in the dim light of the room.

"Precisely."

"Do you know where it is?"

"I do." Josie jumped off the desk and crossed to the large window on the outside wall. With a flourish, she threw the drapes wide. A cloud of dust billowed out, and both girls dissolved into coughing fits.

Ashley, who was farther away, recovered first. Waving a hand in front of her face, she croaked, "Well, I can see those curtains haven't been aired since the time of your grandfather. Is the X in the dust?"

Josie's eyes were watering, and she wiped away the moisture before replying. "No. I was attempting to show you that." She pointed out the window at the white bricks of the neighboring town house.

Ashley rose and squinted at the window through the hazy light. "Who is he?"

"Not who, but where," Josie corrected. "That is where I suspect the other half of the map to be hidden."

Ashley raised a brow. "In that house?"

Josie gave her a mischievous smile. "Do you know who lives next door to this, my grandfather's house?"

"Don't tell me." But Josie could see by the look on Ashley's face that she'd already made the connection.

"That's right. Stephen Doubleday, the new Lord Westman. Grandson of my grandfather's partner."

"That must be who that man is, then." Ashley pointed at the window, and Josie followed the path of her finger.

And found herself staring directly at Lord Westman, standing at his library window. Josie clamped a hand on Ashley's arm and pulled her down to the floor, then hastily tugged the heavy draperies closed again.

"What was that about?" Ashley coughed from the dust she'd kicked up when she landed on the floor.

"Shh! I don't want him to see me."

"Then why—"

"Shh!"

Ashley sighed. "Stop shushing me. He can't hear us, and if you didn't want him to see us, then why were we standing in front of the window directly opposite his library?"

"I didn't know that was his library." Josie got to her knees and made a small slit in the window coverings. "I've never seen his drapes open before. I rarely open these." She peeked through the slit until she caught sight of Westman again. He'd moved away from the window and was standing at his desk, looking down. His shoulders were broad and his waist narrow. His wavy brown hair fell in a queue long past his collar. Josie licked her lips.

She felt Ashley beside her and moved over a bit, so her cousin could see as well. "Now, that is a handsome man," Ashley said finally.

"I know."

Ashley poked her. "What are you about saying '*I know*' in that tone of voice? I thought your families disliked each other."

"We don't dislike each other. We hate each other with a passion. We're sworn enemies."

"Hmm." Ashley looked back out the window, and Josie followed. Westman was in his chair now, his feet propped on his desk and a snifter in his hand. He'd loosened his cravat and Josie thought she could see an inch of the bronze skin at his throat.

"So you're sworn enemies," Ashley said. "There's something about a man who is off limits that makes him irresistible. Don't you agree?"

Josie grinned. This was why she loved Ashley. "I do. And what makes him even more irresistible is that he has the other half of this map."

Ashley's eyes narrowed and she sat back on her heels. "Oh, no. I know that look. What have you planned now?"

"I'm going to sneak over there and steal the other half."

"But you aren't even certain Westman has it, much less whether he keeps it at his town house."

"That's why I have to sneak in and rifle the place. Care to join me?"

Ashley laughed. Josie frowned. She'd been certain Ashley would be excited at the prospect of such an adventure, but it should have been her cousin Catherine here with her. The two had schemed to run away together, find the treasure, and use part of it to help Catie escape her horrible father. But now Catie was married, and Josie needed a new partner. "Why not?" she asked Ashley. "You love adventure."

"Because this is a crusade, not an adventure."

Josie shrugged. "A crusade is just an adventure for a good cause."

Ashley laughed. "Well, it's your cause, not mine. Besides, I'll only be in the way when Westman catches you. You can seduce him far better on your own."

"Ashley! I'm not going to seduce him."

"Well, you should. After all, you've been looking for a lover—in particular, one who would never want to marry you."

"I made a pledge," Josie said.

"Pledge?" Ashley shook her head. "The Spinster's Club was a game we played when we were children."

"The ideals of our club still stand. I plan to be an independent woman, and once I have the treasure, I won't answer to anyone for my actions. Until then, I need a lover who won't trap me."

"There you go." Ashley gestured out the window. "Westman is a safe enough choice. With your families' history, he'd never want to marry you."

"But you think he'd take me to his bed?"

Ashley laughed again. "He's a man, isn't he, and a rake at that."

"A reformed rake, now that he's the earl," Josie added.

"A rake is a rake is a rake." Ashley stood. "How's that for poetry?"

"Horrible."

"It's the best I can do on short notice, and now, I'm going home."

"And I'm going to call on my good neighbor, Lord Westman. Sure you don't want to come along? I think between the two of us, we could figure out a way to get from this window into that." She pointed at the Westman's town house again.

"Not tonight. But give the earl a kiss for me."

Josie watched with annoyance as Ashley opened the door and went out. Now what was she supposed to do? She'd been counting on Ashley to give her courage.

Josie sighed. Some pirate she was. Afraid of heights. Afraid to steal a map that was rightfully hers to begin with. Her grandfather would have been mightily disappointed.

Josie parted the curtains again. It was evening now, and her mother would be sitting down to tea before long. Westman's window was dark. He'd probably gone out for the evening. Josie smiled.

"Grandfather," she whispered, easing the window open. "This one is for you."

Chapter 2

Stephen put his head in his hands. The worry and the fear and the feeling of impotence twisted around themselves and clenched his gut. The feelings were so knotted up, he had no hope of untangling them.

His feelings were not unlike the ledgers, bank statements, and assorted investment documents spread on the desk before him.

Reaching across the desk, Stephen lifted the decanter and poured a full glass of brandy. It was going to be a long night, and before he even began adding profits and subtracting debts, he knew the final sum.

His family was deeply in debt.

And he'd helped put them there.

Stephen sipped the brandy, closed his eyes, and fingered the papers detailing his recent investments. Very profitable investments. Five years working with the East India Company had taught him something of business. Stephen was going to repay all he'd lost and more.

Maharajah stood and growled, the hackles on his neck rising into a spiky collar. Stephen opened his eyes to see what had roused the dog who had been sitting so patiently beside him all afternoon, but the room had grown dark without him realizing it. He hadn't thought to light a lamp or a taper, and now he could see little more than the familiar shadows.

But Maharajah was growling at something. The dog let out a small yip, and Stephen closed his hand on Maharajah's fur. "Quiet, boy," he murmured. Without the benefit of his sight, Stephen strained to hear and was rewarded with the sound of something scraping against the outside of the house.

Rising and moving toward the window, Stephen used the stealth techniques he'd learned from trackers in India. He moved silently and steadily while his thoughts flew. What was out there? A thief? With the rampant crime in London nowadays, it shouldn't surprise him that the thieves were so brave as to attempt to enter private residences in Mayfair. The house was not terraced, which made the exterior more vulnerable, but there was a gate around the perimeter, and no one had ever attempted to breach it before.

He'd sent his housekeeper away earlier when she'd tried to bring him tea, so the library curtains were open, exposing the window and the room to the night. Stephen stared at the window and blinked when a hand appeared at the glass. Bloody hell. Someone was going to break in.

His eyes had adjusted to the darkness, and he glanced around the room for some sort of weapon. There was a pistol in the drawer, but it would take too much time to go back to the desk, unlock the drawer, and extract the piece. Instead, he hefted a solid candlestick.

Ducking down, he moved to a place beside the draperies, crouching in the shadows just as the thief managed to slide the window up. Stephen stared in disbelief. No wonder thieves were targeting Mayfair. Even his own windows weren't locked. Talk about an open invitation.

Stephen heard a faint, "Yes!" from outside and deduced that the thief was pleased by his good fortune as well. Not for long.

There was the sound of boots scraping against the exterior. As Stephen watched, the thief hooked one arm inside the casement then thrust a leg inside. Stephen raised the candlestick and prepared to strike. His other hand was clamped on Maharajah's muzzle, but the dog, though tense, was silent. Even the animal appeared to understand the importance of surprise in this case. Every instinct in Stephen wanted to move now, but he held himself in check.

Move too soon, and the thief would escape the way he'd come in. That would not do. Stephen intended to catch the man.

The thief's foot touched the floor, and then he swung his head inside, crouched low to fit his shoulders, and pulled the other leg over. Both feet on the floor, the thief stood still for a moment, surveying the room. Stephen frowned. Why, the thief was just a kid, far too small and slim to be a man.

Stephen raised the candlestick but hesitated. How could he hit a kid?

But it was too late. The thief had seen his movements and emitted a small gasp before turning back for the window.

Stephen was on his feet, candlestick raised, a growling Maharajah held by the scruff of his neck. "Stop. Do not move, or I'll loose my dog on you."

Maharajah gave a bark of warning, but the thief seemed to debate—escape or attack? Decision made, the thief was moving, both hands on the window ledge, one foot outside the casement. Stephen gave Maharajah a sharp command to stay and lunged for the window. He caught the thief by the collar of his coat and pulled him back inside.

The kid was really no threat. He was so light that Stephen easily dragged him halfway across the floor. Feeling sorry for the boy, Stephen released him, but as soon as the would-be thief was free, he was on his feet again, running for the window. With a muffled curse, Stephen caught him around the waist.

The kid struck back, kicking Stephen so viciously that he almost let go. He held on, ducking some of the fiercer blows.

Determined little bastard.

Stephen lifted him off the floor easily, but the child continued to kick and claw and bite.

"Bloody hell. Stop fighting or I'm going to hurt you." Maharajah growled and Stephen barked, "Stay!"

The kid seemed undeterred. He elbowed Stephen in the jaw.

"Bastard," Stephen said as his head was knocked back. The metallic taste of blood washed over his tongue. He adjusted his grip, trying to hold on, but lost his balance and stumbled. They went down. He and the thief were on the floor, rolling, both fighting for the top position. With a final burst of strength, Stephen won, rolling on top of the kid, straddling him, and catching his arms. He pinned them to the ground, and for a long moment there was nothing except the sound of panting.

Then the thief said, "Well, this is one way to make an introduction."

It was a woman.

Stephen jumped off her as though he'd been burned. His foot caught on the rug, and he went tumbling down again. He scrambled backward until he felt the lion's foot of his desk. Maharajah was right beside him, in the way, but somehow Stephen managed to find his feet. A moment later, he was squinting from the burst of the lamp's flame. He shook the temporary blindness off, and peered at the thief, still sprawled on his floor.

Bloody hell. It was indeed a woman, though one wouldn't have known it from her dress. She wore trousers and a loose white shirt under a large coat. But her low cap had tumbled off in their struggle, exposing her face and hair, and though she wore her hair cropped, there was no mistaking the delicate bones and lines of that face. This was a woman. A beautiful woman.

"Who the hell are you?" he demanded. Maharajah barked as if emphasizing the question.

She sat and blinked at the dog and then him, her dark green eyes huge and mischievous in her pixie face. "Well, that's not much of a welcome."

He touched his tongue to his lip. At least the tender flesh had stopped bleeding. "Perhaps because I don't recall inviting you."

"You didn't." Climbing to her feet, she brushed her trousers off. "Rather rude of you, too."

"Rude? Madam, you just broke into my library."

She frowned at him, but the look did not fit her face. She had a small, delicate face, high cheekbones, and a pert, straight nose. Her forehead was high and her eyebrows swept across the bottom of it like wings. Her eyes were what truly struck him. They were almond shaped, dark green, and positively sparkled. She was one of those women whose expressions—her playful smiles, her teasing laughter, her impish looks—made her beautiful. She was tall and thin, not much shorter than he, now that she'd risen to her full height. She put her hands on her hips in a challenge.

"Well, I would not have had to break into your library had you sent me an invitation. As it was, I was curious."

"Curious?" Stephen shook his head, certain he was not hearing the chit correctly. This was turning into one of the most frustrating conversations he'd ever attempted—even more frustrating than trying to communicate with the Indians in his limited Punjabi. "I'm supposed to believe you broke into my house because you were curious," Stephen said. He was going to get answers out of her if it took all night. "Madam, I suggest you tell me why you are really here. Now."

Her hands slipped from her hips, and she looked almost saddened by his words. Inexplicably, Stephen found himself feeling guilty for having hurt her feelings. Bloody hell. The woman was some kind of fairy with powers of enchantment.

"I told you why I was really here," she said, her big green eyes filled with sorrow. "I wanted to visit you. After all, that is the neighborly thing to do, is it not?"

And once again, Stephen felt the conversation jump out from under him. Now what was the chit going on about? She couldn't possibly mean . . .

But as he stared at her, the slopes and lines of her face became clearer, rearranging themselves into someone familiar, someone—

"Miss Hale."

She beamed at him and clapped her hands together. "Lord Westman! You remember me!"

"Remember you? Madam, we have not been formally introduced."

She shrugged and smiled. "We have certainly been introduced now." She looked about his library, her shining eyes lighting on the books, then the desk, then the worn furniture near the dark hearth. "What a lovely room you have here."

He almost thanked her before he realized he had not invited her and therefore did not care if she liked the room. "Miss Hale, if you were thinking to form a connection with my family, would it not have been more appropriate for you to call on my sister?"

She snorted. "Mrs. Withrow? Ha! She would never have received me. I'm the granddaughter of Nathan Hale, the pirate. Our families are enemies, you know."

Out of patience and lacking the strength to follow the twists and turns the girl continually threw at him, Stephen sunk into his chair and lifted the snifter of brandy. The girl moved closer, raising an eyebrow when he drank. He looked at the glass, then at her, and said, "What? Would you like a glass?"

"Oh, you are too kind." She took a seat in the chair opposite his desk. "Yes, thank you."

He thought about refusing her. A girl of her age

should not be drinking anything stronger than watered wine, but then again, he had offered. What had he expected her to say? With a shrug, he reached for a clean glass, filled it half full, and moved it toward her. She eyed it, then him, then pushed it back at him.

"Ahem."

Clearly, she did not appreciate only being given a half measure.

Stephen almost laughed, something he could not remember having done in years. Instead, he nudged the glass back with one finger, and said, "Drink it."

"You are certainly bossy." She lifted the snifter and took a dainty sip. To her credit, she did not screw up her face. But her eyes watered.

"And you're certainly forward. I know who you are and who your grandfather was. In light of that knowledge, I must ask why you are here. You realize that we will never be friends."

"Oh, but I don't want to be friends," she said, lifting the brandy and taking another small sip. "In fact, I could not be more pleased that our families are enemies. It serves my purpose."

Stephen's hand itched to pour another glass of brandy, but he restrained himself, not wanting to have to offer the girl one as well. "And might one inquire as to your purpose, Miss Hale?"

"Of course. I've been trying to tell you."

That was debatable, but Stephen held his tongue. She lifted her glass and took another drink, this time downing the last remnants. With a thwack, she set the snifter on the desk, rose, and put both hands between them.

"Lord Westman, I have come to be your mistress."

Chapter 3

Josephine frowned at her choice of words. *Mistress* was not the term she wanted. Perhaps she should have used *lover*? To be one's mistress implied control and protection. Josie didn't need Westman's protection, and she certainly wouldn't allow a man to control her. But becoming Westman's lover was a good way to get close to him and discover where he'd hidden his half of the treasure map. Not to mention, Ashley was right. He was delicious to look at and beyond the pale as a potential husband.

"Oh, good God." On the other side of the desk, Westman fumbled for the decanter of brandy and poured himself another glass. He poured carelessly and sloshed a good bit over the rim, staining the documents on the desk. Josie hoped the map was not sitting there. She watched him down the liquid and scrub a hand over his face.

He had a nice face. It was oval with a square, straight nose and generous lips. The lines at his mouth were fine and added character, as did the faint brown stubble on his upper lip and chin. His eyebrows were thick and dark and his long eyelashes framed pale blue eyes.

Josie could have looked into those eyes forever. They were so beautiful, so expressive. His long hair was dark brown and fell in an unruly mop over his forehead. He had either taken the tousled look of the dandies to the extreme or he had not bothered to brush his hair today. Josie was betting on the latter.

Undoubtedly, this man would make a wonderful lover. He was obviously not vain or self-absorbed, and he was handsome, intelligent, and she'd heard him described as witty. He'd been quite the rake in his day, and that meant he probably had the experience she lacked. Best of all, even if her affair with Westman was discovered, there was no way she would ever be allowed to marry him. She could have a torrid affair and find the map, then be free to search for new adventures.

Westman set his glass down and cleared his throat. "I'm sorry, Miss Hale, what did you just say?"

"I said"—she ran a finger along the crystal rim of her glass—"well, what I meant to say is that I want you as my lover."

He reached for the decanter again, but Josie put a hand over his.

"I'm sure this must be something of a surprise to you."

Scowling, he lifted her hand. "You could say that. And while your offer is a very tempting one, I'm afraid I must refuse." He dropped her hand back on her side of the desk.

Unperturbed, Josie smiled. "I knew you would say that." She had expected him to refuse at first. Any man with a modicum of honor would refuse her . . . at first.

He frowned at her. "I assure you I am in earnest."

"Of course you are," she said to placate him. "My cousin says you are a rake, but I told her you reformed when you became the earl."

"I think you mean that as a compliment." He stood and paced behind his desk.

"I do. I know why you wish to reform, and I understand your desire to keep the appearance of such. I have no need to expose myself." She tapped a finger to her lips. "My lord, may I be frank with you?"

He halted and spun to face her. "You haven't been thus far?"

She leaned back in the chair and crossed her legs, though her mother said it was not ladylike. But Josie was wearing trousers and a man's coat. What was the point of being ladylike now? "I have been forthright to a point," Josie told him. "I am eighteen, and I am ready for my life to begin. I am ready to take a lover, and I thought you might suit."

He blinked at her. "What in bloody hell gave you that idea? We're enemies."

"Precisely! No emotional attachment. No chance of a marriage proposal. Really, Lord Westman, can you think of a woman who would make a less suitable bride for you than me?"

"No."

"Well, there you go." She folded her arms triumphantly over her chest.

"Oh, no, we don't." He leaned his hands on his desk, palms spread over the documents. "Just because you offer to be my mistress doesn't mean I have to agree. I don't want or need a mistress."

Josie sighed. "You have one already. Don't you?"

Oh, now why hadn't she considered that possibility? She was much too impulsive by far. She should have spied on him for several days instead of leaping over here at the first chance she had.

He opened his mouth then, appearing speechless, shook his head. "That's not your concern. Not to mention, a lady like you has no business talking of lovers. You should be looking for a husband."

Josie yawned and waved her hand. "Oh, now you're being tiresome. I don't want to be told what to do."

"That's too bad because you obviously have need

of a great deal of guidance. What are you about, sneaking into my house, offering to be my mistress? If your parents knew—"

Josie clutched the threadbare arms of the chair. "Leave my parents out of this. They know I am not a conventional miss, and they long ago ceased giving me advice I don't need."

Well, her father had anyway.

"Perhaps I should have a word with them."

Josie's heart skipped. Her mother would murder her, slowly and painfully, if she knew Josie had even looked at Westman. To cover her fear, Josie laughed. "*You* speak to my parents?" her laugh was brittle. "Oh, yes, because you are the paragon of wisdom and good sense. I came to you because I thought you were the kind of man who could appreciate a woman like me. I did not come to be lectured and scolded." She rose.

"Then I am afraid you have sorely misjudged me."

"Obviously." She moved back toward the window. Just like a man to prefer lecturing to lovemaking. And now how was she supposed to get hold of the map? Angry and more than a little embarrassed, she made one last swipe at him. "But before you pass judgment on me, take a look at yourself. Who are you to give me advice? Your family is so deep in debt that I'm surprised you haven't fled to the Continent yet."

He jerked to attention and glared at her. "Who

the bloody hell are you? What do you know about it?"

"I know plenty, and if you'd been nice I might even have helped you."

"*You*? You help me?" He was coming toward her now, his long legs making quick work of the distance between them. Josie thought about ducking back out the window. She still had time to get away.

On the other hand, she rather liked the flash of his blue eyes and the color temper brought to his cheeks. Perhaps she should stay put just to see what happened. But he approached so fast, her instinct for self-preservation took over and she backed up until she felt the hard, flat wall graze her shoulder blades.

And still Westman came closer, stopping only when his face was mere inches from her own. He imprisoned her, one hand on either side of her neck. Josie felt her pulse kick and the heat flood into her face. Or perhaps it was his heat that was making her so warm. He was so close she could smell the sweet brandy on his breath and feel the tension radiating from his legs and chest.

"And how exactly is a little girl like you going to help me?"

"I—I—"

He shot her a pitying look and stepped back. "Get out."

But Josie wasn't going anywhere. "You don't scare

me," she said. "Nor do you intimidate me. Is that the best you can do?"

"Stick around and find out." The contemptuous look in his eyes let her know he thought she'd run if he said *boo!*

"Very well, then," she spat, half out of anger and half from too much pride, "Mock me, but you'll never know if the treasure could have saved you."

He frowned. "Treasure? What treasure?"

Josie bit her lip. Oh, no, she had done it now. She had not meant to say so much. She had not meant to tell him that she intended to search for the treasure. Drat! Drat her pride and drat the bad-luck treasure. Why couldn't she keep anything to herself? "It's nothing," she said, inching toward the window. "I'm talking nonsense."

He grabbed her elbow just as she reached one hand out for the casement. "You knew exactly what you were saying. What treasure are you babbling about? Not our grandfathers' treasure?"

She frowned.

"Oh, bloody hell. That *is* what you're talking about. It's a myth, Miss Hale. A fabrication."

"No, it's not. My grandfather told me about it before he died."

He ran a hand over his face again. "Bedtime stories."

"If it's only a story, then how did your grandfather buy this house? Why do I live right next door?"

"Oh, I'm not saying that our grandfathers weren't

acquainted. I think they were the best of friends."
He crossed his arms. "Until your grandfather killed
mine."

Josie shot forward and rapped him hard on the
chest. "That's not true. That's the fabrication. My
grandfather would never have done something like
that."

Westman raised a brow. "And yet, my grandfather is dead. He died right here in this room, a bullet in his brain."

Josie ogled the study with renewed interest. This
was where the fabled argument had taken place?
This was where the map had been severed in two
and where, years later, the men had argued and the
pistol had discharged, accidentally killing Westman's grandfather. Josie cleared her throat. "That
was an accident. They were arguing and—"

Westman waved an arm. "More fairy tales. Save
them for your nursery, Miss Hale. They're not
wanted here."

Josie huffed and hefted herself onto the window
casement. "Very well, then I shall return home to
my cradle and my nursery rhymes, but when I find
the treasure, don't think I will share any with you,
odious man."

"Ha. And a moment ago, you were begging to
be my mistress."

Josie was perched on the ledge of the casement,
but now she practically flung herself back into the
room. "Begging? Begging!" She marched toward
him and poked a finger at his chest. "As though I

would ever deign to beg a man like you for so much as a shilling. You bastard."

"Is that the best you can do?" he mocked her.

She raised her hand to poke him again, to push him back, to propel him out of her way, out of her very existence, but he took hold of her hand and yanked her hard against him. "Don't push me."

Josie blinked, too surprised by his sudden defense to wrench away. And then, when she was flush against him, she hardly wanted to. His chest was solid and broad, his body lean and hard and so wonderfully male. He felt male, he smelled male. She looked into his eyes, and there in the watery blue depths she saw something hungry and primitive that the feminine in her instantly recognized as its masculine counterpart. "Let me go," she said, but she didn't mean it. She didn't even sound like she meant it. "I mean it," she tried again, and still her voice was breathy and low. "I don't—oh, bother." And she grasped him by the back of the head and pulled his mouth to hers.

He wasn't a good kisser.

Josie realized that fact immediately. She'd had one or two passionate embraces in dark gardens during *ton* balls, and Westman's lips felt cold and lifeless against hers.

She felt as though she were kissing a frog, and not one destined to turn into a prince. But Josie wasn't the kind of girl who gave up easily. Pulling back slightly to readjust her angle, she went in again.

Perhaps Westman had just been unprepared the first time.

She pressed her lips against his again, and then, when she felt a flicker of response from him, slipped her tongue into his mouth. That had driven her other suitors to heights of rapture. It was a dangerous move, what with her in Westman's study, unprotected, and in danger of his unrestrained impulses. Normally, she would never have attempted something this daring when she wasn't certain of an easy escape, but the danger, the uncertainty, and her treacherous position only served to heighten her excitement.

She *wanted* Westman to try something ungentlemanly.

Instead, her tongue darted into his mouth while his own sat sluggish and uninterested. "Are you done, Miss Hale?" he asked.

Except his words were muffled by the impediment in his mouth. It took Josie a moment to realize his words were not pleas for more, and then she pulled away.

He wiped his mouth. Josie hissed in a mortified breath, and even though she had been described in the *Morning Post* on no fewer than two separate occasions as "The Unflappable Josephine Hale," she felt her face burst into hot flames of shame. Westman had not liked her kisses. Westman found her disgusting.

"If you are finished mauling me—"

Josie took a horrified step back.

"Kindly leave me in peace. I have work to do to-night."

"Of course. I'll go." She dove for the window, hooking her legs over in record time and jumping to the ground with an ungraceful thud. She straightened, standing between the two houses, but before she could look up at Westman's window and contemplate the fool she'd been or her lost opportunity to find the treasure map, the window slammed shut and the lock fell into place.

Josie climbed through her own window and closed the drapes, but when she stepped back into the library, she felt as though the ground beneath her feet was crumbling away, inch by inch. She stood on the edge of a vast precipice, and she wasn't sure it would have been too much of a tragedy if she'd fallen in and disappeared forever.

Stephen stood behind the drapes in his library, one hand fingering the heavy brocade. He'd seen the girl land safely beneath his window before shutting the sight of her out. He heard her scrambling across the way, and flicked the drapes open a half-inch with one finger.

There she went, her round bottom disappearing over the window casement. When she was safely inside, he allowed the material to close again and stepped away.

Maharajah, who had been sitting under the desk, awaiting his master's command to attack, trotted over and licked Stephen's hand. Stephen patted him absently before lifting the lamp and carrying it out of the study and upstairs. But when he reached the landing, instead of turning right, to his own bed-chamber, he turned left, walking all the way down to the far end of the hall, where he never ventured. He paused before a large painting and raised the lamp to shed a beam of light on the man pictured there.

James Doubleday, his grandfather, had been a handsome man. He had the blond haired, blue-eyed good looks of most of the Doubleday family. Like the men who had carried his name, James had an easy smile and a look of affability. Stephen peered closer to the portrait and saw the date of the painting was 1760. Those were the days when his grandfather and Nathan Hale had been sailing the high seas, wreaking havoc on the Dutch and Spanish ships.

The painting had been done only three years before James would be shot dead. What the hell did the man have to look so cheerful about?

Stephen stared harder at the picture, but try as he might, he could see no resemblance to himself in the young man painted on the canvas. In his youth— and Stephen had to laugh at the sad fact that at thirty-two years of age, he was no longer in his youth—he had often been told he was his grandfa-ther all over again. His brother, James, might have born the physical resemblance, but Stephen had all of the spirit and passion for life that his grandfather had possessed.

This comparison had not always been given in such a complimentary fashion. Stephen's father, the late Lord Westman, had called Stephen's womanizing, gambling, and constant state of drunkenness a disgrace to the family. His mother had come away from reading tidbits about her younger son in the morning papers with red-rimmed eyes. In those years, she never called him a disgrace.

She'd never needed to.

His parents might hate him for shaming the family, but even their disgust was better than the indifference they'd showed when he was a child.

James was the golden son, and if Stephen couldn't be golden, he'd be black.

The Doubleday's black sheep had consoled himself with the knowledge that through his grandfather, he came by his dissolute life honestly. His friends loved him, the women adored him, and what would the *ton* do for gossip if he were not there to cause one scandal after another? But Stephen supposed that the sweltering, diseased, filth of India would cure any man of his predilection for scandal and attention.

And then his brother had died. When Stephen returned to England, prepared to assume the title and responsibilities of earl, he'd been a man who wanted nothing but Society's respect.

He wanted to forget his past and become the man his father and mother had always wanted him to be. He relished the opportunity to restore the Doubleday name and fortune. The *ton* didn't think he could do it. No wonder, as he'd been the one to lose most of it at the faro tables. But Stephen knew better than most that the *ton* was full of fools. Stephen's grandfather had built the family fortune. How appropriate that Stephen would be the one to restore it.

He lowered the lamp, thrusting his grandfather's portrait back into darkness, where it belonged. God help him if he allowed one pixie-faced girl to dredge up the past again, to send him on a wild chase for pirate treasure that didn't even exist. Investments, the Doubleday estates . . . that was where his fortune lay.

He paced along the hallway until he reached his room, thrust open the door, and, setting the lamp on the table, fell onto the bed. He had no valet—though he could probably afford one now—and so he need not worry about being interrupted.

He stared up at the deep purple tester. He'd heard stories of the pirate treasure before. He'd even believed some of them, when he'd been particularly drunk. But he hadn't ever seriously considered that the treasure might be hidden somewhere, waiting for him to find it. Stephen rubbed his temples and tried to recall the old story.

His grandfather and Hale had supposedly stolen a fortune in gold doubloons from one of the Spanish ships. On the voyage back to England, they'd sailed their ship into a hidden cove and hidden half the treasure.

It was a wonderful tale, and Stephen had begged

his nurses to tell it to him when he'd been a small lad. But as he'd told Josephine Hale, it was a bedtime story. He closed his eyes, and her face came clearly into view. She had seemed so sure of herself, though. Her small face with its pert nose had radiated confidence when she'd talked of the treasure. And Stephen found that he could not so easily dismiss the myth of the treasure now.

Did Josephine Hale, Nathan Hale's granddaughter, know something Stephen did not? Something had driven her to climb into his window tonight. But perhaps she climbed into men's windows all the time? She was no novice window-climber. She'd had experience. Considerable experience.

She'd said she'd come because she wanted to take a lover. He snorted. A woman who looked like her could certainly find a lover without going to the trouble of climbing through his window. There were younger men, handsomer men, richer men.

Unless she had come to him because she had an ulterior motive. Unless she'd come because she thought he knew something about the treasure. Stephen sat up and pushed his hair out of his eyes. He was James Doubleday's grandson, and she was Nathan Hale's granddaughter. He supposed if anyone knew the secret of the treasure it was the two of them. Actually, if anyone knew the secret of the treasure, it was probably Josephine Hale. While Stephen had never known his grandfather, Miss Hale had reportedly known hers quite well. He'd lived a good forty years after James Doubleday's death. Had he told his granddaughter something, given her something that revealed the secret of the treasure?

Stephen knew the idea was ludicrous. There was no treasure. It was a myth. A fable. But, goddamn it all to hell, what if it wasn't?

What if there was a fortune in gold doubloons waiting for him? He'd more than restore his family's finances then. He'd double them. As quick as the flash of gold from one of those doubloons, he'd be redeemed in the eyes of the *ton*, and more importantly, his family. His older brother's name would no longer be revered. Stephen would be known not as the rake and the dissolute son, but as the man who'd saved the Doubleday name from ruin.

But Josephine Hale . . .

How was Stephen to put his faith in that willow of a girl, a girl known for her recklessness, her impulsivity, and the behavior of her equally outlandish cousins? What kind of woman was she? She couldn't even be twenty, and yet she'd had the audacity to creep into his home and then proceed to make him an indecent proposal. What kind of woman did that sort of thing?

Stephen flopped back on the bed again.

Just the sort of woman that had always attracted him. But had he learned nothing from the past? Had his sins and those who'd paid for them taught him so little? Josephine Hale was the kind of woman that encouraged a man to sin. With that luscious mouth and that mischievous smile, those long, lithe legs and huge green eyes, she was the kind of woman he could bed again and again and never tire of.

She was trouble.

He'd known it the moment he pulled her into his arms—an action that had been more out of long habit than desire. And then, when she should have run away screaming, she'd done the unthinkable. She'd kissed him.

She was no novice kisser either. Stephen had felt his blood heat when her mouth touched his. And when her tongue, small and moist, had touched the tip of his own, he'd felt his pulse quicken, and his cock harden, and he'd been so tempted to toss her onto his desk, flip up her skirts, and plunge into her.

But he had not. It was enough that he'd wanted to, that he'd felt the old need, the familiar lust. He could have given into it. He could have ruined Josephine Hale as he'd ruined another before her.

Guilt slammed into him, sharp and piercing as always.

He wanted Josephine Hale, but he could not act on that. She might never know how hard it had been for him to refuse her offer, to refuse her when she gave herself to him so openly, so freely. She might never know how hard he'd clenched his jaw to keep from calling her name when she'd slipped back out his window.

She would never know how he'd forced his reluctant arms to push the window shut. She would never know the yearning and need she'd left him with.

And she might think she'd left him for good, but Stephen knew now that he would see her again.

Soon.

Chapter 4

~~~⌒◊◊⌒~~~

"There he is," Ashley's voice hissed in her ear. "I cannot believe he had the audacity to attend."

"I cannot believe the ladies-patronesses granted him a ticket," Maddie replied.

"Don't be a goose. They granted him a subscription. He's eligible and an earl."

Josie didn't need to look over her shoulder to know her cousins were speaking of the Earl of Westman. She'd heard the tinkle of female voices echoing through Almack's din, and there were only a few men in England who could achieve that effect simply by entering Willis's Rooms. "He's not that eligible," Josie said, feeling peevish.

Why did everyone care so much about the Earl of Westman?

He couldn't even kiss. Some rake *he* must have been.

"You know that his family is practically destitute," she said, letting her ill humor show.

"All the more reason to grant him a subscription," Ashley retorted, rising on tiptoes to see over Josie's shoulder, presumably to follow the earl's movements. Josie had to dig her nails into her palm to keep from turning and looking as well. "The ladies-patronesses love to play matchmaker," Ashley continued. "No doubt they have some unwitting heiress in mind for him."

Josie scowled. "No doubt."

"My, but you're in a foul mood all of a sudden," Maddie observed, flicking her fan closed. "Josie, you don't harbor a *tendre* for Westman, do you?"

"Of course not! What utter rot."

"Utter rot." Maddie blinked several times, then notched her head up. "So sorry to have offended you."

Josie knew the signs when she'd hurt Maddie's feelings. "Maddie, you didn't offend me. In fact, I'm sorry I'm so awful to be around tonight."

Maddie was instantly all compassion. "You're not awful. Don't talk so." She put her hand on Josie's shoulder, and Josie tried to smile.

Then, when Maddie wasn't looking, Josie shook her head in disgust, mostly at herself. She didn't care if Westman was in attendance or not. So she had made a fool of herself with him. It was not as though he were going to spread the story about. No one ever need know.

In fact, Josie told herself, she was one of the lucky ones. If she hadn't crept into Westman's library and kissed him, she too might be mooning over the earl. As it was, she had no reason to be even the slightest bit interested in him. She could concentrate on finding another eligible man to be her lover.

A man who could kiss.

With the object of forgetting Westman foremost in her mind, Josie turned to the assembly room at large and surveyed the couches full of guests. It was nigh eleven, and the dancing would undoubtedly begin any moment. The room was quickly filling, five hundred elite from the upper ten thousand dressed in their best and assessing one another as she assessed them.

At the far end of the room, the ladies-patronesses had taken up residence on a large couch that gave them a superior view of the room as a whole. It was a large room, over one hundred feet long and forty feet wide. At the end nearest Josie, the orchestra from Edinburgh was tuning their instruments in the little balcony overlooking the dance floor.

Josie's gaze roamed quickly over the large, sparkling chandeliers, the gold wall sconces, the gleaming floor of the room. From habit, she noted the Greek statues and the lavish, heavy draperies hanging from the ornate molding at the ceiling. Usually, she enjoyed looking at all the finery, but tonight she was far more interested in the people. In particular, she studied each of the men that came into her line of sight. That one was a duke, looking to marry and produce an heir. That one she'd had a brief flirtation with last Season. He no longer interested her. That one might do, except he was rather short, and she preferred tall men. Her gaze moved on, until it was torn back to the handsome figure of a man in a blue coat, with brown hair in a queue down his back. She could not see his face, but his stance, his form, everything about him riveted her. Right height. Right build. And his attitude was that of languid indolence. Oh, now she wouldn't mind an introduction to that one.

And then he turned, and Josie almost gaped. It was Westman, of course. He saw her immediately and before she could turn away, he gave her one lascivious wink.

Disgusted, she rounded back on her cousins, only to find both in conversation with her older brothers, John and Joseph.

"Looks like you're going to end up a wallflower tonight, Jojo," John told her with a wink. "We've just asked these ladies to partner us."

"I'm sure I'll do fine," Josie said, trying to manage a smile. Couldn't her brothers find other partners? Josie wanted to grasp her cousins' hands and beg them not to leave her, but they were already allowing her brothers to lead them onto the floor.

Wonderful, she thought. Now she was partner-less. Surely the earl, who appeared to suffer no shortage of female companionship, was across the room laughing at her lonely state.

The dance began, and Josie watched John and Maddie and Joseph and Ashley execute the forms. She knew she could have danced if she wanted. A smile in the right direction would have brought several men running, but what was the point when they'd be the same overbearing, conservative-minded men she already knew?

She stepped back and allowed the milling crowd to obscure her from the eyes of potential dance partners and the gaze of Lord Westman. She hadn't glanced in his direction again, but she swore she could feel those blue eyes on her. She was probably imagining it. He'd made his disinterest patently clear last night.

Josie drifted through the crowds, not even bothering to look for eligible men anymore. Not withstanding Westman, who was trying to reform, the rakes didn't come to Almack's. She'd have to look elsewhere to find a man suited to her purposes. She'd have to look elsewhere for a way to repair her grandfather's reputation as well. Westman was not going to help, that much was clear.

Josie paused at the far end of the assembly room and turned back to watch the end of the dance. Westman wasn't going to voluntarily help her find the other half of the treasure map either. Perhaps she could watch his house for a few days, ascertain his movements and his schedule, and sneak back when he was not at home. She *knew* that treasure map was in his house somewhere. A safe? The attic?

"Now what mischief are you planning?"

Josie spun and looked directly into the stunning blue eyes of Lord Westman. "I'm not planning any—"

He held up a hand. "Don't bother. I can see your brain churning and plotting from across the room. Still scheming how you can get your hands on the treasure?"

Josie blinked, caught off guard. Good Lord, was she really that transparent? "I don't know what you're talking about," she finally managed. "Excuse me." She began to move away, but he stepped in front of her. A few people looked in their direction.

"Sir, kindly step out of my path."

In response, he gave her another of those lascivious smiles and reached for her hand. "Will you grant me the pleasure of the next dance?"

Josie had no intention of allowing him to touch her, but something about that smile rendered her knees and her self-control a bit wobbly. When she had it back, he was leading her toward the dance floor. Oh, Lord, help her! If her mother saw this, Josie would never be allowed out of the house again.

She dug her heels in, but that didn't slow her

progress whatsoever as the floors at Almack's were notoriously slippery. "Sir, cease. I cannot dance with you."

"Haven't you heard? I'm reformed and eligible. One dance won't hurt your reputation."

"No!" Something in her tone must have finally touched him because he paused and looked into her face.

"Goddamn it," he muttered and began dragging her back toward the edge of the room. There was a potted palm in one corner and he pushed it aside and thrust her behind it. Then he released her and stood, hands on hips, appraising her. "I can see there's no point in arguing with you. You're stubborn as a mule, aren't you?"

"A mule. How romantic. And I'd heard you had a silver tongue."

"Not everything you've heard about me is true."

"Oh, I realized that last night. Now, move out of my way." *Please, please, please God don't let Mother have seen us.*

"Not unless you agree to dance with me."

"Are you mad?" she hissed. "I cannot dance with you. I cannot even be seen with you."

"Funny you should say so after crawling through my window last night."

"The fact that we cannot be seen together was precisely the reason I climbed through your window. Now, I must go before my mother hears of this."

"A brazen girl like you worried about your dear mother?"

Josie snorted. "You would worry too, if you knew her. Good evening."

He took her arm again. Josie suppressed the shock that went through her at his touch. Oh, what was wrong with her? She didn't want him anymore.

Westman leaned closer, his breath tickling her cheek. "Miss Hale, we need to talk."

Josie couldn't stop her gaze from focusing on his lips. Perhaps he might be taught to kiss better.

"About the treasure," he added.

That snapped her attention away from his mouth. "Shh!" She glanced furtively about, hoping no one had heard. "I thought you didn't believe in the—in *it*."

"We need to talk."

"Not here and not now. Release me." *Stay away, Mother, just for one more moment.*

"Meet me downstairs in ten minutes."

Josie gaped at him. "No! I cannot leave with you. I cannot even be seen with you. Now move away."

"I'm not asking you to leave with me. I don't want your virtue. We need to talk."

Josie shook her head. Did the man understand anything she was telling him? Any moment her mother was going to see her and Westman. If that happened, Josie's next social event would be her own funeral. "What is wrong with you? People will gossip if they see us together."

"People always gossip. I don't care about that."

Josie wished she didn't care either. It would be

such fun to throw all restraint to the wind and thumb her nose at Society. And she would.

One day.

But right now, her mother was lurking, and Josie valued her life enough to be cautious. "Well, I do care. Now, go away."

He didn't move.

"Lord Westman! Are you listening to me? Are you mad?" He frowned in annoyance, and she pushed her advantage. "Oh, dear. I forgot you were in India, and you have one of those horrid tropical diseases, don't you? The kind that rots your brain from the inside out." She wished he had a disease. That might explain why he'd turned her down last night. His brain was slowly turning to mush.

"What the bloody hell are you talking about?" he said, sounding remarkably lucid for a man in his condition. "I don't have a disease."

She waved his protest away. "It's perfectly all right if you do, but as you are mentally incapacitated, you must listen to me. I. Cannot. Talk. To. You. Here. Understand?"

His eyes blazed blue fire. Time to make her escape.

"Must. Go." She made a good-bye motion with her hand. "Understand? Bye. Bye."

He finally released her arm, and she scooted past him. She walked away quickly, not looking back. Thank God, she'd fled before he'd managed to make a scene. She was safe now.

And then because she couldn't help but give

Westman one last look, she peered over her shoulder and smacked right into her mother.

"Josephine, I've been looking for you."

"Wh-why?" Josie prayed to God that Westman had walked away and was now out of sight.

"I noticed you weren't dancing." Mavis Hale took Josie's arm and twined it firmly with her own. "I found a partner for you."

"I can find a partner," Josie protested. She tried to extract her arm, but her mother yanked her closer.

"What was that, Josephine? Are you arguing with me?"

Drat! "No, Mother. No." *Lord, please don't let Mother make me write another fifty-page essay about obeying one's parents.*

"Good, then come along. Lord Crutchkins is waiting."

"Lord Crutchkins? Mother, no."

Mavis rounded on her, her brown eyes small and determined. "Are you certain you are not arguing, Josephine? Because I promise I can make your life far worse than one dance with Crutchkins."

Josie bit her lip and forced a smile. "You're right, Mother. Crutchkins it is."

She saw the elderly, weasel-faced man waiting for her and tried not to lose her dinner. Lord, the man was older than her father.

He waved a bony hand covered with age spots and grinned his toothless smile.

It was going to be a long night.

* * *

When she was out of his sight, Stephen muttered, "And she thinks *I'm* an imbecile."

Maybe he was. After all, he couldn't stop thinking about that damned treasure. A treasure that probably didn't even exist. How was a fantasy supposed to make him rich? Better to stick with his very real investments.

But what if the treasure was real? He'd come to Almack's tonight with the express intent of quizzing Miss Hale on what she knew of the gold. But with his chance to talk to Josephine Hale gone, Stephen had no intention of remaining at Almack's. The place was just as bland and proper as always. If he were an intelligent man, he would stay, dance with eligible young ladies, and find himself a woman to take the title of countess and give him an heir. But Stephen had never considered himself particularly intelligent.

He had proof of it thirty minutes later when he scaled the Hale town house. Earlier that day, he'd asked his housekeeper to talk to the Hale servants and discreetly determine which room was hers. Now he was hanging outside it, attempting to push the window open. It would be just his luck if she locked it. It would be just his luck if he fell and broke his neck going after a fairy tale treasure.

The window finally gave, jutting up so quickly that Stephen lost his balance. For one precarious moment, he hung by a single hand, and then he hooked his other arm over and crawled inside.

Josephine Hale's room was very much what he'd expected. That was no great reflection of his knowledge of her, he'd simply been in enough young lady's rooms to know what they looked like. This one was no different. It had a small bed with a pink coverlet, and the curtains he brushed past matched the bed. The furniture was simple, a dressing table, an armoire, and a pretty escritoire.

Nothing else was as it should be, however.

A lady's room was to be neat and free of clutter. Josephine Hale's looked like it had been ransacked. The bed was half-made, and dresses, petticoats, and stays littered the bed and the dressing table chair. He stepped inside the room, lowered the window, and stared at the mess. Stockings and shawls, gloves, and hats—there was hardly a space free of feminine accoutrements. He tried to push through the room without disturbing anything, but he'd taken no more than two steps before his foot crunched on a fan. Bending, he swept the fan and a pair of stockings into his arms and made his way to the dressing table.

It took only a moment of poking through the detritus there to see that it contained nothing related to the treasure. He pushed aside three brushes, two small mirrors, and a bevy of combs, along with a nest of hair ribbons, and found nothing but hairpins and the subtle cosmetics allowed an unmarried young lady.

Dumping the broken fan and the stockings on the dressing table, Stephen moved on to the escritoire.

It too was a jumble of half-begun letters, opened mail, and several books. He read the titles of a few and snorted. Obviously Mrs. Radcliffe, Shakespeare, and Lord Byron were among Miss Hale's favorites. No wonder the woman climbed into men's libraries. Her reading material was appallingly loose. He stacked the books in one corner and the unfinished letters in another, and then he sifted through what remained. A few letters from her friends and one from her cousin Catherine, but nothing . . .

Wait.

Stephen pushed the letters aside and lifted the yellowed parchment. Though a low fire burned in the hearth, the light was insufficient for reading, and Stephen had to move closer to make out what was written on the parchment.

It was a map, or at least half of one. There was a coastline, wavy lines representing water, and three ovals that might be anything. At the bottom of the map was a smeared compass, and at the top of the map—what should have been the middle— was the clean rip.

Stephen stared at it. Could this be the fabled treasure map? Was this what made Josephine Hale so confident the gold actually existed? Stephen stared at it for a long time. It certainly looked authentic. Folding the map, he placed it in his pocket and continued to poke through her things. He found nothing else of interest, though, and when he next checked his watch, it was half past one. She would be home soon, and he settled back on her small bed to wait.

He was dozing when he heard her voice. He knew it was her because she had a voice one would not easily forget. It sounded almost like a song, the lilt of it rising and falling melodically with her words. And then she laughed, and he felt his heart swell. When had been the last time that he had laughed like that? Had he ever been so alive and so free? It had occurred to him earlier that her maid would follow her upstairs, and now he moved to the armoire, where he had to crouch. He was taking a chance that no one would open the furnishing. If he knew his girl, she would dismiss her maid after she'd been unlaced and undressed, then toss her dress on the floor.

He was in the armoire, the door open a sliver, when the maid and Josephine Hale entered. She was still talking animatedly about the ball and her plans for the morrow, and the maid was making small sounds of interest. A lamp was lit, and Stephen had a moment of concern when he caught the look on the servant's face at the state of the room, but then her charge turned her back, and the woman began to unpin her dress.

"Oh, and then Mother made me dance with Mr. Southmore. Lord, he is such a bore. All he can talk about is corn. After twenty minutes, I wished I had a cob of corn to stuff in his mouth."

"Miss!" her maid remarked, but without much

heat. She was obviously used to statements like this from her charge. And then the dress was free. Stephen held his breath, hoping this was not the night Josephine Hale would choose to order her life and her room.

But she said, "Just loosen my stays, Williams, and then go to bed. I know you must be tired. I'll clean up in here."

The woman made a harrumphing sound but didn't argue, and Stephen relaxed once again. Finally, the stays too were off, and the maid was waved away. As soon as the door closed, Josephine Hale dropped her dress and her stays on the floor. She loosened and dropped her petticoat as well, then bent, slipping her shoes off, and padded in her chemise to her dressing table. The table was closest to the armoire and provided him an excellent view of her.

She was far from indecent. Her shift was thick and serviceable cotton, and the light behind her revealed little. But Stephen was aroused nonetheless. It had been a long time since he'd seen a woman in only her shift. It had been a long time since he'd looked upon delicate shoulders and a long stretch of arm. It had been even longer since he'd glimpsed a woman's ankle or pretty pink toes. The sight of so much milky white skin, once as familiar to him as his own home, was almost too much.

Inside the armoire, Stephen took a deep breath and let it out slowly. Outside, Josephine Hale began to unpin her hair, allowing the hairpins to lie where they fell. Her hair was not long, and it did not fall down her back as most women's would have. But it was curly, and when she ran one of her brushes through it, the curls uncoiled and the brown mass fell in soft waves to her chin.

That task accomplished, she removed her jewelry, taking care to put it away, and then crossed to her desk. She flipped idly through the papers and letters, seeming not to notice that they had been rearranged, and then she picked up a book and thumbed through it, looking for her page. She took two steps toward the bed, and then halted, and Stephen knew that was the minute she realized the map was missing.

Spinning away from him, she dove for the desk and began tossing papers here and there. Silently, Stephen opened the armoire and stepped out. "Looking for this?"

Chapter 5

⌒◯◯⌒

Josie screamed in surprise as the man crossed the room, his hand coming over her mouth to cut off her cry. She tried to fight against the arm that came around her shoulders, but he pulled her snug against him. "Good evening, Miss Hale."

Recognition dawning, Josie let out a whoosh of air and sagged against him. "Westman," she mumbled, though her words were unintelligible.

"Don't scream," he whispered and relaxed the hand cupping her mouth. "Promise?"

She nodded and made no sound as he slowly drew his hand away. The callus on one finger trailed along her cheek, tickling and tantalizing the skin. He put his hands on her shoulders, and she allowed herself to be turned until she faced him, until she was once again looking up into his handsome face.

"I should have known you'd be here," she said.

He shrugged. "You said we couldn't talk at Almack's. You didn't say we couldn't talk here."

"I see the malaria has already begun to rot your brain."

He frowned. No sense of humor, she decided.

"Do you know how much trouble you caused me tonight?" she asked. "Because I couldn't account for my time with you, my mother took it upon herself to find me eligible dance partners, which means I danced with every ugly, boring, foul-smelling man in attendance. Do you know what she would have done had she found me with you?"

"I can only imagine. I didn't anticipate that a girl like you would care so much for the social niceties."

Josie straightened. "What does that mean? 'A girl like me'? What kind of girl do you think I am?" She took a step back, but he caught her shoulder before she moved too far away.

"Don't get all huffy now, Miss Hale. I mean no disrespect. I like you. We're two of a kind."

She crossed her arms. "And that's not disrespect?"

Westman grinned.

"I'm glad you find this amusing, Lord Westman, but I am in no mood for games." She took a quick inventory of his hands and the floor around him but didn't see her treasure map. She held out one imperious hand. "Kindly return the map to me and climb back out my window."

"Forceful. I like it." He took her outstretched hand.

"I mean it, Westman. Give me the map and go."

"That's not what you really want me to do." Still holding her hand, he drew her closer. And then when she was flush against him he backed up, taking her with him. Josie's head started to swim. "You don't really want me to go, do you Miss Hale?"

She felt his legs bump her mattress, and she willed herself to break free. He wasn't keeping her against her will. His touch was so light that she could easily escape.

But she didn't want to. No, now that they were against the bed, she wanted to see what would happen.

Josie swallowed as she allowed him to push her down on the bed and then sat next to her. She'd never had a man in her bedroom before. Even her brothers and her father did not cross this room's threshold. Her bed and her room seemed so small with Westman beside her. He was everywhere she turned—his body, his scent, his soft voice. She shivered, and then made a valiant effort to regain her wits. She was no milksop miss who would faint the first time a man tried to kiss or touch her. She was in control here. This was her room, and he had her map.

"I suppose," she began, testing her voice, "the

question, we should be asking, Lord Westman, is what do you want?"

Good. That was better. Her voice was cool and controlled, but also low and seductive. She watched as the pupils of Westman's pretty blue eyes widened.

"You mentioned the treasure earlier this evening. Is that what you've come for, or do you have something else in mind?" She let her tongue flick out to wet her lips.

She heard Westman's breath catch for a moment. Ah-ha! So he was not entirely immune to her. But his voice was cool when he answered. "I have a great deal in mind for you, Miss Hale. But for the moment, I'm hunting treasure."

"And what makes you think I can help you?"

"The same thing that made you think I could help you. You need the other half of this map." He patted his coat pocket. Josie's eyes widened. So that was where he'd secreted it.

Without thinking, she reached forward greedily, but he caught her wrist before she could touch his coat. She tried to wrench free, but this time he was not so gentle. With persistent, steady strength, he eased her back, following her down until her wrist and her body were pinned on the bed.

He was above her, his face so close she could see every long eyelash framing his blue eyes. He held her effortlessly, using one arm and his body to pinion her. Josie was not so foolish to believe that if she tried to free herself with her other arm, he would not catch that one, too.

And would she really have minded that? She was afraid she would rather enjoy being at his complete mercy. But her pride forced her to keep her free arm out of his reach.

"Tonight *I* have a proposition for *you*," he said, his nose touching hers.

"What's that?" she said, but her voice came out as a husky whisper.

"I propose"—his free hand moved along her hip, touched her waist and continued higher—"that we work together."

Josie had to gulp to take a breath.

"I propose we become partners in this treasure hunt."

His fingers brushed the underside of her breast, and Josie bucked. The shock of pleasure from his touch was so raw, she hadn't anticipated it. His warm hand closed over her breast, and she could not help but moan. She'd been expecting this; she knew he would touch her. And she'd been touched there before. But this was not like it had been with other boys. When Westman squeezed her breast and flicked her hard nipple, she could not stop herself from moaning and arching with pleasure.

She wanted him. She looked into his eyes, so blue and so full of promise. She almost moaned again when he lowered his mouth to the fabric of her chemise. She felt the heat of his mouth through the cotton, and she bit her lip to stifle her scream. In that moment, she would have done anything he asked if he would just lower her neckline and take her aching breast into his mouth.

"Tell me about the treasure," he murmured, and Josie snapped back.

She'd do anything but give him the treasure.

Her free hand came up, and she pushed his head away. Hard. The look on his face was full of surprise, but he recovered quickly. "Am I to take it that you do not wish to be partners?"

"The treasure is mine. I don't want your help."

He leaned close again, whispering in her ear, "But you need my help, Miss Hale. You need me."

Oh, Lord, she did need him. Why couldn't he just agree to be her lover last night? Then she would never have mentioned the treasure, and she would not be in this position. If she told him no now, would that be the end of this pleasant seduction? And if she said yes, could she trust him enough not to double-cross her and keep the treasure for his own?

His mouth lingered against her ear, and she wondered if, at this point, she really had any choice. "This is hardly fair," she said finally.

She heard him chuckle, and the low rumble had her pulse racing again.

"You were not exactly fair last night. I am simply better at this game than you."

She couldn't argue with that, and she didn't try. "Do you want to be my partner?"

"Yes," he breathed in her ear.

She shivered. "For better or worse?"

He chuckled again. "For richer or poorer, Miss Hale."

"Those are the easiest of my terms."

"Give me your worst."

She turned her head and met his gaze. "Get off me and I will."

And to Josie's disappointment, he released her faster than a hot coal.

When Stephen sat back, it took him a moment to regain his bearings. He'd intended to play the part of the rake with Josephine Hale, but somewhere in there, he'd forgotten he was only acting. Sometime between when he'd first touched her and when he'd pushed her down on the bed under him, he'd gone from seducing her to being seduced by her.

Bloody hell. The woman hadn't even been trying to tempt him tonight. It was her reaction to him that did him in. Her low moans and the way her body writhed under his had warped what started as his best intentions. He hadn't been lying when he'd said he thought they were two of a kind. He could tell she would complement him perfectly in bed. She would be an adventurous lover, eager to please him and eager to be pleased.

And as he lay on top of her, as his body hardened and he filled his palm with her soft breast, he wanted her in his bed. He wanted to sink back into the gluttony and unbridled debauchery of his past life. She was the kind of woman who could bring it all back, who could remind him how it felt to live again.

Thank the devil she had finally agreed to his terms. When he wasn't touching her, he could think again. He could remember why he was doing this— why he was chasing this ridiculous treasure myth. He needed to restore his family honor. He needed to restore his family finances. He may not be the best son for the job, but he was the man to whom the task had fallen. And Stephen would be damned if he'd disappoint again.

Her gave her room, and Josephine Hale sat and, after scooting a respectable distance from him—if any distance could be called respectable when they were alone in her bedchamber—she began straightening her chemise. She made a tempting picture in her virginal white with her fiery, disheveled curls about her face. Her eyes were a mossy green and slightly glazed.

Stephen looked away—tried to remember that he was dangerous to this woman. "You mentioned terms," he said, still not looking at her. Better to keep their relationship as impersonal as possible. From now on, he would use his charms only under the direst circumstances.

"Terms," she said. From the corner of his eye, he caught her nodding as though to remind herself. "I have several. First of all, I don't trust you. I want some assurance that when we find the treasure—"

"*If* we find the treasure."

"That *when* we find the treasure, you aren't going to run off with it."

Stephen didn't have much of a temper, but now he felt his anger begin to simmer. He spoke softly, meeting her eyes. "Are you implying I'm the kind of man who cheats women? Are you questioning my honor, madam?"

"Now who is huffy?" she shot back. "I only want some assurances, not only that we split the treasure equally between us, but that you will not leave me behind."

Stephen stood. "It's an insult to be presented with these terms. I'm a man of honor."

"But you are also a man. I have two brothers, Lord Westman. I know how overprotective and irrational men can be."

Stephen snorted and then, angry all over again, turned away. He had to keep his temper below boiling because the amusing part was that, when he was angry, he could be rather irrational. Chalk up another point to the pixie.

But she did not know him. She didn't know him at all, and who was she to question his integrity? He supposed he deserved this treatment. He had not behaved entirely admirably with her, but he did wish that for once in his life, he would be given the benefit of the doubt. "Since you seem to need it, you have my word," he ground out finally. "We share the treasure."

"Good, then—"

"But I also have terms." He rounded on her. "We share all information. If you have any knowledge in addition to this map"—he patted his coat pocket again—"you will share it all."

She bit her lip and looked away, considering. Finally, she nodded. "Very well."

"And we share all the work. I'm not going to crawl about attics and sort through dusty papers alone only to have you sweep in at the last minute and take half the glory. You'll work as hard as I."

She raised one thin swallow's brow at him. "You have a rather low opinion of women, don't you?"

"No lower than yours of men, Miss Hale. Do you agree?"

She licked her lips, and Stephen had to shutter the bolt of arousal the action produced in him. She was an accomplished flirt; he would give her that and more. He wondered just how many men she had conquered. And he wondered if it was only for the treasure that she had chosen him to join their ranks.

"So you're saying you want me to spend hours upon hours with you in small cramped spaces getting all dirty." She rose and took a step toward him. Her tone made the whole plan sound lurid and licentious, and as Stephen's thoughts were headed in that direction anyway, he decided he had better go.

He had what he wanted.

"I'm asking for your complete cooperation," he said.

She cocked her head. "Oh, you'll have it, my lord."

Stephen nodded and moved toward her window. "One other thing, Miss Hale. This partnership is to be entirely business. Entirely impersonal. We will not become lovers. We're business partners."

Josephine Hale shook her head. "I cannot agree to those terms, my lord. I will share all my information and give you every spare moment of my time. I will do all that you ask and probably push you to do more, but I will not agree to keep our relationship impersonal. I rather fear we've gone beyond that point already."

She was not making this easy. Here he was, trying to protect her virtue, and she wanted none of it. Little fool. If she only knew . . .

"Take it or leave it, Lord Westman," she said when he didn't answer. "You'll have the bulk of what you want, but I won't agree not to become your lover. Surely an experienced rake like you can resist one naive, inexperienced miss like me."

He snorted. "Undoubtedly."

"Then we have a deal. I'll meet you tomorrow night."

It was only after Stephen had climbed down the house and was back in his bedroom, thoughts of Josephine Hale creeping unbidden into his mind, that Stephen realized he had no idea where or when they were to meet.

He had a bad feeling that, as long as he had the

map she wanted, the naive, inexperienced miss would not let him out of her sight.

Josie lay in bed the next morning, pondering the long day and what to do with it. She could not possibly sneak over to Westman's until her parents believed she was abed.

Unfortunately, she tended to keep late hours, so that meant she could conceivably retire no earlier than eleven, and even that might raise eyebrows. Perhaps if she feigned a headache?

It was quite likely that by the time she was done with Westman, she would have a headache in truth. The man was decidedly vexing. The more she knew of him, the less she liked him, and the more she wanted him.

And that was exactly what he wanted.

He made no move to make himself agreeable to her, but he did not shrink from seducing her. Of course, he made it quite clear his seduction was naught but a pretext to get information and cooperation from her. She'd be a fool to think he was interested in her as anything more than a means to an end. He wanted money, not a lover, and he'd use all his skills at seduction to achieve his aim.

But as her efforts to reclaim the map had failed, and Westman still had it in his possession, Josie had to admit that his skills were far more numerous and more refined than she had first judged.

Josie was treading on treacherous ground, beginning to imagine sharing Westman's bed, when a knock sounded on her door, and Ashley poked her head in.

"Are you still in bed? Lord, you must be the laziest girl in London."

Josie sat and made room on the bed for her cousin. "I'm tired. I had a late night last night."

Ashley raised a brow. "No later than I. We left Almack's together, and I saw no need to sleep past noon."

Josie looked down at her hands and fiddled with the small gold and emerald ring she always wore, a bequest from her grandfather, which she had been given on her sixteenth birthday. "Perhaps my evening did not end after Almack's."

The corner of Ashley's mouth turned up. "I would ask if your mother then dragged you to Lord Effington's ball, but I do not think you would be smiling were that the case."

"Lord Effington? If I'd been forced to attend his do, I would probably have spent the night casting up my accounts. He is truly horrid. I pity the girl he marries."

Ashley scooted closer. "Then what, Miss Hale, were you doing all night?"

"I had a visitor."

Ashley nodded, a gesture for Josie to go on. Josie paused for a moment, uncertain how much she wanted to tell Ashley, and then decided she might as well tell it all.

"He was waiting for me when I arrived home."

"He? I'm intrigued. Where was this gentleman"—

she raised a brow in question, and Josie nodded—
"this peer"—another brow, another nod—"waiting
for you?"

Josie spread her arms, indicating her bedroom.

Ashley's eyes widened. "May I ask the gentleman's name?"

"Perhaps it's best if we simply refer to him as
Lord W."

"Really? The same Lord W you told Maddie you
cared not a jot for at Almack's?"

"Perhaps. A girl can have a change of heart."

"Oh, most assuredly. But might one ask why the
change of heart? Might one even inquire, rather in-
delicately, but forgive me, have you taken a lover?"
Ashley whispered the last, and Josie felt a small
shiver of excitement run up her spine at the idea.

"Not yet. And it won't be him. He's all wrong for
me. Too small-minded and controlling. He actually
threatened to tell my parents I'd sneaked through
his window."

"Well, he wasn't threatening that last night. I
call that progress."

Josie turned her ring and said nothing.

"Don't you call that progress?" Ashley asked.

"There's a small problem," Josie mumbled.

Ashley's eyes, green like her own but with rather
more blue, widened. "Is he—" She cleared her throat.
"Can he not perform?"

"No, nothing like that. At least I don't think so,"
Josie said. "It's just that I think he's more interested
in the treasure than in me."

"The treasure?" Ashley held up a hand when Josie tried to go on. "How does he know about that? Yesterday you told me you sneaked into his house, kissed him, and that he was a horrible kisser, and you didn't want him. Is that the whole truth?"

"Not exactly. I might have mentioned the treasure on accident."

Ashley gasped. "Josie! You told me you weren't supposed to tell anyone."

"Well, I didn't mean to, but now that he knows, he's intent upon finding it. You know his family needs the money. He wants us to be partners."

"And you agreed?"

"Well, he's very persuasive . . ."

"Josie! It's one thing to take a man as your lover, but it's quite another thing to work with a man. You know how men are."

"He agreed to all my terms."

"And you believe him? He's a man. Lord, Josie, it's almost like you're married to the man already!"

Josie laughed. "You are overreacting, Ashley Brittany. I wouldn't marry Stephen Doubleday—I couldn't marry him—even if wanted to. Which I don't."

Ashley scowled at her. "I don't like it, Josie. And what about your grandfather's honor? How are you going to prove him innocent with the very man who'd like to vilify his name throwing obstacles in your path?"

"Westman doesn't know that part, and as long

as he doesn't, he won't know to throw obstacles in my path. In a way, having his help searching for information on the treasure almost makes it easier to also find information exonerating my grandfather."

"And if Westman becomes suspicious?"

"Then I'll kiss him and make him forget."

Ashley laughed. "I'm sure you will, too. You're a wanton woman, Josephine Hale."

Josie shrugged. "I do what I can."

"What are your plans today?" Ashley said, switching the subject. Josie didn't mind. After all of Ashley's protests, she preferred almost any topic to that of Westman.

"I thought I would lie here all day until it was late enough for me to sneak over to Lord W's. Why?"

Ashley closed her eyes. "Do not tell me these things. I'm going to be up all night worrying."

"You worry? Ha!"

"Do me a favor, cousin." Ashley pulled Josie up and out of bed. "Get up, get dressed, and come with me to Gunther's. I'll buy you an ice and then we can visit Maddie. She made me promise to help at the orphanage. Or the widow's home. Or whatever her latest charitable endeavor."

Now it was Josie's turn to scowl. "Oh, no. I love Maddie, but she has far too many causes, and they're all in Seven Dials. You know my mother will not allow me to go."

Ashley crossed her arms. "Has that ever stopped you before?"

"No, but I was never this close to losing my virginity before. I have to stay alive, or I'll be a maiden forever."

Ashley shook her head. "Get dressed fair maiden. I promise to have you back in time for your rendezvous."

Chapter 6

Seven Dials was at the northern end of St. Martin's Lane and was so named for its column, from which seven sundials radiated, each facing one of seven streets that branched from the center. For an area named after sundials, there was very little sunny about it. Seven Dials was a place of trash-filled gutters below and fetid air above. On every corner one could see skinny dogs watching skinny children with hungry eyes. Men loitered about aimlessly, without work, without hope, their eyes shifty and prowling. Women and children fared no better, and possibly worse. The lucky ones had a hovel somewhere to crawl back to after a day of hard labor. The unlucky slept on the streets.

It was no place for a gentleman of the *ton*, but

that didn't stop many of them from slumming in search of cheap gin and cheaper women. Stephen had spent considerable time here when he'd been a youth. He knew its twists and turns, where to find the cleanest whores and the dirtiest fights, where to pawn a ring to pay off a gambling debt and where to find the highest stakes games to lose it all again.

There were other pleasures to be had as well, but Stephen, though once an unrepentant libertine, did have standards. He would not buy a child. He would not attend dog fights, cock fights, or bear baiting. In Stephen's opinion, those pastimes were more accurately labeled crimes. He'd never had any wish to hurt anyone or anything, though he'd done just that nonetheless.

And now here he was again, walking the old streets, smelling the old stench, but for once he wasn't interested in sin. His thoughts were on redemption.

Stephen was careful not to allow himself to become too optimistic. He was pursuing an item of interest, no more. He wasn't entirely convinced that Miss Hale's treasure was anything more than a figment of her imagination, though the map in his pocket gave him some reassurance. That did not mean, however, that if there had been a treasure, said treasure was still waiting for him to stop by and scoop it up. It had been more than fifty years since the treasure had been hidden. Surely bandits, smugglers, even tide and time could have absconded with the gold doubloons by now.

He'd thought about mentioning these possibilities to Josephine Hale the night before, but why dash her hopes? He was tired of being the man who dashed everyone's hopes. Miss Hale could learn for herself some of the harsher realities of life. He needn't be the one to teach her.

He turned down Queen Street—a street he doubted Her Majesty had ever set foot upon—and glanced down at the crumpled paper in his hand. Josephine Hale was not the only one with resources and knowledge. Stephen had done a bit of digging through old papers himself, and he'd found a receipt for a warehouse in Seven Dials among his grandfather's things. He didn't expect the warehouse to still be standing, and he really didn't expect it to hold anything of interest, anything of his grandfather's. But he had nothing better to do in the hours before his sweet neighbor called on him—if that was the appropriate term—and so he'd sent for a hack and traveled back in time, to another time in his life, to Seven Dials.

He glanced at the paper again and scooted aside to avoid a snuffling pig. "Can I 'elp you, gov?" a young man, presumably the owner of the pig, asked. Stephen turned to him, and the scrawny, grime-covered youth looked him up and down. "You lost or something?"

"I'm looking for this building." Stephen held out

the paper, pointing to the name and address of the warehouse.

The boy shook his head. "Can't read. Wot's it called?"

"The Queen's Palace, and it's supposed to be here on Queen Street."

The boy snorted. "Now that's a good one. The queen's palace 'ere in Seven Dials."

"There's a shilling in it for you, if you find the place for me."

The boy's muddy eyes widened. "Be right back, gov. Watch me sow, will you?" And he was off and running, calling out to the men slouching here and there to ask if they knew of the Queen's Palace. The replies were far from helpful, and Stephen kept moving, scanning what few signs there were.

He was so intent on his work that at first he didn't hear the tinkle of laughter from farther up the street. And then the sound of mirth, so foreign to this place, penetrated, and he turned and looked. His eyes narrowed when he caught sight of a pink muslin gown housing a familiar feminine figure.

Stephen rubbed his eyes. He told himself it couldn't be. That it shouldn't be. But when he opened his eyes again, there she was.

"Josephine Hale," he barked.

A few yards away, the tall flame-haired woman with cropped curls, cocked her head. Then shaking it as though she'd made a mistake, she looked back at her companions, and Stephen was even more shocked to see that she was in the presence of two other ladies—one blond and one brunette. They were not alone. Stephen counted four footmen, but it didn't matter. They should not be here.

He started for them, then noticed that the sow he was supposed to be minding wasn't following.

"Pig," he called. "Pig, come here."

The pig snuffled at the dirt and meandered farther away.

"Bloody hell." Stephen went after the sow, trying to ignore the jingling laughter of the women. Finally, he managed to catch the rope leash tied around the pig's neck, and he led her up the street.

All three girls stared at him, the blond and Josephine trying to hold back giggles. The brunette had managed to regain her composure.

"Lady Madeleine," Stephen said, bowing to the brunette woman he now recognized as the Earl of Castleigh's daughter. His bow thrust him a few more feet than anticipated as the pig was not as keen to stop as he. But finally he had her under control. "This is an unexpected pleasure," he said after backing up.

"My lord," Lady Madeleine curtsied. "Truly, this is an unexpected sight. Have you—er, come to make a donation? Or is your business purely . . . agricultural?"

"Donation?"

"He's not here to make a donation to the orphanage, Maddie," Josephine said. "He's here for other reasons—undoubtedly disreputable reasons."

"Perhaps he's a pig thief," the blond woman said, covering her mouth to hide a smile.

"Am I correct, Lord Westman?" Josephine asked.

"No, Miss Hale," he said, telling himself not to notice how pretty she looked in her pink gown, her cheeks pleasantly flushed and her lips red and ripe for kissing. "As a matter of fact, I am here on a matter of legitimate business."

"What business?" she demanded. "Pig business?"

"Personal business," he answered, trying to shake off the sow who was pushing her nose into his boot. "What the devil are you doing here? This is no place for ladies."

"Or gentlemen," the blond added. Stephen gave her a tight smile, then glanced impatiently at Josephine Hale.

"My cousin," she said in answer to his look, "Miss Ashley Brittany."

"Of course," Stephen bowed and gave her his best rogue's smile. "I've heard of you, Miss Brittany. The rumors pale compared to the real thing."

Ashley fluttered her eyes at him—a true flirt. "Thank you, my lord. And the rumors I've heard of you, well"—she looked at the sow—"clearly I have not heard the whole story."

"Oh, bother." His beguiling next-door neighbor sniffed. "If you want to simper and make love to each other all day, I'll be off. Maddie and I have things to do." And she swept past him, headed for the entrance to a dingy building with a simple sign reading "Foundling House" above it. Stephen almost laughed. The little chit was jealous. Not a moment ago, he'd been thinking about kissing those ripe lips—an act that would surely ruin all his good intentions—and she thought he wanted her cousin. If Miss Hale only knew how much he wanted her. He wasn't about to enlighten her, nor could he allow her to escape, so with a quick nod to Lady Madeleine and Miss Brittany, Stephen went after her.

Or at least he tried. It took a good half-minute to convince the pig to stop eating his boot and trot toward the building.

"What the devil are you doing now?" Stephen said, tugging at the pig to make her keep up. "I insist that you and your friends go home at once."

She kept walking. "Go home? You can't tell me what to do. You go home."

God, she was so pretty. Infuriating, but pretty. What would it be like to kiss her when she was all riled up like this? Would the heat of anger melt into the ardor of passion?

Before she could escape into the orphanage, he stepped in front of her. To his pleasure, he saw the pig wind its way behind her, trapping her. "Does your mother know that you're here?"

She crossed her arms. "Does yours?"

"That doesn't matter. I'm a man."

He knew immediately it was the wrong thing to say. Her green eyes turned hard as emeralds. She stepped close to him, and spoke through clenched teeth. "You, sir, are an ass." She looked as though she had more to add, but the youth picked that moment to dash up to them.

"Hey, gov! I found it. I found the building ye wanted. The Queen's Palace."

"Good," Stephen stepped away from her, handing the pig's leash to the boy. "Excuse me." He gestured to the youth to walk with him, but Miss Hale was having none of it.

"What's the Queen's Palace?" she asked, following them.

The boy turned to speak to her, but Stephen put his hand on the kid's shoulder and propelled him forward. Josephine Hale quickened her step as well. "Is it an inn? A brothel?"

"No, miss! Nothing like that." The youth turned to speak to her, clearly upset that a lady such as she would think so lowly of him. "My mum would whip me good if I 'ad anything to do with those—ahem, ladies."

"As well she should," Josephine Hale said with a nod. "You seem like a good boy, uh—"

"Charlie, miss."

Before Stephen could stop him, he'd unattached himself from Stephen's hold and was sticking his hand out. "The name's Charlie."

Stephen watched in astonishment as she took the boy's grimy hand in her clean white gloves. "Josephine Hale. A pleasure to meet you. Now, pray tell, what is the Queen's Palace?"

"Well, I don't rightly know. Ye'll 'ave to ask this gent 'ere. 'e told me 'e'd give me a shilling to find it. It looks like some kind of warehouse."

"A warehouse?" she said with a suspicious look at Stephen. "How fascinating. Do lead on, young Charlie."

The boy did as he was told, urging his pig on with them. Josephine Hale gave a quick wave to her friends and then followed their guide. Irritated, Stephen fell in step beside her. He should have just kissed her senseless when he had the chance. Maybe that would suspend her constant interference in his life. "I don't recall inviting you to accompany me," he growled. "I told you this was personal business."

"I'm not accompanying you," she said staring ahead. "I'm accompanying Charlie, and he doesn't mind. You don't mind if I come along, do you, Charlie?"

The boy looked back. "No, Miss 'ale. I'm right 'onored."

She gave Stephen a superior smile. "There. He's honored to have me along. Would that your manners were as pleasing."

"I was charming last night." And just the thought of that encounter had his breath quickening.

He could have sworn her cheeks colored, but she turned away from him. "I didn't think it very charming of you to steal from me."

"It's just 'round this corner!" Charlie said, pointing past a man selling brownish apples.

"I don't steal." For the second time in less than

twenty-four hours, Stephen felt his temper surge. What was it about this woman that rankled him?

"I distinctly remember asking you to return my property," she said, her voice haughty. "As it is still in your possession, and there without my approval, I think I am well within my rights to complain."

"A complaining woman. What a surprise."

She turned, most likely to verbally flay him, but Charlie came to his rescue. "That's it, gov. Do I get me shilling?"

Stephen handed it to him, and boy and pig were gone. Stephen surveyed the old building, making a mental note of its location. "Well, there it is, Miss Hale. As you see, nothing much to look at. Now, if you'll allow me, I'll find you a hack and see you safely home."

Ignoring him, she started forward. "I'm not going home, especially not with you."

Stephen made a dash to catch her before she could enter the building. He was rather tired of dashing after her. "You're not going in there."

He caught her by the wrist, and she looked up at him. "Yes, I am. I find I have a sudden interest in this warehouse."

"*Why?*"

She leaned close, and once again those rosy lips taunted him, begged him to be kissed. "You tell me, Lord Westman. What's your business here? What are you trying to hide?" Her green eyes flashed.

"Bloody hell. I'm not trying to hide anything."

"Then this warehouse has nothing whatsoever to do with the—the you know what?"

Stephen didn't answer.

"My lord?" she pressed. "Does this place have anything to do with our grandfathers?"

Stephen wanted to say no. His mouth worked, his throat worked, and his hands clenched. Why the hell was it so difficult to lie to her about this? Because he'd given his word last night to include her?

But damnation! That didn't include a foray into London's underworld.

"I can see by the look on your face that the answer is yes." Her hand snaked out and smacked him on the chest. "You lying rogue. And to think I trusted you!"

He grabbed her arm before she could strike again. "You didn't trust me. You gave me a litany of terms."

"And you gave me a lecture about how you were a man of honor. Where's that honor today, Lord Westman? Or does it only surface when you're trying to woo a woman into your bed?" She spat the last, her tone harsh and unyielding.

Stephen's was equally so. "If I'd been trying to get you into my bed, Miss Hale, you would have been there." And he wouldn't still be wanting her right now. "And I was going to tell you about the warehouse."

"After the fact!"

"Yes. Seven Dials is no place for a lady."

With a mutinous look, she spun away from him. He watched her march back and forth before the warehouse's entrance, her hands clenching and unclenching. "Just like a man," she spat at him on one pass. "Liar!" she hissed on the next.

He grabbed her arm again. "I am not a liar."

"You promised me that you would not leave me behind. That you would share all knowledge."

"And I would have."

"After you left me behind!"

"I told you, Seven Dials—"

"I don't care whether we have to descend into the pits of Hell, my lord. If you go, I go. Understood?"

He glared at her. If he had to listen to one more word . . .

"Do you think you can get that through that thick male skull of yours?"

"Do you think you can get this through that hard skull of yours?" And then he pulled her against him, lowered his mouth to hers, and took her sweet, round, complaining mouth with his.

It was the only way to get her to shut up. It was the only way to prove he was in charge here, not her. And it was the only way to get his mind off all the other wicked things he wanted to do to her. He should have throttled her, but how could he when she stood before him in that pretty pink dress, her cheeks flushed, her eyes flashing, and her small, round bosom heaving.

Stephen couldn't remember the last time he'd wanted a woman so much. Wanted to kiss her or throttle her, he wasn't sure which. But once his mouth met hers, he knew he'd made the right decision.

She was shocked at first. Her mouth was tight and her body rigid, but then she let out a soft sigh, and she was all his. Or, rather, he was hers. Her arms came around his neck, her body melted into his, and her tongue plunged into his mouth, at once beginning an erotic duel with his own. She was telling him that he hadn't won this battle. That she wasn't surrendering one inch to him.

And Stephen loved it. He loved having it proven, once again, that this woman was his match—and more.

"I don't have rooms," a creaky male voice said. "This isn't that kind of establishment."

Josephine broke the kiss first, jumping away from him with lightning quickness. Her cheeks were red with heat and passion, her breath came fast, and Stephen found that he was irrationally proud of the fact that he'd done that to her. And now that he was once again in possession of his wits, he was also disgusted with himself. Kissing her on the street corner. What had he been thinking?

Stephen cleared his throat. "We're looking for the Queen's Palace."

"You've found her. I'm the owner. What do you want?"

Stephen glanced at Josephine, and she looked right back at him, one eyebrow rising.

"We're looking for items my—"

Josephine cleared her throat.

Stephen blew out a slow, measured breath. "Items *our* grandfathers might have left here. The name is Westman."

"And Hale," she added.

At that revelation, the man's bushy gray eyebrows rose a good half inch. "Westman and Hale, you say? Oh, now that's an interesting pairing. Yes, it is. Come in Lord Westman, Miss Hale. Let's see if we can't find what yer looking for."

He motioned them inside the dark building, and despite her earlier assurances of traveling to Hell with him, Stephen felt his companion scoot closer. He put a comforting hand on her arm and watched as the old man motioned, with one bent finger, for them to follow.

The elderly owner led them toward what appeared to be the only source of light in the place. All around them giant shapes loomed, and there was the faint drip-drip-drip of water. Josephine Hale put her hand in his. Stephen took it, willing all unclean thoughts from his mind. It wasn't easy, what with his blood still thudding in his ears and his cock slightly stiff from their kiss.

What was the use, really? He was a rake at heart. But he could rise above it. He would be the heir his family needed, the man his brother was. He would not take advantage of an innocent, foolish girl. Not again.

There was the screech of a cat, and Josephine Hale jumped into his arms with a tiny scream.

"We're almost there," the owner told her. Stephen could feel her trembling, but he also felt her straighten her shoulders and walk on. She was no coward; he'd give her that.

"It's rather dark in here," she said.

"I don't imagine the price of a candle or lamp oil means much to a lady like you," the man said, steering them around a tower of what looked like Turkish rugs. "But outside of Mayfair, we make do with a lot less."

Stephen felt her shoulders straighten even more, a defensive gesture, or so he assumed, until she said, "I'm sorry. It was thoughtless of me. I should keep my mouth shut."

To Stephen's amazement, the man chuckled. They'd reached the office and the source of the dim light. The man waved them inside. There was a small desk and two chairs and a door to an inner office behind the desk. "You're Nathan Hale's granddaughter, all right," the owner said, following them inside. "You don't have a proud bone in your body."

Stephen tried not to guffaw.

"Ah, Lord Westman disagrees." The warehouse's owner took the seat behind his desk and Stephen allowed Josephine Hale the other chair. He took up guard behind her.

"I think she might have one proud bone," Stephen said. Josephine shot him a glare, and he added, "Or two."

"Can we please get on with the business?" she said.

"By all means." Stephen extracted the yellowed paper from his tailcoat. "I found this among my grandfather's papers."

Below him, Josephine Hale snatched the paper from his hand. "Why didn't you show it to me before?"

"I only found it this morning," Stephen added, uncurling her fingers and handing the paper to the warehouse's owner. "As you see, it has this name and address."

The old man looked at the paper. "And you were wondering if we might have something of your grandfather's still here."

Stephen shrugged. "I didn't think it would hurt to check."

"It's unlikely." The man leaned back and steepled his fingers. "I remember your grandfather." He looked at Josephine. "Yours, too. They came here sometimes in their seafaring days. I was a boy, couldn't have been much older than one and ten, but I remember them. That's a long time to keep something in storage."

"Is there any way we might search?" she asked. "We'd be careful not to disturb anything."

The man gave her an incredulous look and

then glanced at Stephen. "Eager, ain't you? It would take you years to search this place, and all you'd get for your trouble are rat bites and dirty hands."

"But—"

Stephen put a hand on her shoulder, silencing her.

"Let me check the files," the owner said. "I'll see if there's anything worth looking for."

With that, he rose and retreated through a door behind him. It was filled with drawers, which were, presumably filled with files. When the man was out of earshot, Josephine looked back at him.

"Don't ever do that again."

Stephen swallowed a laugh. "Miss Hale, I fear I've committed so many transgressions in your eyes, that you will have to be more specific."

She glared at him. Lowering her voice, she whispered, "Don't ever kiss me again, especially not in public. If that behavior gets back to my mother—"

"Do you really think your mother has friends in Seven Dials?"

"My mother has friends everywhere. Very little escapes her. If you're going to be my lover, you will have to learn to be discreet."

Stephen clenched his jaw and tried not to yell. "I am not going to be your lover, Miss Hale. I only wanted to shut you up. That's the extent of my interest in you."

She leaned back in her chair and assessed him for a long moment. Their gazes met and held, and she stared so long Stephen thought she had forgotten what she'd intended to say. But finally, she said, "That's too bad. Your kissing today was much improved. I might actually be good for you. I might even teach you a thing or two."

Stephen stared at her in horror, wanting to correct her, but unable to find the words. She thought him a poor kisser? She thought herself above him in the art of seduction? It was too ludicrous, too ridiculous to be believed. He wanted to haul her into his arms and show her how absurd she really was. He was reaching for her, too, when he heard, "No, don't start that again." Stephen glanced up and the owner was heading toward his chair. "I found something you might like to see."

The man held a smooth wooden box in his gnarled fingers. It was the size of a bread loaf with tarnished gold latches and hinges. Stephen reached for it, but Josephine Hale was before him. She took the box into her hands.

It was the most beautiful box Josie had ever seen. No matter that the wood had once been intricately carved but was now smooth with wear. No matter that there were scratches marring the wood and that it smelled like a used chamber pot. She loved that box. It had been her grandfather's, or at least something he had touched or used, and she loved everything that had to do with him. Turning it this way and that, she found the gold latch keeping it closed and lifted.

Nothing happened.

Josie frowned, tried again, and then she saw the keyhole. "It's locked," she said, holding the box up for Westman to see. He took it from her, tried opening it himself, but when he too failed, he didn't hand it back. She grit her teeth. Just like a man.

"Do you have the key?" Westman asked the warehouse's owner.

"No key, just a box. Here's the inventory log." He held out an ancient ledger, and Josie had to stand to peer at the words noted there.

Contents: One wooden box.
Storage Fee: Paid in full
Signed: J. Doubleday

"That's all there is, then." She glanced at Westman. "We'll have to break it open."

"Not here," the proprietor said, rising. "I got better things to do than watch you two open a box. There can't be nothing in that box but trouble. Yer grandfathers were trouble, and I can see you two are trouble. Ye got what you came for. Now be gone with ye."

Westman nodded. "Can I pay you for your services?"

The man shook his head. "You saw the ledger. Paid in full. Ye can take the box and be gone."

"Thank you," Josie told him, following Westman out the door, back into the black warehouse. But this time the inky shapes and unfamiliar sounds didn't frighten her. She had the box. Nothing could frighten her.

Chapter 7

Josie started back the way they'd come, but Westman put a hand on her shoulder. "Where do you think you're going?"

"To open the box, of course," she said and reached out, taking it from him. "Thank you."

"This isn't the place—"

Josie fanned a hand at him. "We'll go to the orphanage. No one will see us there." She smiled. "And, as an added bonus, Maddie told me some of the city's best child pickpockets live there—reformed, of course—but I imagine they will make quick work of this lock."

"Pickpockets. Splendid," he grumbled.

Less than five minutes later, she opened the foundling house's door. Maddie peered into the entryway from one of the main rooms. "You're back. Can you help me set the table?"

"Oh, not now, Maddie! We found something—a box. Is there anywhere we can go to take a closer look?"

Ashley's head appeared above Maddie's. "We? Oh, you've returned with Lord Westman."

Josie wondered when her cousin had started restating the obvious. Westman didn't seem to mind. He doffed his hat, then settled it under his arm. He was being remarkably tolerant—at least for him. Perhaps he had finally given up fighting her.

"I suppose you can use the parlor," Maddie offered. "Are you certain you can't help with the orphans? It would be a wonderful way to prove how reformed you are."

Westman gave her a tight smile.

Josie sighed. "Stop trying to recruit more members for your benevolent society."

Maddie looked unrepentant.

"Just one more thing." Josie knew this request would not go over very well, but she had no choice. "Could we borrow one of the children who used to run in Finnegan's gang? We don't have a key for the box."

Maddie's mouth tightened. "The benevolent society doesn't like to encourage the children—"

"I know. But just this once," Josie pleaded. "I'll explain how the box belongs to me and that I need help opening it. It's all right if the box is mine, isn't it?"

Josie thought she heard Westman mutter a comment questioning her ownership of the box, but then Maddie said, "Fine. I'll call Johnny."

"Thank you!"

Josie led Westman to the parlor, and Ashley scooted inside before Josie could close the door. When Josie gave Ashley a look, indicating they wanted privacy, Ashley said, "I just want to take a peek." Then she whispered, "I'm not going to steal your beau."

"He's not my beau," Josie hissed back. Ashley laughed.

"I'm standing right here, you know," Westman said, taking a seat in one of the tattered chairs.

"A gentleman wouldn't listen," Josie said. She lit a lamp and set the wooden box on a small lamp table.

"So that's it?" Ashley asked, coming to peer at the box. "What's so important?"

"It belonged to my grandfather," Westman told her. He glanced at Josie, apparently uncertain how much to reveal.

"It might have a clue to the treasure," Josie finished for him. "Ashley knows about the treasure map, but no one else outside of my immediate family."

Westman nodded. "Good. Let's keep it that way."

There was a light tap on the door, and Josie moved to shield the box from view. "Come in," she called, and the door swung open, revealing a short, skinny girl who could not yet have celebrated her eighth birthday.

"Miss Maddie says you need to see me." The little girl stomped into the room. "But I didn't do it. I didn't touch Sarah's doll. I swear." She crossed her thin arms over her scrawny chest and stuck out her lower lip.

"Are you Johnny?" Josie asked.

"I'm Johnny," she said. "But I didn't do it."

"Of course, you didn't," Ashley said. "We never thought you did. We asked for you because we—well, they need your help."

The little girl brightened. "My help? Really?"

Josie added, "Do you think you could help us?"

The girl nodded. "What do you need?"

Josie could remember being that age and having her mood change from one instant to the next. She glanced at Westman, but he was eyeing the child as though she were a tiger. He was curious but wary.

"Do you see this box?" Josie asked the little girl.

She bobbed her head, blond curls bouncing.

"We own the box." She motioned to Lord Westman, including him. "But we seem to have misplaced the key, and now we can't get it open. Miss Maddie said she thought you might be able to help."

The little girl narrowed her brown eyes, then looked at the box, then back up at them. "I don't think that's a good idea."

Josie silently cursed Maddie. Her cousin had

done such a good job reforming these children that they viewed everything as a trick to get them to misbehave.

"This isn't a trick," Josie said patiently. "I know Miss Maddie told you not to pick locks and pockets anymore, but we really do own this box, and we really need to get it open. Can you please help?"

Johnny looked at her, then Westman. Westman shifted, and the chair suddenly looked too small for him.

"This is your box?" the little girl asked.

He glanced at Josie, and she stared right back at him. *Answer.*

"Ah, yes." He shifted again. "It was my grandfather's box. Now it's mine."

Josie kicked him.

"Ours."

"So it's not *really* your box?" Johnny said.

Westman rubbed his brow. "It's mine now that my grandfather is gone."

The girl looked uncertain.

"Look," Westman said, leaning forward. Josie prayed he wasn't too intimidating. "Can you help us or not? If you don't open the box, I'll have to break it open. Miss Hale would hate it if I broke her pretty box." He winked at the little girl. "Please help?"

Josie rolled her eyes. Now the man was flirting with orphans. But she couldn't complain when his attempt worked. The little girl took the box from the table and peered at it intently. Josie was aware that she held her breath, that all of them did, as the girl studied the lock.

Finally, Johnny looked up. "I need a hairpin."

Josie fumbled in her curls, but Ashley was faster. "Here, use mine."

The little girl took it, inserted it in the lock, and fumbled. The room was so silent that Josie could hear the ticking of the clock and the little girl's breathing. Johnny bit her lip and kept working.

"I have to catch the lock," she said, through her teeth clenched in concentration. "It doesn't usually take this long." She gave them an apologetic peek. "I don't practice anymore."

"That's okay," Josie said.

Johnny glanced up at them, then looked at the door, probably worried Miss Maddie would find her and scold her. Josie spoke to distract her.

"Johnny is an interesting name for a little girl. Is that your real name?"

The girl went back to the lock and the hairpin. "No."

"What's your real name?" Ashley asked.

The little girl clamped down on her lip again. "Joanna."

"That's a pretty name."

Johnny wrinkled her nose. "It's a baby name. I like Johnny. There!"

Even Josie heard the click as the lock turned. Johnny handed the box back to Josie, and she eased the top open. Three heads peered over her shoulder.

"Dinner is served!" Maddie called from the dining room. There was the thunder of feet on the stairs as a herd of orphans charged toward the food.

"Oh, drat!" Ashley said. "This always happens when something good is taking place."

Josie lowered the lid again. "Maybe it's better for right now. I'll tell you if we find anything interesting."

"Oh, very well." Ashley held out her hand to Johnny. "Ready for dinner?" And the two joined the rampage, shutting it out as Ashley, with a last wistful look, closed the door behind them.

Josie glanced at Westman. "Do you want to do the honors?"

"And be accused of not sharing information? I think not."

"Fine." With a flourish, Josie flipped the lid open and stared at the red velvet lining. She put her hand inside, ran it along the soft, worn material. "Nothing," she whispered.

Westman took the box and peered at its empty contents.

"I cannot believe this!" Josie wailed. "All this effort for nothing. It's empty! Why would our grandfathers store an empty box? Oh, I knew this treasure was bad luck."

"Perhaps the box wasn't empty when they stored it. It may have been looted." He set the box on the table, and Josie heard the faint thunk.

"Or perhaps they hid the contents inside the

box." She reached for it again and shook it lightly. Something rattled, and she felt a burst of sunshine in her heart. "Give me something sharp."

"I'm not the footman, Miss Hale."

Josie just managed to keep a frustrated sigh from escaping. Westman must have spent his tolerance measure for the day. "Very well. Your lordship, may I please have something sharp?"

Standing, he reached into his boot and withdrew a slim all-purpose knife. Josie took it and used it to slice the crimson lining. It parted easily, and she saw the glint of something gold. Her heart sped up. A doubloon?

The lining opened and Josie grasped the gold . . . key? It was an old-fashioned skeleton key with intricate curlicues in the bow. The blade was long and thin with a rectangle at the base.

"Is that it?" Westman asked.

Josie handed him the box, so he could search for himself. A key. She licked her lips. It wasn't as good as a doubloon, but it could prove promising.

Westman set the box down. "It's empty," he said. "Just the key. Try it. Let's make sure it doesn't fit the box."

Josie tried to fit the key in the hole, but the blade was too large. She smiled, loving the mystery. "So, we have a key without a lock. I wonder what else we'll find." She looked at Westman. "You said you found the information about the box in your grandfather's things. Did you see anything that needed a key?"

"No. Just a few papers."

"What other papers? Oh, never mind. I'll come over tonight, and we can go through everything again."

"Oh, good," he drawled.

"I don't know when I'll arrive. I have to wait until my parents go to sleep, then climb out the window."

Westman stared at her. "Climb out the window? No, madam. There will be no more going in and out of windows. Come to the servants' entrance in the back. I'll be waiting for you."

Josie reached up and ran a finger along his cheek. "I like the idea of you waiting for me."

Westman caught her hand, and his blue eyes were icy. "Stop flirting with me. You aren't prepared for the consequences."

"Why don't you let me decide that?"

"I've already decided."

She swung away from him, and he said to her back, "Don't be too late tonight, Miss Hale. I won't wait long."

Westman paced the small landing in front of the servants' entrance, then pulled out his pocket watch and checked the time again. How much longer was he going to have to wait? It was after one, and he'd seen Josephine Hale home over eight hours ago. Of course, he hadn't actually seen her to the door. He'd hired a hack and escorted her and her blond cousin home, then he'd had the hack take him to his club. It was unlikely anyone had seen him with the women as no one paid much attention to the myriad of hacks driving about the city, but he'd been careful to keep his hat low and his coat collar high.

After dinner and a game of whist at his club, he'd returned home at ten, as promised, and proceeded to wait for his neighbor for the next three hours. She'd said she had to wait to escape until her parents went out or went to sleep. What were they doing over there?

Stephen poked his head out of the servants' door again. The Hale town house was dark, and there didn't appear to be any movement inside. Had Josephine fallen asleep and forgotten her mission?

Tired of waiting inside, he paced the yard in front of the servants' door. It was a cool night, clear skies—if London skies could ever be considered clear—and Stephen thought he saw a star somewhere in the heavens above.

"Ouch!"

Stephen froze, cocked his head to the side, and peered once again in the direction of the Hale town house. Nothing.

"Drat!"

He clenched his jaw. He might have mistaken an owl's hoot for *ouch,* but owls didn't say *drat*. Stephen peered at his neighbor's town house again, and this time he saw her.

Hanging from her third story window.

"Goddamn it!" He threw open the side gate and

crossed the space between their houses in five long strides. "Miss Hale!" he hissed when he was below her. "What are you doing?"

She looked down at him and frowned. "Hush! My parents will hear you!"

He could see now that her gown had caught on something sharp protruding from the window, and she was having trouble freeing the gown and keeping her handhold. She had one leg balanced on the trellis and the other perched precariously on the window casement. She tried to free herself and pinwheeled her arms when she lost her balance.

Stephen felt all the blood in his body drop to his toes. "Miss Hale!" he shouted, trying to get under her. "What the devil are you about?"

"Shh!" she hissed back. "What do you think I'm doing? I'm trying to sneak over to your house."

Stephen began climbing up, using the tree and the trellis he'd availed himself of the night before.

"Don't come up here!" she shouted.

He ignored her and continued climbing. His arms protested. It had been some time since he'd climbed into a lady's window, and his muscles were still sore from the activity of the night before.

"I thought I told you no windows," he said. His breath puffed out as he pulled himself up to a higher limb. Why didn't anyone grow trees with branches close together?

"And I would have been more than happy to oblige," she said through clenched teeth. "Believe me."

He could hear the fury in her voice. Perhaps now wasn't the best time to point out that she'd made a mistake.

"But how do you expect me to sneak into your house without using windows? I can't walk through walls."

Stephen groaned and pulled himself up again. He was within three feet of her now. If he'd stretched, he could have touched the hem of her gown.

"No one"—he hauled himself up again—"expects you to"—he scooted out on the tree limb, faltering for a second then regaining his balance—"walk through walls. You could"—he held out his hand and fumbled with the trapped piece of her gown—"use the door."

She smacked at him, and he almost lost his balance.

"Hey!"

"Hey, yourself. Do you not think I would have used the door—any door—if I could have? My brothers just came in, and the servants are in the kitchen. This was my only option."

"Lovely option," Stephen muttered. Finally, he located the obstruction. Her gown had ripped, and a nail pierced the thin muslin fabric. He leaned out farther, teetering on the edge of the limb, and yanked at the material.

"You're going to rip it," she said.

He peered up at her. "Do you want me to free you or not?"

"Fine. Just hurry up."

"At your service, madam." And he tugged rather viciously, loosing the material and ripping it a bit more than was probably necessary. Bossy woman.

She started to move down, her slipper on the window casement finally finding a foothold on the trellis. Her hand followed, and she wobbled slightly as she found a place to settle.

Stephen held his breath, watching her negotiate the descent. He could just see the headline in the *Times* when she fell: "Westman finally takes vengeance on Hale." He shuddered. Killing Josephine Hale would not bring him the respect he desired. He doubted even India would be far enough to recover from a scandal of that magnitude.

"Miss Hale," he hissed when she was steady again. "I'm going to climb down. I want you to watch and then follow. Place your foot where I do. Place your hands where I do. Understand?"

"I can climb down on my—"

He grabbed her ankle and squeezed it tightly. "Miss Hale. For once—for bloody well once—don't argue. Just do it." Trusting that she was not as stupid as she acted most of the time, he began his descent, making sure to exaggerate his movements so she could see. He glanced up to ensure she was doing well and realized—purely by accident—his angle provided him a perfect view up her dress.

He looked away. Of course the chit would pick tonight to wear a gown rather than the trousers he'd met her in. Had she done it on purpose? He glanced up again, this time studying her face. Her expression was intent, her eyes studying the tree. She didn't appear to have any idea the view she was affording him.

Not that he could see everything. Her dress, though simple and light, was voluminous, and she was wearing a chemise underneath. Still, when she moved just right, when his angle was right, and when her skirts swayed just right, he had an eyeful. His mouth felt dry.

"Why are you stopped?" she asked, tearing him away from his admiration of her firm white bottom rising above her pale garters and stockings.

Feeling like a naughty schoolboy, Stephen looked away and quickly climbed down the last few feet. She came after him, and he took a deep breath and counted backward from thirty-seven to keep his eyes from roving back up. It was the hardest, longest thirty-seven numbers he'd ever tallied.

A moment later, she was beside him on the ground, wiping her hands on the dress. Stephen watched the movement, unable to stop imagining the treasures that lay beneath the thin material.

Looking up at him, she pursed her lips. "What's wrong?" She looked down at her dress and then back up at him.

He took a step back and—bloody hell—he felt his face flush. "Nothing. Why do you ask?" Damn it! He even sounded guilty.

"Because you're standing there staring at my gown. Don't you like it?"

"It's fine. I—I didn't even look at it. Not that I

was looking elsewhere—" Oh, this was no good. He cleared his throat. "Let's go inside." Taking her by the wrist, he led her through the servants' door and into his home. She went willingly, preceding him as they crossed the threshold.

Stephen watched her, knowing that if he followed her, his resolve would falter and fail.

For a moment, the image of another young, impetuous woman flashed in his mind. Smiling, teasing, moaning in pleasure . . . crying in shame.

Jaw clenched in determination, Stephen closed the door behind him.

Chapter 8

It wasn't fair, Josie thought two hours later when she'd gone through every paper James Doubleday had left behind. Westman had told the truth when he'd said that the only thing of interest in the stack of papers was the warehouse address. But it wasn't fair that they should come so far now, find the key, and then go away empty-handed.

Especially after she had nearly killed herself climbing out of her bedroom window. Much as she'd tried over the years, she'd never gotten past her weakness: fear of heights. She was such a ninny, which was all the more reason to keep pushing herself to overcome her cowardice.

Truth be told, she would have chosen just about any other way out of her house tonight.

But she'd faced her fear, hiding the terror and hysteria she'd felt from Westman, only to end up with nothing to show for it. Why, they hadn't even found the other half of the treasure map yet! Josie knew it must be here somewhere.

She'd gone through her own house too many times to count. It was not there. There was no other explanation for its absence. The map had to be here, in Westman's house. She was willing to bet on it. And she had. Involving Westman like this had been a risk, and it was still a risk. She still didn't know if she could trust him, not only with the treasure, but with the second and more important aspect of her mission—to clear her grandfather's name.

And then there was that other, rather stickier, issue. The more time she spent with Stephen Doubleday, the more she needed him as her first lover. Certainly, his ridiculous attempts to protect and shelter her annoyed and aggravated her. Certainly, he made her want to smack him when he began to lecture her about what young ladies should do.

But he also made her want to kiss him. His kiss outside the warehouse yesterday had been nothing short of . . . eye-opening. She had never been kissed like that. Never. Her heart had beat so fast and her pulse had raced so hard that she'd feared she would explode. And that had not been the worst of it. The quick shot of arousal that hit the pit of her belly and descended as a slow trickle of heat, lower and lower, had almost undone her.

No boy had ever made her feel like that before.

And she'd kissed quite a few boys. Several men, too. She was not a loose woman—despite the fact that she was now looking for a lover. She didn't allow men liberties, though her definition of *liberty* was probably somewhat broader than, say, Maddie's. But Josie's grandfather had taught her to be precocious. "Experience life and love to the fullest," he'd said.

And she was beginning to think that if she didn't have Stephen Doubleday as a lover, her life would be incomplete. She had to be kissed like that again. What would her life be if she never experienced sensations like those again? It wasn't that she wanted to marry him. She hadn't changed that much. She hadn't all of a sudden decided she wanted to be tied to a man *for life*. Even Stephen Doubleday, as intriguing and adventurous as he was, was still just a man—overbearing, domineering, and arrogant. Men like that were a shilling a piece among her circle. She didn't want to spend the rest of her life leg-shackled to Westman, but that didn't mean they couldn't enjoy a few hours together.

In bed.

Except that Westman, with all his noble reforms, wasn't going to touch her. And if he did, she half feared he'd try to force a marriage. And so she'd returned to where she had started.

She put down the last of James Doubleday's papers and sat back in the desk chair. Nothing about this search for the treasure or her partnership with Westman was easy. Maybe it was the bad luck associated with the treasure or maybe it was just her own impatience, but Josie felt further from finding the answers to her questions than ever.

She'd made Westman go through the books in his library, opening them to check for forgotten slips of paper, but he'd finished some time ago, and was now sitting on the couch across from her, eyes closed.

"That's everything," she said. He opened his eyes and Josie saw that they were red with fatigue. He looked so tired. "I've looked at each paper twice. I don't see anything relating to the treasure."

Westman rubbed the bridge of his nose. He had a very nice nose, Josie thought. It was long and straight and fit his face. But it was not so big or long as to get in the way when he kissed her. She'd kissed men with noses like that before, and the experience had been less than enjoyable. Not like yesterday with Westman. Everything about that had been enjoyable.

Josie bit her lip and tried to force her thoughts away from the tantalizing topic of kissing Westman.

"What do you say we go upstairs?" Westman said then, and Josie almost jumped out of her skin. She snapped her gaze to his face, but he was still lounging with eyes closed on the couch.

How could he make an offer like that and still look so unperturbed?

She cleared her throat, not trusting her voice. "You want to go upstairs?"

He nodded. "It seems the next logical step. There's nothing we can use down here."

Josie considered that statement carefully. She'd heard of men with strange perversions. "What do you want to use upstairs?" she said cautiously.

"What do I—?" Westman gave her a long look. "What I meant, Miss Hale, was that we might go upstairs, to the attic, and search through its contents. It's the next most logical place to search."

Josie stood, mostly to have something to do. "I see. Yes, you should have said so before. Let's go."

Westman stood and motioned to the door. She preceded him, but from behind her, she heard him murmur, "What did you think I meant?"

"Nothing." Josie walked faster. "Exactly what you said."

"No, you didn't. You had a look on your face, like a doe who's just heard the snap of the hunter's foot on a nearby branch."

"What a strange analogy."

"Appropriate, I thought."

"Not really." She walked faster, until Westman grabbed her elbow and yanked her back. He motioned her toward the stairs she'd just passed, and with a sheepish look, she started up them. There was absolutely no way she was going to reveal to Westman what she had really been thinking. Why give the man another opportunity to tell her he didn't want her?

They continued up the stairs in silence, but Josie was all too conscious that Westman was behind her. Was he laughing at her behind her back? Was he thinking she was the last woman he'd take to his bed?

Was he—oh, yes, please God—was he watching her bottom sway as she climbed?

She peeked back at him, but—drat!—he was looking over the banister at something below. Of course he was. Why would he pay any attention to her?

Finally they reached the stairs to the attic, and this time Westman took the lead. He carried a small lamp, shining light into the stuffy, uppermost room. Josie followed him. Obviously, she had far less willpower than he because she was unable to keep her eyes from his lovely rear view. He may not want her, but that didn't mean she couldn't look at him.

The attic was not exactly the kind of place that would further her romantic notions either. It was dusty and cobwebbed from disuse and held a faint dead roses smell she associated with her great-aunt Una. There was a small bed and a mirror in one corner, probably a servant's at one time, and quite a few framed paintings stacked against the walls. Josie caught her reflection in the mirror and winced. She looked a fright. Her hair was in wild disarray, her dress was wrinkled and torn, and she had a smudge of dirt on her nose.

She tried to wipe the spot off as she observed the stacks of furnishings—chairs, side tables, lamps, and decorative pieces—placed here and there. They were older pieces, nothing that might be considered fashionable now, but they were in good taste. Along with the furnishings were dozens of crates, stacked one on top of the other. The crates were generally unlabeled, and Josie foresaw hours of work ahead of her and Westman.

She glanced at him and knew he saw it too. Was he annoyed at the prospect of spending so much time with her or only annoyed at the large number of crates to sort through? Surely, he had better ways to spend his evenings than with a rumpled girl and a stack of crates.

Josie only wished she did.

But if spending the next few nights alone with her in a cluttered attic, going through crates bothered Westman, he didn't show it. Without hesitating, he went to one of the crates, pulled it forward and searched for a crowbar to use in opening it. There was one against the far wall, next to a crate that had once been opened and never resealed, and Westman took the tool in hand and heaved the lid off his chosen crate.

Straw spilled out, and out of courtesy, Josie waited for him to set the crowbar down before she began to dig through the straw. It was full of carefully packed porcelain figures—what might have once been a little girl's collection of shepherdesses and dairymaids. Josie brushed the straw from her skirts, sighed, and watched as Westman opened a crate of old linens next.

She watched him sort through the sheets, opening them and shaking them out. She thought about helping, but her mind was preoccupied. Had Westman guessed what she'd been thinking in the library? And why did it bother her so much to think that he had? After all, he was the one who'd seduced the map away from her last night, and he was the one who'd kissed her yesterday in Seven Dials. If he didn't want her to think of him as a lover, then why did he encourage her?

And—drat! a thousand times drat!—*why* didn't he want her for a lover? What was *wrong* with her?

She watched him shake out another sheet, and she couldn't stand it anymore. "Why don't you want me?" she said finally, much more forcefully than she'd intended.

"Huh?" Westman stopped shaking the sheet and gave her an uncomprehending look.

"I said"—she rose and brushed the dust and packing straw from her skirts—"why don't you want me? You can tell me, you know. It won't hurt my feelings."

"Tell you what?" Westman still held the sheet, raising it almost as a shield.

"Is it my hair?" she asked, fingering the cropped locks. "I know men tend to favor long hair, but it just gets in my way. Is it my hair? If it is, just tell me."

He stared at her, his eyes flicking to her hair, and then back to her face.

"My nose, then? You can be honest with me," she told him. "I know it's a bit sharp. Family trait, but I have nice lips. Or at least I've been told so, but"—she narrowed her eyes at him—"you hate my lips, don't you? *Don't you?*"

He shook his head. "What are you blathering about, Miss Hale? There's nothing wrong with your lips or your nose."

She opened her mouth, but he held up a hand.

"Or your hair. Now, can we please get back to work? It's late, and I'm tired."

"I'm tired, too, which is why I'd appreciate you just being honest with me. If it's not my hair or my face, is it my body?"

She glanced down at herself. She didn't usually give her figure much thought. Like all the Hales, she was tall and thin, with long legs and a graceful neck. She thought about Ashley, who men always called beautiful, and her cousin Catie, who had recently married. "It's my bosom, isn't it?" Josie tried not to be embarrassed at mentioning her breasts. She tried to behave as a woman of the world might, but it was rather difficult when she was not yet a woman of the world.

Westman blinked at her again. "Miss Hale, I don't—"

"They're too small." She cupped the offending flesh. "That's it, isn't it? That's why you don't want me as your lover. I'm too flat-chested."

"Miss Hale—"

"But I'm really not that flat. It's just this dress is a bit big for me, and these aren't my best stays."

"Miss Hale!"

She was close to tears now. Lord, had she ever debased herself so much? She must be more tired than she'd realized. She should just go home now, before she said anything truly mortifying. "I'm going home," she said, turning away from him. "I'm sorry to be such an idiot. Maybe that's why you don't want me."

She hadn't taken two steps when she glanced in the mirror directly across the room and saw him coming for her. He hesitated at first—his face a mélange of confusion, aggravation, and indecision— and then he moved so quickly that his arm came around her waist before she could even cry out. He hauled her against him, taking her breath with him so that she let out an unladylike, "oof!"

But then he was holding her. She was enveloped in his arms, and she hadn't realized before quite how thick his wrists were or how solid his chest was. And she didn't remember him smelling so good either. She wanted to lean back against him, but she didn't dare degrade herself further. Was he touching her just to show her what she could never have?

"God help me, but I do want you, Miss Hale," he said, and his velvet voice almost brought her to his knees. And then she deciphered the words.

Josie's head shot up, and she felt it smack into his chin. "Oh!" She craned her neck slightly. "I'm so sorry. What did you say?"

He rubbed his chin.

"Can you say it again? Please?"

He looked down at her with those hypnotizing blue eyes. "I want you."

"But my bosom—"

He chuckled. "There's nothing wrong with your breasts. Bloody hell, but I wish there were."

She felt his hand loosen from around her waist and inch upward. Her breasts tingled in anticipation.

"In fact, I wish I'd never met you."

"Why?"

"Because if we keep on like this, I'll ruin you." His hands caressed her abdomen as he spoke, and her belly tensed. "You'll lose your reputation, your family, your place in Society. You want adventure? This one might be your last."

"No reward without risk, Westman," she whispered. "That's what my grandfather always said."

He stared at her for a long moment. "You're so naive. So young. I'm a fool to want you. But I do want you."

"Why?"

"A hundred reasons." He kissed her nose. "Your mischievous smile." His breath was so warm and soft against her ear. "Your tempting lips. Your perfect breasts." His hands inched upward.

"You—you shouldn't say such things," she replied, but she didn't mean it. Not at all. She didn't want him to stop. Ever. His hand brushed against the underside of one breast, and Josie didn't want him to stop that either. But though this was what

Josie had wanted all along, she found now that it was happening, she was half scared out of her mind. Her legs had turned to jelly, and she could barely stop them from wobbling.

"They are the perfect size." His hand closed around her breast, kneading the sensitive flesh until her nipple puckered and hardened. His hand kneaded again, and this time she gasped at the heat that shot through her. "The perfect size for me."

And when she looked down, she saw that he was right. Her breast fit neatly into his hand, filling it but not spilling over. He flicked at her hard nipple, and she moaned. "Westman, I want you," she murmured, unable to stop herself. "Please."

She felt the uncertainty in him. She felt the way he tensed and the rigidity in his hand on her. And then she felt him give in. His body seemed to relax, to curve to hers, until she was a part of him. He held her, supported her, lifted her up.

And then his hand moved, lowering the bodice of her gown, lowering the top of her stays, and freeing her breasts to his touch. Josie sucked in a breath. She had allowed men to touch her breasts before, but she had never allowed it to go this far. She had never stood as she stood now, naked before a man's eyes. She could feel his gaze over her shoulder, feel him looking at her. And then she glanced straight ahead, and she was looking at him looking at her.

She had forgotten the dusty cheval mirror, clouded with age, but not so old that she could not see Westman and herself reflected in it.

Lord, the image was truly wanton. She stared at her breasts, exposed in the glass. They were round and pale, and the nipples were dusky rose. She stared at Westman's hand, resting just below her left breast. His skin was darker than hers, his arm holding her where he wanted. She loved the power in his posture. She loved the reckless woman she was in his arms.

And when his gaze met hers in the mirror, she loved the way he looked at her. It was almost a welcome home. She could see the longing in his eyes—the same longing she felt.

His hand moved, and he cupped her breast, pushing it up as though he were testing its weight. And then his free hand snaked about her waist, and he cupped her other breast, so that both his hands were on her. The pleasure was almost more than she could take. The pleasure of his touch on her breasts and the promise of his touch in other places. The place between her legs began to ache, and she shifted to ease the need there.

But just when she had succeeded, his fingers took her nipples between them, and he pulled the already tight buds tighter. Josie took a fragmented breath. She wanted to close her eyes, but she couldn't stop watching the picture in the mirror. She couldn't tear her eyes from the way Westman was looking at her.

He really did want her.

And then he released one breast, and Josie blinked from the loss of his touch. But no sooner did she open her mouth to protest, than his hand began to glide lower, and her every muscle tightened with anticipation.

"Oh, yes. Touch me," she moaned.

His lips were beside her ear. "Where do you want me to touch you, Miss Hale? Here?" He pressed against her belly, and she shook her head.

Lord, she was so wanton in his arms, so shamefully wanton, but she couldn't seem to stop. She didn't want to stop. "Lower," she whispered. "Touch me lower."

He glided lower, touching her pelvis. "Here, Miss Hale?"

She looked at him in the mirror, looked at his hand hovering just above the juncture of her legs.

"You know what I want," she said, her voice low and husky.

"Show me," he said against her neck, and she did. She took his hand, skated it over her pelvis, and buried it deep between her legs. She didn't need to tell him what to do then. He worked her through her skirts, stroking her, teasing her, making her moan.

And then he too moaned. She heard his breathing come faster and harder, and he spun her around, his hand never leaving off pleasuring her. "I have to touch you," he whispered. "I have to have you in my mouth."

Josie was almost afraid to know what that meant, but then he lowered his lips to her, took one long, hard nipple in his mouth and sucked.

"Oh, God," Josie said on a gasp. "Oh, yes."

He buried his head between her breasts and then after he'd kissed and touched and tasted to his satisfaction, he peered up at her. "See how little I want you? I've thought of nothing but this since you climbed from your window."

She frowned. Maybe it was the incessant, tantalizing movement of his hand, but she was confused. "Climbed down from my window?"

"I could see up your skirts," he admitted, his look unapologetic.

She almost laughed. "You're a bad man."

"Let me show you how bad."

And with one movement he flicked her skirts up and his hand touched bare flesh. Josie almost screamed. "Oh, God. Yes!"

His hand played her flesh, stroking and teasing until she was slick and pulsing with heat. And then, when she knew she could no longer stand, he lowered her to a bed of straw and knelt between her legs, spreading her knees. Josie didn't mind. She wanted him to look. She wanted him to see how wet she was, and how much she wanted him.

She opened her legs wider, loving the way his gaze on her felt. She was so hot, so coiled up, so ready to explode.

And then he bent and touched his mouth to her.

Josie bucked, unprepared for the exquisite torture. His tongue flicked out, and she bucked again. He tapped his tongue out again and again, and then he drew back. "There it is," he murmured with admiration. "The bud I've been coaxing out."

He lowered to her again, and this time when he touched his tongue to her flesh, the pleasure was so strong that she did scream.

"Come for me, Miss Hale," he said against her thighs, his mouth alternately sucking her and his tongue darting out to flick the nub of pleasure. "Come in my mouth."

He sucked and he flicked, and Josie writhed against him, coiling further, her muscles bunching, her toes going numb, and then she exploded.

Not quickly.

She exploded slowly and completely, her pleasure rising and rising, taking her hips with it, until she was so high she could hear the angels singing.

Except that wasn't the sound of angels. It was the sound of her own screams of pleasure.

Chapter 9

Stephen lifted his head, feeling as though he'd just downed a bottle of gin. He was drunk. Drunk on the woman in his arms. Her smell, her taste, the very sound of her voice had intoxicated him. That was the only explanation for the incredibly poor judgment he'd just exercised.

Unless one considered that Stephen Doubleday was the earl of poor judgment.

Stephen felt like slamming his head against the floor. Why did he keep doing things like this? Why did he keep mucking everything up? He'd promised himself he wouldn't get involved with Josephine Hale. He'd promised himself he'd not seduce another innocent.

And what had he done now? Gone and debauched

the most unsuitable woman in the entire country of England. At least unsuitable for him. He should be searching for a bride, a mother to bear him sons to continue the Westman title, not dallying with his family's enemy.

And she, well, she should be searching for a husband of her own. Except—

He glanced at her. Her eyes were closed, her breathing deep, and he could see the rapid-fire pulse at the base of her neck. She'd been magnificent. Really, truly, stunning. He wanted her in his bed, and imagining her with another man was not a pleasant thought at the moment. She should be his. But for their goddamned fool grandfathers, she might be.

"We should both be ashamed," he said, when she finally opened her dark green eyes and blinked at him. At his statement, she blinked again.

Stephen ran a hand through his hair. Perhaps he should begin again.

"What I mean is that we are becoming distracted from the task at hand. We should be spending our time searching for the treasure, not involved in this—" He tried to think of a word that would not offend her. "This debauchery."

Her eyes narrowed, and her eyebrows slammed together.

Stephen coiled for escape. Wrong word. Again.

She threw down her skirts, temporarily blinding him, and when he found his way out, she had her bodice put to rights, and her arms crossed over those small, perfect breasts. She was fuming.

"Now don't—"

"Don't be huffy?" she said, cutting him off. "In the space of half a minute, after the most wonderful experience of my life to date, you mention both shame and debauchery? And you don't want me to be huffy?"

Stephen raised a brow. "Miss Hale, you said you wanted a lover. Were you not prepared to engage in a bit of shame and debauchery? It would hardly be worth it if you did not."

She grunted and stood. "Well, you would know, wouldn't you? And you should be the one who's ashamed. All this time telling me you didn't want me as a lover, and then, when you have me feeling ugly and vulnerable, you seduce me!"

Stephen opened his mouth to protest, and then closed it again. It was a perfect seduction plan, only he hadn't actually thought of it. But he took one look at her now and knew she was in no frame of mind to be rational.

He had better stick with the basics.

"We are not lovers, Miss Hale."

She stopped pacing and cocked her head at him. "If we're not lovers, then what was that?" She gestured to her skirts and then to the floor.

"That," he said, rising from the floor she'd just accused, "was a mistake. I acted on an impulse. One impulsive act does not make us lovers."

"One impulsive—!" She stared at him, then backed away. Two steps. Three. "Oh, I see now." She nodded, still backing away. "I see how it is.

That was nothing to you, was it?" She shook her head, and said, almost to herself, "Silly me. The most wonderful experience of my life, and he thinks it's a mistake."

"Miss Hale," Stephen said, taking a step toward her.

"No." She held up a hand, turned, and began to descend the attic stairs. "I can see myself home. I'm certain you have better things to do than to waste your time with a mistake like me."

"Miss Hale!" he called, but she was gone.

Bloody, bloody, bloody hell.

He sank down on the crate beside him and put his head in his hands. Perhaps he was not as bad as he thought. How much of a rake could he be when he'd obviously lost his touch with women? They used to run to him, not away from him.

No, he amended, they'd always run away in the end. No woman stayed too long. He'd made sure of that. He didn't want commitment, didn't want emotion. He wanted companionship, varied companionship, and when one woman became too familiar, he made sure she wanted to go.

The scenes had not been unlike tonight's with Josephine Hale. But tonight was worse, far worse. Josephine was not some woman he could ignore on the street or in a drawing room. She was his partner. She was going to make him a hero—or at least her treasure was.

He could send her a letter of apology. He could send flowers. He could climb into her window and beg her, on one knee, to forgive him, but he knew none of it would work because there was one variable he'd forgotten.

She was a virgin.

"Damn." He stood and paced back and forth across the attic floor. He'd known it all along, but tonight confirmed it. In her anger, she'd said twice that their lovemaking had been the most wonderful experience of her life.

Now, Stephen knew he was good. He knew he could please a woman, but he wasn't vain enough to believe he was the only man talented in this area or even the best lover in London. Certainly his ministrations tonight had been intended to give her pleasure, but they were nothing compared to what he could do. Her pleasure had been minuscule compared to what he could have given her.

And himself, he thought, feeling the longing rise up inside him. Just thinking about her made him want her again. He wanted to hear those little mewing sounds again, he wanted to feel her tense and jump at his smallest touch, he wanted to taste her again, hear her laugh.

"Bloody hell," he roared, slamming his fist down on an old chest and slamming the emotion out of himself as well. He was beginning to sound like a besotted schoolboy. He didn't have *feelings* for Josephine Hale. He was not ever going to have those feelings for her. He didn't have the time or the leisure to fall— To have feelings for an unsuitable woman.

What he needed to do was to find that treasure and restore his family before all the shaky walls he'd built came crashing down. He'd repaid so much of his debt, but he still owed so much. If his investments failed, if his estates didn't produce, the creditors would descend on him and devour him and his family honor without compunction.

So to hell with his promises to Josephine Hale. He didn't need her to find this treasure. She was the one who'd left, not he. He'd find it without her and then, just to show her how magnanimous he could be, he'd give her the Hale half anyway. In fact, Stephen thought, picking up the crowbar and sliding it under the edge of another crate, he would probably work faster and more diligently without Josephine Hale to distract him. He'd go through the rest of these boxes and if they yielded nothing, he'd search his mother's house. The clue to that key had to be here somewhere. Maybe the other half of the map held the secret?

True, it was her map, but there was nothing wrong with him borrowing it for a day or a week or two. He patted his tailcoat absently, reassuring himself that the map was still there.

It wasn't.

Dropping the crowbar, he patted again, then removed the tailcoat all together and shook it. Still nothing, but Stephen could not believe it. He searched the coat again, and still nothing. How could that be? There was no way Josephine Hale had picked his pocket. Had he dropped it or—

And then he had a mental picture of his library. He had an image of his hand placing the map on the table near the couch he'd been lounging on. He hadn't wanted to wrinkle the map. Stephen sighed with relief, and then he remembered Hale's penchant for windows.

Swearing, he rushed down the stairs, all three flights, skidded through the entryway, threw the library door open, and stared.

It was gone. Of course.

She'd taken it. Of course.

He was a fool. Of course.

The next afternoon, Stephen tried not to look like he was pacing outside the bakery on Bond Street. He tried to look like he had an inordinate interest in the cakes and pies on display. He tipped his hat to the ladies who came and went and cursed the random footman who had told him Miss Hale had been seen inside.

Stephen craned his neck, trying to get a look through the glass and inside once again. But there were too many people inside, all ladies and all wearing bonnets. How was he supposed to distinguish Josephine from the rest?

The bell to the shop jingled again, and Stephen glanced dejectedly at the lady who emerged, carrying a white baker's box. It wasn't Miss Hale.

And then he looked again and jumped in front of her so quickly that he startled her.

"Miss Brittany! Forgive me," he said with a quick

bow. "I didn't mean to startle you. But, I own, I am glad to see you."

Ashley Brittany raised her blond eyebrows and gave him an amused smile. "I am glad to see you as well, Lord Westman. But never say you have been waiting outside this shop for me."

Stephen opened his mouth, prepared to flirt, and then decided he couldn't stomach it today. He wanted answers, and he wanted them fast. "Actually, no. I was told Miss Hale was inside. In point of fact, I was hoping to see her. Is she still inside?"

Miss Brittany shook her head. "She never was inside. I'm afraid your information is bad, Lord Westman."

"But you know where she is."

She glanced down, and he realized he was clutching her arm, his grip rather tight. He pried his fingers loose, and she continued to smile at him. "Lord Westman, might we walk a little way together?" She looked about herself, indicating the numbers of people passing them and, no doubt, taking note of their conversation.

"Oh, of course." He took the box from her and offered his arm. In fact, he was glad to leave the busy shops behind. No telling when one of the owners would recognize him and come out demanding payment on some familial debt.

Not to mention, lately a feeling he remembered well from his time in India had begun to niggle at him again. He felt watched. Followed.

With her footman trailing, they strolled a block

or two in silence, and then Ashley Brittany said, without looking at him, "What is your interest in my cousin, if you don't mind my asking? Is it still to do with this treasure map?"

"We are partners in that venture, yes," Stephen said carefully.

She nodded. "I only ask because back there, at the bakery, you seemed rather frantic to find her. My understanding is that the treasure has been lost for over fifty years. Surely a few more days will not disturb it." She gave him a sidelong look, her blue-green eyes full of mischief.

Stephen saw the family resemblance immediately. The cousins might not look alike, but they had the same mischief-making attitude toward life.

He continued to walk with Miss Brittany directing him occasionally, and Stephen thinking how to answer her question. He did not know how much her cousin had told her. Did she know everything and was now pretending not to in order to trap him in a lie? Or did she really think he and Josephine Hale were still just partners?

"Miss Brittany," he said finally, "I don't know what Miss Hale has told you, but I need to speak with her. If you could tell me where to find her away from home, I would be much obliged to you."

"Well, she's away from home right now," Miss Brittany said. "In fact, I'm taking you to her. You see, our cousin Cat—Lady Valentine—has just returned from the country with her new husband. We are all at her home."

Westman's hopes immediately rose, then sank. He had a passing acquaintance with Lord Valentine. But passing was not enough to warrant a visit to the politically powerful earl: a man who would one day be the Marquess of Ravenscroft and some even said the nation's prime minister.

"You see, Lady Valentine is planning a huge ball for her husband's political friends. Of course, she is terrified of balls and social affairs, and so we are helping her." She pointed to the baker's box. "I am in charge of the food. That is a cake sample I want the girls to try. It's absolutely divine."

Stephen was half listening, his own thoughts racing. If Josephine was going to be working with her cousin on a huge ball for the next few days that would mean she would be unlikely to have any time free to search for the treasure. And, of course, she had the map.

"I may be able to place your name on the guest list," Miss Brittany said. "You might speak with her there."

Stephen nodded. "That is very kind of you." Pausing to give her the box back, he bent and gave her a sweeping bow. "Good afternoon. If you could possibly do me one more favor. Might we keep this conversation between us? Would you mind not mentioning to Miss Hale that we spoke?"

At his suggestion, she pursed her lips and looked

past him. "I cannot make any promises, Lord Westman, but I shall try."

"Good enough." He bowed. "Good day,
madam."

Josie listened without interest as her cousins de-
bated the merits of the food arrangement at Catie's
ball. They were in Catie's bedchamber, the only
room not piled floor to ceiling with extra china and
linens, and Catie was holding court. They'd been
over the location for the ball, the invitations, the
guest list, and the cake—thanks to Ashley. Now
Catie had drawn a large diagram of the tables she'd
have placed in the dining room and she was attempting to decide where each dish should be placed.
She had placed various circles and squares on the
tables and wanted the girls to help her label them.

Josie sighed. She didn't really care if the straw-
berries were beside the pineapple and where the
roast beef fit in. She didn't know why any of them
cared because they would all probably be far too
busy to eat anything anyway. Poor Catie was so
frazzled and so terrified the ball would not go well
that Josie knew one of them would have to be beside her all night.

Catie was deathly afraid of social events. She
became short of breath and started to shake whenever she was forced to attend one of the *ton* func-
tions. She began to feel as though everyone and
everything was closing in on her.

Which was why it was such a beautiful statement of her love for Valentine that she was hosting this ball for him. If someone had told Josie a month ago that Catie was poised to be one of Society's most glittering hostesses, Josie would have laughed. Of course, she would have laughed if anyone had told her Catie would have married her sister Elizabeth's betrothed.

Catie was the first in their circle, the first in their childhood Spinster's Club, to break her vow and marry. Not that she'd intended to marry. She had been tricked, and yet, she did not appear at all unhappy with her husband. Well, he obviously frustrated her at times, but that was to be expected. Still, as difficult as Valentine could probably be—and Josie doubted he was that difficult, not as compared to *some* men, anyway—Catie had a look about her. She had a peace, a glow. She had adamantly denied being in love with her husband, but Josie didn't believe her for a moment.

Catie was in love, deeply in love.

Josie sighed as Catie started talking about the fish. Watching Catie, with her rosy cheeks and her eyes only for her husband, Josie almost wanted to be in love. Watching Catie, Josie almost wanted to marry. Almost.

It had been the right thing for Catie. Her father was a horrid brute, who would have sold Catie for ten pounds and beat her for less. Josie was glad Catie was away from him and in the arms of a nice man like Valentine.

But Josie herself had no such inducements to

marry. Her father was kind, if somewhat negligent, and though he wanted her to marry, he would never trick her into a union nor demand she do her duty. He had two sons. He would have grandchildren.

Her mother was not so kind. She was controlling and bossy, and her punishments were legendary. Once when she'd caught Josie sneaking out of the house at night, she'd made Josie stay in her room and read the entire Bible, cover to cover. Since Josie had only been ten, it had taken her over a month.

Another time Josie had been in trouble, her mother had made her write a twenty-page apology. Another time, she'd forced the twelve-year-old Josie to spend the summer learning to sew rather than playing outside with her brothers. The punishments would have been minor for most of Josie's peers, but to a girl who thrived on movement and fresh air, they were torture.

And Josie assumed marriage would be as well. Even though Valentine looked wonderful, Josie could not get past the problem that, while she liked Lord Valentine, he was nothing special. He was just a regular man. That was fine for most women Josie knew. It was fine for Catie. That appeared to be what she needed, but Josie would need much, much more to persuade her to marry.

She wanted a man who was unconventional. A man who treated her as an equal. A man who craved adventure like she did. A man who didn't insist she bear him a child every year and plan his lavish balls. She wanted a man she could confide in.

A man she could laugh with and dance with and make love to.

An image of herself in the mirror, a man's hands on her, flicked in her brain, but Josie shoved it away. No, Westman was not that man. She still wanted him as her lover, but it would have to be on different terms. She hadn't been prepared last night, and she'd made a mistake with him. She had allowed her feelings to interfere with her mission. Now she saw her own folly. She placed her hand protectively over her reticule, where she'd placed her half of the treasure map. She was not so much a fool as to leave it out of her sight again.

Restoring her grandfather's name and finding the treasure were the most important things. She wanted Westman, true, but she had to keep that separate. He was right. The treasure, their lovemaking, these were business ventures. She could not let her heart interfere. She needed Westman. All the clues were locked in crates in his attic. If she was going to have access to them, she couldn't afford to throw a tantrum because giving her the most amazing sexual experience of her life meant nothing to him.

"You don't look like your mind is on the punch bowl," Ashley said. She was sitting on the bed next to Josie, and Catie and Maddie were on the chaise longue at the end of the bed.

Josie blinked and sat up. "Of course my mind is on the punch," she whispered back to Ashley. "It's just that the punch doesn't occupy my every waking thought. I have other things to consider as well."

Ashley smiled at her, and Josie frowned. She didn't like that little smile of Ashley's. Her cousin looked like a cat with a feather sticking out of her stuffed mouth.

Drawing back slightly, Josie said, "And why are you smiling like that?"

"Like what?" Ashley's smile never faltered.

"Like you know something you shouldn't."

"Well, by all means," Maddie said, interrupting, "if Ashley knows something she shouldn't, then she should tell the rest of us."

"Either that or let us get back to what's really important." Catie shook her drawing. "The table configuration."

Josie felt like ripping the table configuration into ten thousand tiny pieces and then stuffing them all in Ashley's mouth so that she would quit grinning.

"Why do you think I know anything of interest?" Ashley asked. "Isn't a girl allowed to smile anymore without it meaning something?"

"Of course, but you're hiding something. I know that smile, Ashley," Josie said. "What is it?"

"Why don't you tell us, Miss Hale?" Ashley shot back. "I think you're the one hiding something." Now all of them looked at Josie, and she felt her face color. How ridiculous was that? Her cousins were making her blush?

But she wouldn't be blushing if she didn't have anything to blush about, now would she? And, really, they were going to find out about her and Westman anyway. What was the point in hiding it?

Then she looked at sweet, innocent Maddie and the happily married Catie, and she just couldn't do it. She just couldn't face all the questions and speculation. "Ashley, may I have a word with you outside, please?" Josie said, hopping off the bed.

"You two need privacy?" Catie widened her hazel eyes. "This is new."

"It's a surprise," Josie said. Ashley still hadn't moved to get off the bed, so Josie grabbed her arm and pulled. "For the ball," she ground out. Lord, Ashley was heavier than she looked.

"Wait!" Catie stood. "I don't want any surprises at the ball. I cannot manage surprises."

Josie sighed. "It's a good surprise, Catie. Nothing that will upset you. Trust me."

And she pulled Ashley through the door and into the hallway.

"What was all that?" Ashley said, pulling her arm back and straightening her skirts. "I'm sure whatever you have to say to me can be said in front of Maddie and Catie."

"But whatever you have to say cannot. Tell me."

"Tell you what?" Ashley's eyes looked big and green in the light of the hall. "I don't know anything." Josie was about to strangle her, when Ashley added, "I promised not to tell."

Josie stepped back, bumping into the wall. "Promised *who* not to tell? Tell what?" Her heart was thudding now. She knew she would reveal her tryst with Westman to her cousins at some point, but surely she should be the one to tell them!

And only them. But if Ashley had already heard, then . . .

Josie grabbed Ashley's arm. "Who told you? Is it all over Town now? Oh, God, please tell me my mother does not know."

Ashley glanced down at her imprisoned appendage. "Do you know that's exactly what he did to me?" She shook her arm. "And he was frantic, just like you."

Josie slowly released her cousin's arm. "Westman," she whispered. "That's what this is about. You saw him."

"I promised not to say," Ashley answered.

"But you did see him, didn't you? Was he looking for me? Oh, never mind." She shook her head. "He wasn't looking for me. He was looking for the map." Josie felt the tension drain out of her shoulders. It wasn't as bad as she'd feared. Her secret was still safe.

"He didn't mention a map," Ashley said. "But he was rather worried. Care to tell me what's going on?"

"Not yet."

"You know I'll find out."

"Not this you won't. Not unless I tell you." She knew Westman well enough to believe he didn't kiss and tell. So if they hadn't been discovered by anyone else, she was safe.

But now it was Ashley's turn to clutch Josie's arm. "You didn't—he didn't—you two didn't—"

Josie sighed in exasperation. This could go on all afternoon. "I'm still a virgin."

"But something happened," Ashley said, the knowing smile back. "Tell me."

"No."

Now Ashley looked hurt, so Josie took her hand.

"I want to tell you, but I just can't right now. Suffice it to say that we argued, and Westman lost." Lost the map and her friendship.

"Of course, he did."

Josie laughed. This was why she loved Ashley. No one but her cousins could be so loyal. "But he lost in a big way, and he's none too happy about it. And yet, I cannot allow him to win, Ashley." She didn't want to give him the map back, nor did she want to lose him as a partner.

But how could she keep working with him if he considered her a mistake and an impulse? Drat! He'd even said she was a distraction from the search for the treasure map. Well, she'd show him that she didn't care about anything but the treasure.

Ashley nodded and stroked a finger along her chin thoughtfully. "Well, then, there's only one thing to do." She motioned for Josie to come closer, and then whispered, "Let him think he's won. Give him what he wants. Do you know what that is?"

A business relationship. Purely professional. That was what he'd said. "Yes," Josie answered.

"Then give it to him. When he gets what he wants, you get what you want, too."

Josie considered this. For some reason, Westman did not want to admit his attraction to her, and they couldn't go back to working together if he avoided her, afraid that what had happened between them last night might happen again. But perhaps if she showed him she could rise above that and treat him purely—well, mostly—as a business partner, then they could both get what they wanted. She could have the treasure and perhaps, in the end, him as well.

"Well, what do you think?" Ashley asked finally.

Josie stepped back and stared at her cousin. "Ashley, you are truly wicked."

She smiled. "Josie, you're the one who still won't tell me what you and Westman did last night."

Chapter 10

❧ ❧

Stephen allowed one hand to glide down her slim, pale neck, while the other lowered her slowly to the library couch. She sighed with pleasure and made quick work of his waistcoat and cravat.

For his part, Stephen was just as eager. He couldn't wait to get the raven-haired beauty naked. She was short, round, and luscious, her breasts so ample they spilled out of her dress and overflowed in his hands. She had a quick smile, dewy brown eyes, and an eagerness that proved she'd done this before.

Many times.

Stephen clenched his jaw and tried to remember that was one of the reasons he'd chosen her. She was experienced enough to know that a night of lovemaking did not a lover make. And she was pretty enough to tempt him. He'd decided, after very little thought, that he had been celibate far too long. If he were going to keep his head with his partner in business, he had better find an outlet for his other needs.

And that was the other reason he'd chosen the voluptuous Alice Keating. She was nothing like Josephine Hale. She didn't sound like her, didn't look like her, didn't smell like her. Not that he was thinking about her—Josephine Hale, that was. He grit his teeth, and Alice, who had just opened the buttons on his shirt, looked up at him.

"What's wrong, Westman? Don't you like this?" She slid one hand in his waistband and tugged his shirt free.

Stephen kissed Alice again, then moved back, and pulled the shirt over his head. "I like it," he said, watching her eyes widen with desire when she saw his chest. "You're just what I need."

Reaching down, he pulled her against him and began to divest her of her own garments. There would be no rutched-up skirts and tugged-down stays tonight. He wanted her naked and warm when he plunged into her. He pulled the tie on the back of her round gown and then flicked the three buttons open. The shoulders of the dress slid neatly down, and he got the first sinful glimpse of her lovely pale breasts.

He bent to kiss them, just to run his tongue over the rounded tops, when he heard something above him thunk. Mouth poised above Alice, Stephen looked heavenward and listened.

One of the servants had dropped something. That was all.

He lowered his head again, but got no closer when he heard Maharajah growl.

Maharajah didn't growl at the servants.

And—wait a moment. What servants? Stephen didn't retain any but his housekeeper.

Stephen had the library door open in an instant. Maharajah was staring at the stairs and growling.

"What's wrong?" Alice asked, her voice petulant and full of disappointment. Well, he was disappointed too. His cock was hard and eager. He was more than ready, and yet he couldn't ignore the fact that his dog was poised to attack and that a noise had come from upstairs. There was no reason for his housekeeper to be moving things about upstairs at—he glanced at the clock on the library mantel—two o'clock in the morning.

Then he heard something else. This time it was a sort of scraping, and he cursed. He sprinted across the foyer—thankful he hadn't removed his pants yet—and took the stairs two at a time. Maharajah followed.

As he'd expected, the first floor was dark and silent, and Maharajah urged him higher. The second floor was equally barren, but Maharajah ran to the door housing the attic stairs. It was standing wide open. "Miss Hale!" he bellowed. Maharajah barked.

Another thunk, followed by a curse and the sound of scrambling. "Stay!" Stephen commanded and was up the stairs in time to catch her squeezing behind an old armoire. "What the devil are you doing?" he shouted when he saw her. It was a rhetorical question. He could see quite clearly what she was doing. Packing straw was strewn about the attic, the contents of a half dozen crates were scattered here and there, and Josephine Hale, dressed in trousers and a man's shirt, was covered with straw.

To her credit, she didn't hide. As soon as he burst in on her, she stood straight and brushed at some of the debris covering her. "Good evening, Lord Westman. I'm sorry to have disturbed you." But her tone was not the least bit apologetic, and she had a look on her face that could only be described as gloating.

Stephen advanced on her. It was bad enough that she had sneaked into his library, bad enough she had involved him in this chase for treasure, bad enough that he'd almost taken her on the floor of this very attic last night, but now she had come again, without his permission—again—and begun going through his private things. The Doubleday things, which were none of her business.

He closed in, his anger peaking, but she didn't back down or even look alarmed. "I can see you are in high dudgeon at being interrupted. Please, go back to"—she gestured absently at his bare chest—"whatever you were doing. I shall be quieter."

"How the hell did you get in here?" he said, voice low and menacing. Given three more minutes, he really was going to kill her. He'd grab her, break the attic window, and push her through. And then he'd jump too, because by the time she was done with him, he was going to be stark-raving mad.

"Don't worry, Lord Westman," she said, her look patronizing. "I didn't use the window. I came in through the servants' door."

He glared down at her. "When?"

She made a show of trying to remember, and then said, "Oh, while you were showing that woman into your library. I suppose with your faces all mashed together like that, you didn't take notice of me."

Stephen swallowed. She had been in the house when he and Alice had come in the door? "Alice has nothing to do with this. With us."

She shrugged, easily dismissing the woman and him. "I didn't say she did. Now, if you've all the answers you wanted, can I get back to business? You can go back to your . . . uh, entertainment for the evening."

Stephen took a deep breath and tried not to think how close that attic window was. He could drag her two feet and have her through in a matter of seconds. Then it would all be over. The misery would end. "I don't want to go back to my entertainment," he began.

"Really?" Josephine asked. "She looked rather pretty and, ah—well-endowed. Is she downstairs waiting for you?"

Damn. Alice. She was still downstairs and probably wondering what the hell happened to him. He looked back at the woman beside him. "You have to leave. Now."

She shook her head. "Oh, I don't think so. I have a lot of work to do here, and I know how you dislike women who don't pull their weight. That was the agreement we made when we formed this partnership. Was it not?"

Stephen opened his mouth and then clamped it shut again. "Are we partners once again? Are you back to sharing the map with me?" Damn it, but if he didn't need the money from the treasure so badly, he would have walked away from her and never looked back.

She pursed her lips. "Perhaps. If you hold up your end of the deal. I can't be the only one slaving away up here."

"Are you implying that I am not pulling my weight?"

She thought for a moment. "Now that you mention it . . ."

"Look, you little hellion—"

She held up a finger. "Language, Lord Westman. Really."

That was it. She was going through the window.

"Stephen?" a sugary voice called from below. "Darling, are you coming back? I'm waiting for you."

Stephen paused in the act of reaching for Josephine Hale. She raised one brow. "Stephen? How sweet. And you call her Alice?"

"Don't move," he said, knocking down the finger she still held up. "Don't even think about moving. I will be back in exactly three minutes, and you had better be right here where I left you."

She gave him a tight smile as he backed away. Damn. He just knew she was going to move as soon as she was through the door.

Josie watched him go, keeping her smile in place until she could hear him thudding down the stairs. Back to his little trollop.

Be calm, she told herself. *No emotions. You have to show him that last night didn't matter to you. You have to keep this partnership professional.*

Josie hadn't lied about seeing the two of them as she came in through the servants' door. She walked in on the one thing she had not expected to see. She should have been glad he was seducing another woman. She could have pilfered the whole house while he was thus occupied, but for some reason his liaison made her irrationally angry.

How dare he! How dare he, when he had just been with her last night? How could he go from her to—that?

Well, Josie had seen the trollop, so she supposed

she knew how he could do so. The woman was everything Josie was not. And didn't it boost her self-esteem to have to admit that?

The real self-esteem crusher was that she had cared so much. Josie kicked a pile of straw out of her way and went back to sorting through the contents of the last crate she'd opened. Actually, she hadn't sorted the contents of any of the crates. She had only opened them, loudly and with as much force and pent-up anger as she could muster. She'd wanted him to know she was here. She'd wanted to interrupt his little plans for the evening.

Not that she wanted to be his trollop. When they finally shared a bed, she would be using him, not the other way around. And she wouldn't feel anything more than pleasure. She wouldn't allow it to mean anything more to her than their liaison last night had meant to him.

But her new attitude didn't imply that, in the meantime, she was going to allow him to swive some woman while she did all the work searching for the treasure. And with all this work, who had time to take a lover? If she wasn't going to take a lover while they searched for the treasure, he wasn't either.

There was nothing but old silver in the crate, so she moved on to the next, filled with books and papers. A spark of hope ignited inside her, and she bent to remove the topmost items. Below her, she could hear the faint sounds of Westman and his trollop. It sounded as though he were showing her out. Good. She didn't want to have to start slamming the crowbar into things again.

On the other hand, she thought as she leafed through one book of poems and then set it aside, she didn't want to see Westman without his shirt again. Lord. She lifted another book. That had been a sight she was unprepared for. She'd never really given a man's chest much thought before. She'd seen her brothers shirtless from time to time and never took much notice. They were thin and tall like she, their chests scrawny and pale.

But Westman—well. She looked up, imagining him again. There was nothing scrawny about the man. His shoulders were impossibly broad and impossibly chiseled. He looked like a statue, each muscle and plane beautifully molded into perfection. His arms were muscled as well, so much so that she could see where one muscle merged into another. He was not beefy, but defined.

Josie forced herself to lift another book from the crate and flip through it. The house was quiet now. Westman would be on his way back, and she really should at least appear to be busy.

And then there was his abdomen. She had never even thought twice about a man's abdomen, but now she could hardly turn the thoughts off. She wanted to touch that hard flat expanse of skin. She wanted to run her fingers over those ridges of muscle and see what happened to Westman's blue eyes when she did so.

She wanted . . .

Frowning, Josie read the sentence her finger was on in the book she held.

"Corsicana was not at all what we'd hoped. In the future, as long as The Good Groom *doesn't need repairs, we'll skip that port."*

Josie's heart was beating so fast she couldn't even turn the page. The words were mere scratches in the leather-bound journal. They could have been written by anyone. She didn't recognize the handwriting, but she knew who had penned the entry.

James Doubleday.

And he'd been writing about his pirate ship—the ship he had shared with her grandfather—*The Good Groom.* She knew the name almost as well as her own. Her grandfather had spoken of that ship like a man speaks of his first true love. With shaking fingers, she turned another page and saw the date above.

12 January 1759.

One year before the treasure had been found and hidden. One year.

"I thought I told you not to move."

Josie jumped at Westman's voice. He was standing in the doorway, holding his shirt, but she barely noticed that he was still bare-chested. Wordlessly, she held out the journal, and he, seeing something of what she was feeling, didn't say another word, but crossed to her and took the book in his hands.

He looked at several pages, then flipped to the front. "My grandfather's journal," he said. He showed her the name on the inside cover, confirming what she already knew.

"We've found it," she whispered. Then, with more excitement, "We've found it!"

He looked at the book in his hands, flipped pages as though trying to believe what he saw was real. All his scowling from a moment before was gone, and his face broke into a huge grin. "We're going to be rich."

She laughed, and he reached down and pulled her to her feet. "We're going to be rich," he said, spinning her around. "We're going to be rich as kings."

Josie started laughing too, her mirth increasing when Westman took her in his arms and danced a little jig with her. Up and down the attic, stepping over boxes, spinning around they went, both of them laughing like loons.

And then suddenly they tripped over the books Josie had left out, and she almost fell. Westman caught her, pulling her close. Close enough for her to remember that he wasn't wearing a shirt. Close enough for her to remember the way it had felt in his arms last night. Close enough that she had to get away.

Struggling, she separated from him and turned, attempting to catch her breath and her lost composure.

"I'm sorry," he said from behind her.

She wasn't sure what he was apologizing for, but she nodded her acceptance anyway. "I found the journal in this crate," she said. "I suggest we search the rest of its contents and see what else we find."

But two hours later, they had nothing to show for their work except the journal. They'd been through almost all the crates, but only the one Josie had searched seemed to hold anything of James Doubleday's. Exhausted, and knowing she had to get home before sunrise, Josie plopped on the floor beside the journal. "I can't look any more," she wheezed, out of breath, her lungs choked from the dust. "I can hardly keep my eyes open, and I have to be at Catie's by ten for more ball preparations."

"Catie is your cousin?" Westman asked, piling items back into a crate. He glanced at her. "The one who just married Lord Valentine?"

"The very same."

Still crouching, he ran a hand through his hair, probably trying to put it to rights, but he left a smudge on his forehead. "There was some interesting talk surrounding that marriage. Something about him being tricked."

Josie kept her mouth closed. As a rule, she didn't gossip. As a law, she didn't talk about her cousins' personal matters.

"I am acquainted with Valentine," Westman said. "I know he was planning to marry Elizabeth Fullbright, Lady Valentine's sister." When Josie still didn't reply, he said, "You have some interesting relatives, Miss Hale. Are all of you troublemakers or only the women?"

At that, she laughed. "I assure you that neither Lady Valentine nor my cousin Lady Madeleine are troublemakers. As for myself and Miss Brittany, I will not venture to say."

"And only Lady Valentine married?" He shook his head. "Unusual family. I would have thought the four of you would be mothers twice-over by now."

Josie snorted. "Not likely. We're not only friends and cousins, but we're also members of the Spinster's Club."

Westman looked unimpressed.

"It's a club we formed as children. We promised never to marry."

"Obviously Lady Valentine broke the rules."

"She did, but don't think it will happen again. The circumstances of Catie's marriage were rather unconventional, as you've said. The rest of us will remain unmarried."

"But not virgins," he said, giving her an appraising look. "Your behavior when we first met makes a bit more sense to me now. But do you really think you'll never marry? How old are you?"

Josie huffed. "As though I would answer an impertinent question like that!"

He rolled his eyes. "Eighteen? Nineteen?"

"Eighteen."

"Why, you're still a child. You'll marry," he said, with a decided nod.

Josie glared at him, then leaned over and poked him in his arrogant chest. "Statements like that are precisely the reason I will never marry. I don't know what decisions my cousins will make, but long ago, I made a vow to myself that I would never marry a man who acted like—well, like you!"

He sat. "What's wrong with me?"

"Nothing. You're exactly like every other man."

"Sweetheart," he said with a rakish grin, "I assure you, I'm not."

"Oh, please." She pushed away from him, fanning her face. The room felt too hot and too small, and her gown felt too small. "You are. I am so tired of arrogant, domineering, bossy men. I am so tired of uninformed, egotistical men like you telling me what I will and won't do. You don't know me," she shot at him, her voice rising more than she would have liked. "You don't know my heart or my mind. If I say I won't marry, I mean it, and all you've done is give me every reason to keep reaffirming that vow."

"For a woman who has her own good measure of arrogance and who is more than a little bossy, you certainly have a low opinion of men."

"No," Josie said, rising. "I don't. I love men. I want to be in love with a man, and I want to be loved by a man. I want what you did to me last night to happen again a hundred times. But I will be damned if I am going to shackle myself to a man so I can have it. I'll be an independent woman, if it kills me."

Westman rose beside her, his face now devoid of the earlier humor. "And exactly how do you intend to be this independent woman? You are a lady, the niece of an earl. You can't go about seducing men all over London. You don't have the same liberties lower-class women have."

"Not yet, but were I to become independently wealthy"—she held up the journal, the key to the treasure and her future—"I could do almost anything I liked, and no one could say a word about it."

Now it was Westman's turn to snort. "And you really believe that, don't you?"

"Listen, Lord Westman, I don't want your opinions of me or my plans. I'm eighteen, and I am ready to start living my life. All I want from you is help finding the treasure that will allow me to do so. Then we can each go our separate ways. You to seduce more trollops and whores, me to find more adventure."

"Perfect," Westman said. "Then we are in agreement."

"Perfect," Josie answered. "Now, I'm going home and to bed for a few hours. I'll meet you here tonight."

"I'll be waiting." As she walked by, he plucked the journal from her hand. "And I think I shall keep this for insurance, in case you read something in it and decide to hale off to parts unknown without including me."

"Do not be ridiculous," Josie said, reaching for the book Westman held out of her reach. Dratted tall man. "I am not going to leave you out. I told you that before."

He shrugged. "You have the map. I have the book. That seems fair to me."

"It would." Josie started down the stairs, then called as she descended, "And let's not invite Alice along tomorrow night, Westman. Either that, or I'll have to start bringing my prospective lovers along. And I know you don't want that."

She heard something crash and kept walking.

Chapter 11

19 May 1759

I hate leaving Margaret.

Truly, 'tis the only thing I dislike about life at sea. I love the wind and the water and the storms and even the dead calm. I love the freedom of owning my own ship, making my own rules, answering to no one. I love seeing new places and tasting new food and buying exotic gifts . . .

For Margaret.

My Maggie. How am I going to make it six months—mayhap more—without you?

As much as I want to stay, I have to go. There are more adventures for me in this life yet, and she knew as much when she married *me. Only, now with little Jamie, for that's what we call James Jr., she's not free to enjoy them with me.*

So I'll sail the West Indies for both of us—all three of us. I'll buy her silk cloth for beautiful dresses and spices for delicious food and rum for us to drink on cold London evenings.

And I'll write in this set of six journals for both of us. This set Maggie gave me on the morning of our departure.

And maybe, if I have a spot of the old Doubleday luck, Hale and I will stumble across a bit o' treasure.

Stephen closed the book and let out a loud curse. Outside his library door, he heard something clatter and winced. He'd forgotten his housekeeper was about today.

But damn, how could he not curse? He had spent the afternoon reading the entire journal, and the first mention of treasure was on the very last page. Westman turned the journal in his hands. This couldn't be his grandfather's only writings. He was a man who obviously felt the need to put his feelings on paper. Stephen now knew he was a man who loved his wife, loved his son, but who also loved his freedom. He'd led a fascinating life, and Stephen had no doubt he'd captured that fortune in gold doubloons.

But where the bloody hell was the story about it?

There had to be more journals. His grandfather had mentioned a set of six. If this was the first, then there would be journals that came after.

But bloody well where?

He'd searched every inch of his house. He and Josephine Hale had searched the entire attic, and this was it. The only journal. These writings and a key that didn't seem to fit any lock were their only clues.

There had to be more, but where?

Stephen ran a hand through his hair and tried to think where else his grandfather's things might have ended up. He'd been sent to India eight years before by his ailing father, the Jamie mentioned in the journal. His father had threatened to have Stephen kidnapped and transported against his will if he did not agree. Stephen was a disgrace to the family—a dissolute rake, who finally ruined one woman too many. And maybe his guilt over that last act forced him to acquiesce to his father's will. He left for India willingly.

He'd been in India when his brother, James, had become the earl. His mother's letter describing James's illness had been followed so closely by the news of James's death, that Stephen had not even had time to think of going home. Given the choice, Stephen would not have returned. It was not as though he were welcome.

When he'd returned to claim the title that was now his, his mother, all her things, and all of his brother's things were gone from the house. But was that all she had taken?

He shook his head. His mother had nothing to do with this. Why would she take her father-in-law's possessions with her? She'd never even met the man.

But his grandmother . . .

The Dowager Countess, Margaret Doubleday.

Stephen hadn't seen or spoken to the woman in years. He had heard that ever since her husband died, she'd been a recluse, preferring to spend the majority of her time in the country. At one time, she had been a belle of Society, setting the fashion, attending every ball and theater. But something had happened, and she'd changed. By the time Stephen had reached a majority, she almost never came to London at all anymore.

His few memories of her were of a woman with haunted eyes, who constantly looked over her shoulder. He could hardly reconcile this portrait to what he read of her in the journals.

And yet, if anyone knew something about James Doubleday, it was his grandmother. Where the hell was the old woman now anyway?

An hour later, Stephen was pacing his mother's drawing room, waiting for her to appear. She had a small house on Mount Street with large windows that gave her a good view of all that passed outside. He did not see her often. She had never forgiven him his youthful transgressions. In particular, she blamed him for losing the family fortune, though it had been her husband who decided to honor Stephen's vowels. Lord Westman could have refused. It would have destroyed Stephen's honor, forced him to flee to the Continent, but at that point, his parents would have been glad to see him gone.

And they did see him gone.

Stephen had hoped, upon returning from India, that his mother's attitude toward him had changed. He was the earl now, and she had always favored his brother, the heir.

But he'd been mistaken. It hadn't been the title she loved, but her first-born, James. And no matter what he did, Stephen couldn't be James.

Now Stephen paced the room a few more times, refused a third offer of tea from Phillips, her agitated butler, and then almost pounced on his mother when she finally opened the door. She held up her hand when he went to her to kiss her cheek, and he had to settle for a formal bow.

"Stephen." She nodded at him and crossed to her favorite chair. The one overlooking the street. "This is an unexpected visit. To what do I owe the honor of your presence?"

Her hair was white and looked heavy in its chignon at the back of her head. Her face, always pale, was even paler now with only the faintest color in the cheek. Her neck was long and regal, her hands small and delicate, her eyes brown and uninterested. Stephen pushed onward.

"Mother, I am sorry I have not called before now. I trust you are doing well." He sat opposite her on the green damask couch.

She waved a hand. "And if I died, would you really care?"

"Of course. But you're not going to die. You're in excellent health."

She gave him a piercing look and went back to her perusal of the street. "There are other things that kill a person besides failing health. Shame, for one."

Stephen looked down at his hands, feeling the sting of her censure. He had done all he could to save the family from social and financial ruin. He'd more than proved he was capable of the task, but she was never going to see that. He was not James, her eldest, her favorite

"Actually, Mother," Stephen said, trying to keep the mood light, "I've been thinking a bit about our family history myself." She hadn't been referring to the shame of that, he knew, but it was as good an opening as he was likely to have today.

"I was in the attic the other night—"

"Whatever were you doing up there? Dallying with one of the maids, I suppose."

Stephen clenched his hand on the chair's arm. "No, Mother. I was going through some of the crates, and you will never believe what I found."

She gave him a look that seemed to indicate he had failed to impress her before.

"Grandfather's journal," Stephen said, holding the book aloft for her to see.

She blinked and went back to her view of the street.

"I was reading it today," Stephen said as though she cared, "and I found at the end the journal ended rather abruptly. I thought I might finish out the memoir, but I couldn't find any other journals. Do you know where they might be? With Grand-mother, perhaps?"

His mother turned to him and gave him an icy stare. "You have come to ask me about journals? In this time of crisis, you have come to ask me about *journals*?"

Stephen shifted in his chair.

"You are worthless. Worthless!" she spat and stood. "Why did I ever waste my time with you? I should have killed you when you were born, you useless scamp."

"Mother, I hardly think—"

"No, you never did. That was the sole territory of your brother. You lie around all day and read journals. Do you realize our family is ruined? Do you realize we are all about to be evicted from our homes? Is that what you want? Do you want your mother living on the streets?" She was screeching now, and Stephen had to fight to keep his own voice level.

"No, Mother, that is not what I want. And we are far from destitute. I'm doing my best to restore our fortune."

"Your best." She sneered at him. "What an oxymoron." She strode toward the doorway, and Stephen rose and went after her.

"Mother, all I want from you is Grandmother's address. At least give me that."

Without pausing, she said, "Ask Phillips. In fact, from now on, if you have something to say to me, say it to him. I am certain he will relay the message." She opened the door and Stephen closed his eyes when it slammed closed again.

"Sir," came a small voice from the corner with the tea tray. "May I show you out?"

It was Phillips. Stephen rubbed the bridge of his nose. "Yes, thank you."

The stiff-necked man led him down the stairs and opened the door. Before Stephen could replace his hat, though, Phillips leaned close. "The Dowager, your grandmother?"

Stephen raised his eyes to meet Phillips's. "You know her address?"

"Twenty-eight Swallow Street, my lord. Just south of Hanover Square. The house is green and brown, my lord."

Stephen nodded. "Thank you." He replaced his beaver hat and turned to go.

"My lord, one more thing."

"Yes, Phillips."

"Her ladyship, sir, your grandmother, is not at

home. We had a letter from her last week, and she won't be in Town for another month or more. Your mother's eyes are weak, my lord, and I read the letter to her. Pardon me, my lord, but I thought you might like to know. In case you"—he glanced behind him—"needed the journals soon."

Stephen smiled. Phillips wasn't half bad. Now if only the old butler could teach his mother some civility. "Thank you, Phillips." Stephen pressed a crown into his palm. "Let me know if you come across any other interesting information."

"Yes, my lord," Phillips said, pocketing the five shillings and closing the door.

"It took you long enough," Stephen said, stepping out of the shadows between his house and the Hales'.

Josephine jumped and whipped to face him. "You frightened me," she chided.

He'd just watched her shimmy down the trellis and the tree outside her bedroom window. He was finally able to breathe again, and he didn't really care if she ever did so again. She'd scared him half to death.

As usual.

But he'd be damned if he'd let her know that. He wasn't the liberal egalitarian she seemed to want in her bed—nor did he want to be—but he could at least spare them further arguments, if he kept his mouth shut and allowed her to think he was somewhat unconventional.

"What are you doing out here?"

"Waiting for you." He took her arm. "I'm taking you on an adventure."

"Adventure?" She gave him a curious look but didn't resist as he led her to the front of the house, where he'd had a hack waiting for the last hour. He paused in the shadows, looking up and down the street. Again, he was reminded of his time in India—felt dark eyes on his back, heard the hiss of whispered words—and yet he saw no one. Still, he hurried Josephine across the way and handed her into the carriage.

He gave the jarvey the directions, then sat back and smiled at his companion. She was wearing an old shirt, trousers, and a coat tonight. Her red hair was pinned under a boy's cap. Anyone who saw them would think she was a lad, unless they came close enough to see the delicate cheekbones or the long, thick lashes of those sparkling green eyes.

"So what is on Swallow Street?" she asked when they were underway.

"My grandmother's house. I read my father's journal today—"

There was a cry of protest from the other side of the carriage.

"—and when I finished, I realized there must be other journals."

"You read the journal. *Without me?*"

"So I went to my mother's house and asked her about them. As usual, she was singularly unhelpful, but another friend was kind enough to give me this tip. My grandmother is not at home, so we will have to sneak in. Your favorite pastime." He finally paused and looked at her.

"You read the journal without me?"

With a sigh, he extracted the book from his coat and handed it over. "I was trying to save us time, not keep the book from you. Read it at your leisure, but start with the last entry. That is the one that mentions treasure."

"Really?" Dipping her head, she began to thumb through the worn pages.

"Unfortunately, the date is May 1759. We need something a bit more recent, and I thought the most likely place for the rest of the journals to be kept was at my grandmother's house."

"Yes, mmm." She was angling the book, attempting to read in the weak light from the carriage lamps. Stephen realized there was no point in trying to speak to her now, so he leaned back and watched Piccadilly go by until they finally turned onto Swallow.

"Miss Hale," he murmured, when he saw the jarvey pass number twenty-eight. "Put the journal away. We're almost there."

He'd instructed the hack's driver to drop them farther down Swallow Street, almost to Oxford, so that none of his grandmother's neighbors would see a carriage stop before her empty house. This way, they could also find a back way inside. Stephen didn't expect any of his grandmother's servants to be about, not with a month or more before the old lady would arrive, but he intended to be cautious.

Stephen had found that Josephine Hale could be quite reasonable—when he wanted her to do something she wanted to do—and she followed him without comment through back alleys, over gates and fences, and finally to the back of his grandmother's house.

He gave each of the windows a try, but they were all locked. He'd been expecting as much, so he pulled the crowbar he'd taken from his attic out of his greatcoat.

"Good Lord!" Josephine took a step back. "What are you planning to do with that?"

Stephen gave her a grin and swung at the window. The crack of the glass was loud, and they both held their breath for several moments. A dog barked and then all was silent.

Easing a hand inside the window to avoid wounding it on the shards of glass, Stephen turned the lock. He raised the window and looked at Josephine. She wanted unconventional.

"Ladies first."

Chapter 12

⌒◯◯⌒

"**L**adies first?" Josie said. Of course, now that there was something dangerous to do, he was the soul of chivalry. But she wasn't about to let a dark night, an empty house, and a teeny bit of breaking and entering scare her. If he wanted her to go first, she'd show him.

Of course, perhaps this was the time when the treasure's bad luck would catch up to her. Maybe there'd be some old butler inside the house, pistol primed and ready to shoot her dead as soon as she was inside.

Bad luck or no, Josie was too close to the treasure to stop now. Hoisting herself up, she crawled through the window, managing not to knock anything over once inside. It took a moment for her eyes to adjust, and when they did, she saw she was in the music room. There was a small lamp near the window, and she moved it aside as Westman came through.

Once inside, they lit two lamps, and he led the way through the silent house. They surveyed most of the ground floor as well as the first floor, and then Westman led them back through the music room to the book room.

"We'll start here," he told her. "We'll check all the books on the shelves and then pull them all off to make sure the journals aren't hidden behind them."

Josie nodded, sighing inwardly. There were dozens of shelves and all crammed with books. She didn't even know Westman's grandmother, but she wished the lady wasn't such an avid reader.

By tacit agreement, she and Westman started at opposite ends of the room. Josie took the ladder and climbed to the uppermost shelf, holding her lamp high enough to read the titles. She shivered. Without a fire, it was cold in the house and musty-smelling. And she was so exhausted that the titles swam together before her eyes. The late nights with Westman and the planning of the ball with Catie meant she'd had about six hours' sleep in the last two days.

But she couldn't let Westman see how tired she was. If she didn't work as hard as he, he'd never let her live it down. And she didn't like how he always seemed to be one step ahead of her. She hadn't even read the journal, and already they were searching for another.

But at least he had proved he was capable of treating her as an equal. He had waited for her before coming here, and she'd been the one to go in first.

Josie took down a row of books, attempting to keep them in the same order. She placed them on a side table and held her lamp to peer into the empty space.

Nothing.

She began to replace the books. So what did Westman's sudden change in attitude mean? Had he actually listened to her when she'd gone on and on about arrogant, bossy men? That was more than she could say for most men of her acquaintance. But perhaps, as she'd heard her mother and aunts say, on occasion, men could be trained.

She began work on the next shelf and glanced at Westman. He, too, was examining books, picking one up, studying it, then setting it back again. His hair had come loose from the thong he used to hold it back, and it fell around his face, making him look just that much more feral than his cohorts.

Lord, she could see why all the ladies were after him. She could see why rooms quieted when he entered. And she could see that it was going to take more willpower and concentration to keep her thoughts where they should be.

She was going to find a clue to the treasure, not ogle Stephen Doubleday. She was going to figure out what lock that key fit, not imagine him without his shirt on. She was going to find the other half of her treasure map, not remember how his lips had felt on her body. She was going—

Drat! She tossed a book down hard enough that Westman looked over at her. She gave him an apologetic wave and went back to her searching.

She was going to go insane if she didn't take a lover soon and get Westman out of her mind.

She lifted another book, studied it, and set it aside. *Focus on the treasure, Josie. Remember what's important.*

She picked up another book, trying her best to focus. There was no title. She couldn't remember if any of the other books had had titles or not, so she hoped this was the first. She flipped the book open, and then almost fell off the ladder.

"Westman," she said, her voice low and breathy with excitement.

"What's wrong?" He was already halfway to her. "Do you feel faint? You should lie—"

"Oh, stubble it, Westman. I found another journal." Like the first, it was small, barely bigger than her hand, and made of tattered leather and yellow pages.

Together, they searched and found three more— identical to the first—and since Josie wasn't about to be last to know this time, she made Westman promise to read them with her.

After restoring the book room to rights and closing the drapes over the broken window in the music room, they went back to Westman's town house. An hour after their arrival, they had their heads together, leaning back against his couch, reading the journals aloud.

Josie had never known James Doubleday, and the more she read, the more she wished she had. He was amusing and passionate and unconventional in just the sort of way a man should be. Until his son Jamie had been born, his wife Margaret had sailed the open seas with Doubleday and Josie's grandfather.

Even after Doubleday had been made an earl, he'd taken his countess with him. The lovely Maggie could shoot, swear, and steal with the best of the pirates. And James knew her value. He never tried to hold her back because she was a woman, and it wasn't until after the birth of their son, that she asked to stay behind. James had wanted her— had wanted them both to go with him—but he knew that Jamie meant more to her now than any adventure on the sea.

Josie found herself looking forward to the arrival of Westman's grandmother in Town. She'd like to meet the adventurous Maggie.

Josie's own grandfather was mentioned often, but the tidbits were rarely personal. Josie knew enough to fill in the lines. Her grandfather's marriage had been more conventional. Her grandmother had never been on *The Good Groom*. Sometimes, before her grandmother's death, Josie liked to think that her grandmother pretended her husband had never had a career as a pirate. She'd certainly never discussed it with her granddaughter. Whenever Josie had mentioned the treasure or pirating, her grandmother had given her embroidery to do and told her to practice.

Josie had sat with needle and thread as long as she could and then ran to play with the wooden cutlass her grandfather had made her brothers—the cutlass in which the boys promptly lost interest but which she cherished.

Throughout her childhood, Josie wanted to be a pirate. Now, through James Doubleday, her family's archenemy, she was reliving her grandfather's adventures all over again.

"This is the last one," Westman said from beside her. His head and shoulder touched hers, and he was a warm comfort next to her. For the most part, he'd been reading out loud, and that was fine by her. She liked listening to his deep, melodic voice. Liked pretending it was James Doubleday's.

She set aside the journal and Westman opened the last one, "Twenty-third May 1759," he read.

Josie closed her eyes. In her mind, she saw the voyage to the West Indies, she could picture the posts where the ship docked to buy supplies and trade goods, and she was there when Nathan Hale and James Doubleday first heard about the Spanish ship, heavy with gold doubloons.

"It's nothing more than a myth," Nathan told me after we left the tavern. "There are

as many myths of gold and treasure as there are blades of grass in the New World. I won't sacrifice the cargo we have to chase after dreams."

I followed through the winding alleys back to the rowboat, where One-Eyed Jack and Scaggs were waiting for us. It was hot and the harbor was full of the smell of dead fish and rotting fruit. But on the breeze coming down from the mountains, I could smell other things too—the perfume of the doxies, the campfire where a black man fried a fish for dinner, the damp, cool air up in the hillsides. And I could hear the sounds of the tropics, which are never quiet as people in London imagine. Insects buzzed, birds sang, and the waves lapped at ship and shore.

When we were in sight of our men, I put my hand on Hale's shoulder. I wanted to say my piece before the men could hear. One-Eyed Jack, in particular couldn't be trusted.

"I have a feeling about this one, Nate. Now, I don't say that often, and I don't say it lightly, but I'm saying it this time."

He was listening, but I could tell he was none too happy, so I said, "If I'm wrong about this one, if there's no Spanish treasure ship heading this way, then I'll give you my share of the profits on this voyage for putting up with me and going out of your way."

Now he was really listening. Hale was a

*shrewd businessman, never one to pass up a
good bargain.*

"And if there is a ship?"

*"And we manage to take her? We split the
treasure right down the middle. There's no
losing here, Nate."*

*"Not unless we get blown out of the wa-
ter," he said.*

But I knew then that I had him.

Westman stopped reading, and Josie looked up
at him. "Would it be terrible of us to skip to the
end?" she asked.

He chuckled. "Don't tell me you're one of those
people who reads the last page first."

But, she noticed, he was already flipping pages,
scanning the text.

"I can be a bit impetuous," she admitted.

"You don't say. Here, this looks like what we
want."

It was a detailed account of how they spotted
the Spanish ship, chased her down, and boarded
her. They'd lost Scaggs and several other men in
the battle, but they'd left the Spanish ship to limp
along, its burden far lighter.

Though the account shied away from mentioning
too many of the gruesome particulars of the battle,
Josie could imagine the crew's state: men with cuts
on their heads, blood streaming into their eyes;
men with stumps instead of arms; men whose

wheezes for breath punctuated the silent night, but who were themselves silent in the morning.

Suddenly she understood why her grandfather had always said, "There is no glory in battle, only relief that it is over."

Sickened at the thought of the carnage and senseless loss of life, Josie reached over and turned the page. Westman, who had been reading, looked up at her.

"We have to know where they hid the treasure," she said and kept turning page after page of descriptions of the voyage home. Finally, on the next to last page, there was mention of their pursuit and the hiding of the treasure, but the man who had painted a detailed map of the islands and the voyage was woefully scant in his details of the hiding place.

"He doesn't even mention the map!" Josie said, thrusting the offensive book at Westman. "All he says is 'Hale and I made note of where we left the doubloons.' That must be the map, right?"

Westman nodded, reading the page again for himself.

"Wonderful! But we don't have the other half of the map—your grandfather's half. What did he do with it?"

Westman was still reading, turning the last page to be certain no other text remained. As Josie watched, a small envelope floated out from the back cover and landed on the floor.

She looked at Westman and they both reached, their heads banging together in the process. Rubbing her ringing head, Josie let Westman take the envelope. He held it up, studied it, then said, "I think I know where we'll find the map."

Stephen stood at the entrance of Thomas Coutts & Company at Number 59, The Strand, and restrained the urge to check his pocket watch. Again.

Josephine Hale was supposed to meet him here at eleven sharp, and it was half past. Thus far, he'd seen no sign of her. The slip of paper with the bank's name was burning a hole in his pocket. Stephen closed his eyes and saw the paper in his mind.

Safekeeping

Coutts

The numbers and letters scrawled in an unfamiliar hand had to refer to the private banker to the *ton*. Stephen was wagering everything that the key from the warehouse in Seven Dials would open whatever his grandfather had left in the bank's vault.

He looked down The Strand again, toward Whitehall and then Fleet Street. But how the hell long was he going to have to wait? If Josephine didn't arrive soon . . .

He peered toward Whitehall, where at the corner of one of the smaller lanes he saw a flicker of a parasol. A moment later he saw the parasol again, followed by a small face, and then both were gone again.

Stephen sighed. Did the woman really think she was being inconspicuous? He began marching toward the corner, reaching it just as she poked her head out again.

"Eek!" she said, when she saw him on the other side.

Stephen reached out and grasped her arm, pulling her and the white parasol into the open. The pretty parasol matched her dress. It too was white with small pink flowers and a light dusting of ruffles and flounces.

God, she looked pretty.

"What are you doing?" he said, ignoring her ripe lips and her pink cheeks, and urging her toward the bank.

"I'm trying to keep out of sight," she hissed, angling the parasol so that it hid her face from passersby. It also knocked him in the forehead. He swatted it away.

"You're going to take an eye out with that."

"It's just until we're inside. If my Mother hears—"

"Yes, I know. The world will end."

She glared at him, closing the parasol as the bank's doorman did his duty. "One day you will meet my mother, Lord Westman, and then you shall see that I do not embellish."

They stepped into the bank, and a small man dressed in black and wearing spectacles approached. "My lord, how may I help you? Making a deposit, perhaps?"

Stephen scowled. He'd been afraid the visit would be less than pleasant. He'd taken out a loan when he'd returned from India to cover his family's expenses, and a payment was due shortly.

"Actually, I would like to take a look at the vault. I believe I have an item in safekeeping."

The bank manager raised his eyebrows and nodded. "What is it, my lord?"

"Something the first Earl of Westman left here," Josephine provided, and the manager's eyebrows rose again.

"Is this the lady's item or yours, my lord?"

Stephen cleared his throat. "Both."

The clerk's eyebrows reached new heights.

"Here, I have the key." Stephen extracted it before the man could ask any more questions or think of reasons to protest.

"One moment." The clerk spent a tense five minutes with another man—perhaps the bank's senior manager. They consulted a large book, conferred, and the junior manager returned carrying a key to the vault.

"Right this way." He motioned toward the back of the bank where there was an impressive set of metal doors. A narrow, spiral stairway led to the bottom floor, which housed the vault and the items left for safekeeping.

Stephen bumped into Josephine, and she elbowed him aside, taking the key from his fingers as she did so. "Ladies first, my lord. So kind of you always to remember that."

Stephen clenched his hands, imagining her pretty white neck between them, and then he followed her through the metal doors the clerk held open for them and locked again as soon as they passed through. Two men stood guard at the bottom of the wrought-iron stairwell, and Stephen looked at them in surprise. They looked more like pirates than guards. One possessed only a single eye.

Ahead of Stephen, the vault was dark and smelled of camphor and old money. The manager paused to unlock the vault's gate and then motioned them both inside, locking the gate again from the inside. Josephine glanced at him, green eyes shining like a cat's in the dim light of the lamps. Her excitement was contagious, and Stephen felt his own pulse quicken.

This was it, the end to all his worries, the end to his reputation as a dissolute younger son.

The clerk walked down what seemed to be miles of boxes and doors, each labeled with a small name or number etched in black.

"That's it," Josephine said, pointing to what looked like a treasure chest. "That must be it."

"Do you have the key, my lord?" the bank manager asked.

"I do," she said and held it up.

"Very good. The chest may only be opened with your key."

The clerk motioned to the box and looked at Josephine. With trembling fingers, she inserted her key and turned it. She heard the lock creak, and it stuck for just a moment, and then with a creak and a smattering of dust, the lock turned.

With exaggerated solicitousness, the manager stepped away toward the opening to the vault, his back to them.

Stephen met Josephine's eyes. They were still shining like glorious emeralds. Her cheeks were rosy, her lips were wet and parted, and her breathing was fast and excited. If the clerk hadn't been only a few feet away, Stephen would have kissed her. She was that irresistible.

Instead, he reached forward and lifted the lid of the chest. It swung on rusty hinges, much in need of an oiling. Something inside gleamed, and Josephine reached for it. But it wasn't treasure, no gold doubloons. Instead, she pulled out an old haversack, one of her long fingers caressing its gold clasp.

"Shall we open it now?" she whispered.

"Better to wait, I think," he said. He gave the clerk a pointed look. "Until we're alone."

"And when will that be?" she murmured. "I have to attend Catie's ball tonight."

"I'll meet you there," he whispered. "I'll bring the sack, and you bring your half of the map. We'll sneak away and open it together."

"No!" she hissed. "No, if you take the sack, how do I know what you'll find inside? I want to open it together."

"We will. I'll wait for you."

She pursed her lips, and he could see the distrust

in the crease between her eyebrows. Her eyes were narrow and wary, like a cornered cat's.

"Are you done, my lord?" the clerk called from the other end of the vault.

Stephen looked back at his partner. "Miss Hale, we are partners. I give you my word I will wait."

She shook her head. "Your word?" She glanced at the clerk and lowered her voice. "The word of a Doubleday means nothing to me. You are a family of liars. You accused my grandfather of murder. Lies, all of it."

Stephen bit out a curse and took her arm, propelling her farther down the vault.

"My lord?" the bank manager said, his voice impatient. "Shall I ask Mr. Coutts to assist?"

"One moment," Stephen answered, then swung to face his partner. "This is not about our grandfathers, Miss Hale. This is about you and me. This is about you not being able to trust a man, even one who has given you every reason to trust."

"Every reason?" she shot back. "What about Seven Dials? What about when you read the journal before me?"

"Josephine!" he growled. "This is getting us nowhere. If we can't trust each other, then we're no better than our grandfathers, and, after all these years, we've come no farther. We're partners. Partners until the end. Together until the end. Look how far we've come working together."

She frowned at him. Frowned at the haversack she still held. And then, with her jaw firmly clenched and her eyes blazing with fury, she held out the sack.

He reached out to take it, but she didn't let go, and he inadvertently pulled her close. "I'm going to trust you, Westman," she whispered. "One time. But I warn you, if you don't show up at the ball tonight, I will personally come and shoot you, then pry the haversack from your cold, stiff fingers. Don't double-cross me."

Stephen held back a smile at her threat. "I'll be there," he answered, taking the sack. "You can count on it."

Chapter 13

"He's not coming," Josie said, pacing the assembly rooms where Catie's ball was in full swing.

"Stop worrying," Ashley said, sipping the glass of punch her last dance partner had fetched for her. "It's still early."

"It's after midnight," Josie said. "He's not coming." She clenched her pretty emerald silk reticule, sewn to match her dress, and could feel her half of the map inside.

"Why does it matter if he comes, anyway?" Maddie asked. "I thought you didn't like him."

"I don't," Josie answered. It was a lie and a blatant one. It mattered very much whether Westman made an appearance, and not simply because she wanted to see the contents of that haversack. It was more than that now. There was more between them than the treasure, the adventure, and her grandfather's legacy. There was trust.

What had Westman said today? *Together until the end.*

She'd trusted Westman more than any other man. This afternoon, it had pained her physically to allow him to walk away with that haversack. She couldn't understand why she had done it, except that she wanted to trust him. She wanted to believe there was one man in the world who would keep his word, who would look at a woman and see her as an equal. All her life she'd wanted to be accepted, to be treated on equal terms with men.

Rising on tiptoes to see the entry stairway, Josie murmured, "He has something of mine." Something just as precious as the contents of that haversack.

"Where's Catie?" Ashley asked. "Perhaps we should check on her."

Maddie nodded, but Josie shook her head. "She said she was fine and shooed Maddie and me away. And then, a moment ago, I saw Valentine lead her across the dance floor and through that servants' door."

Ashley raised her eyebrows. "Really? How wicked."

"How wonderful," Maddie said. "I'm so glad that she's happy."

Josie sighed. If only Westman would show up,

she too would be happy. Not as happy as Catie probably was on the other side of that door, but happy all the same. She craned her neck to search the room once more, caught her mother's eye, and quickly looked the other way. Was it just her imagination, or was her mother watching her even more closely than usual tonight?

"What does he have?" Maddie said, and Josie tore her eyes away from the other guests to glance at her cousin.

"What?"

"I said, what does Westman have? You said he has something of yours."

"Nothing." Josie shook her head. "It's not important."

"Then why are you—?"

Josie clamped a hand on her cousin's arm. "He's here," she breathed. "He just walked in."

"Well, if he doesn't have anything you want, Josie, I can see a few things I like," Ashley said. "Look at him."

Josie was, and he was as gorgeous as her cousin intimated. Dressed in his evening black, his hair brushed back, his face a mask of social politeness, he looked every inch his title. Indeed, he looked like a king. He was that regal, that imposing, that exciting.

That trustworthy?

He'd come, as promised. She saw him look around the room, saw his eyes light on her, and she couldn't help but sigh. Handsome, trustworthy, exciting. How was she going to keep her emotions from getting the better of her?

"Excuse me," she said to her cousins and made sure Westman saw her angle for the dining room, which was all but empty now. She peered back and saw him threading his way through the crowds. In the dining room, a few servants were busy mopping up a spill of red punch, but other than that she had the dining room to herself. Leaning against the wall, she clutched her reticule to her chest and breathed deeply. She knew the other half of the map was in the haversack. Tonight she and Westman would put the two halves together, and they'd finally know the location of the secret treasure.

"Dreaming about silver, Miss Hale?" a low, velvet voice asked.

She opened her eyes and stared into his lovely blue ones. "Gold doubloons, Lord Westman." She was so excited, so eager, she could have kissed him.

His eyes warmed in response, and he smiled. "Did you bring the map?"

She nodded. "Where's the sack?"

He patted his tailcoat, and she saw that the lines of the form-fitting garment were not quite as sleek as usual.

"Good. I've already found us a secluded place to open it. Follow me."

Westman raised his brows. "Follow you? How do I know this isn't just a ploy to steal my virtue?"

Josie laughed at Westman's role reversal. "I promise your virtue is safe with me," she said, then motioned for him to follow. They wound their way through the kitchen, which was a hive of servants cleaning dishes and loading silver trays with full glasses of champagne. And then they were out a back door and into an alley where several grooms were crouched, playing dice.

They stood and doffed their hats when they saw her and Westman. "Go play somewhere else for a quarter hour," Westman said, tossing a few coins in the midst of the game.

The men scrambled for the coins and, without protest, gathered up their blunt and disappeared back to their horses and coaches.

The men had left a wobbly three-legged stool with a small lamp on it, and Josie pulled her map out of the reticule and spread it on the ground, in the yellow spill of light. Westman was busy removing his coat. It was no easy feat without the aid of a valet, and when he was done, he tossed it to Josie.

"Here, sit on this." The coat wasn't as nice as some she had seen, but it wasn't cheap either, so she spread it carefully beside the map and knelt on the wool. She looked up in time to see Westman pull the haversack off his shoulder and over his head.

Josie wanted to reach for it, but she held back, watching with impatience as Westman fumbled with the old clasp. Finally he had it, and he crouched beside her, dumping the contents on the coattails.

Josie gasped at the bounty that spilled forth.

"Jewels," she said on a breath.

Westman blinked, his eyes wide, and lifted the

small rubies and the emerald as big as her thumb-nail. There was also a jeweled dagger; a sextant; a compass; a yellowed parchment that reminded her very much of her half of the map; the sixth, and presumably last, journal; and a large bronze key.

Josie lifted it. The once shiny blade was now dulled with green, but it was still intact. The bow was fashioned into a skull and crossbones. Josie shivered. "It's the key to the treasure box," she whispered. "I'm certain of it." What else but the bad-luck trea-sure would have such a macabre key?

Westman was a step ahead of her, unfolding the yellowed parchment to reveal the half of the map Josie had never seen but imagined so many times. Josie lifted her half of the map and frowned. It didn't fit right.

Westman reached out, took her map, turned it, and fitted it to its lost partner. The halves came together like lovers, the frayed edges melting into one another, forming a near seamless picture of the landscape. And now Josie saw that all her life she'd thought the map had been torn horizontally, that she had the lower half. Now she realized the map had been torn vertically, and she had the right half.

"Cornwall," Westman said. "I'd recognize that shape anywhere."

"Are there islands off the coast of Cornwall?" Josie asked. She pointed to the map. "I always thought these shapes were islands."

Westman nodded. "That's what I thought as

well, but now that I see the whole, I think they're too close to shore. They must be markers of a different sort."

"Guides to the treasure," Josie whispered, tracing a finger over the drawing until she touched the X near the shoreline and directly opposite the three small island-shapes.

"Perhaps rocks jutting out of the water near a hidden cove or a cave. Smugglers use them all the time."

Josie shook her head, her confidence in the treasure suddenly shaken as well. "Smugglers? But if they've been using Grandfather's hiding place, then they might have discovered the treasure." Lord, there'd been so many reports of smuggling the last few years. Since the war, every ruffian with a ship was looking to make money smuggling French goods.

"It's a risk, but I won't know until I see the hiding place myself. Before I go, I'll read all the journals again to make sure there aren't any more clues."

Josie glanced up sharply and almost rapped Westman on the chin. "Before you go? Before *we* leave, you mean."

"Miss Hale, please be reasonable. You cannot ride off to Cornwall with me."

Josie took in a sharp breath. Oh, no. No, no, *no*. The man was not going to do this to her now. Not when she had just begun to trust him. She stood, taking the map with her. "Oh, yes, I can, and I will."

"But your parents—" He seemed to flounder for a moment, and then his eyes lit. "Your mother. What would she say?"

"Oh, she'll murder me," Josie said, "but the important thing is that she does so after I have the treasure. Why do you think I've insisted on behaving so well this past fortnight? I don't want to be locked in my room before I have a chance to escape and find the treasure."

He blinked at her. "Miss Hale, I hate to be the one to say it, but you probably should be locked in your room. You cannot travel with me to find the treasure. Your reputation—"

"Doesn't matter. The only thing that matters is the treasure." She'd be an independent woman, and then she'd have the freedom to vindicate her grandfather. "Once I have the treasure, nothing can touch me." Not her mother, not Society, not arrogant, overbearing men like Westman. Why had she ever thought he was any different? When was she going to learn?

Westman bent over and lifted the haversack. He began piling the jewels and instruments back inside.

"What are you doing?" Josie asked.

"We'll talk about this tomorrow." He lifted the journal and placed it in the sack. "Perhaps you'll be more reasonable then."

"Westman—*Stephen*," she said, grabbing his arm before he could take the map. "I told you from the start that I won't be left behind. Not during the search for the map and not now when we have it. You agreed to my terms. Now you have to fulfill them."

His eyes blazed cold blue fire. "You don't understand what you're saying, and I'm not going to help you ruin yourself." He gave her a contemptuous look. "I'm sure you can accomplish that on your own."

"And if I do ruin myself, what's it to you?"

He went back to filling the sack.

"Oh, why did I ever trust you? In the bank today you said we were partners. 'Together until the end.' Was that another of the famous Doubleday lies?"

"No, I only meant that you have to trust me." He put the map in the haversack and slung it over his shoulder, then reached for his coat, shaking the dust off.

"I did trust you," she spat with eighteen years of venom. "I trusted you, and look what's happened."

"Miss Hale—"

"Leave me alone. I knew this would happen. You men think you're the only ones entitled to have adventures. I won't give this up so easily." She turned to the kitchen door, reached for the doorknob.

His hand shot out before she could scoot away. He yanked her back, so that her shoulder was jammed into his chest. "Stop talking nonsense. This isn't about your misguided, overblown sense of adventure, Josephine," he hissed, anger making his body tense and his grip cutting. "This isn't about fun. This is about your life. You're going to destroy it, and I'm not going to be the one who helps you. Not this time."

She glanced down at his hand. "Don't touch me."

He released her as though she were some vile insect.

"Don't ever touch me." She reached for the doorknob and stepped back into the kitchen. Head held high, she reentered the ball.

Inside, nothing had changed. Inside, everyone laughed and drank and danced. But Josie's heart was heavy and cold.

Vile man. She should have known he was as much a liar and a deceiver as the rest of his vile family. The more fool her. She'd trusted Westman. He'd tricked her into believing he might be different.

No, that wasn't even true. She knew he was no different than every other man, but she had wanted him to be. If she should be angry at anyone, it was herself. But how could she help it? She'd watched Catie fall in love, and she wanted some part of that—lust, desire—for herself.

When was she going to realize that the perfect man for her was nothing more than a shadow in the fog?

Stephen stood in the empty alley and tried to shrug on his tailcoat. It was bloody near impossible without his valet. He shoved an arm through the sleeve and cursed again.

Why the hell was he so angry anyway? Why the hell did he care if he'd disappointed Josephine Hale? She was ridiculous. She needed to be disappointed.

Why couldn't the woman understand that once her reputation was gone, she couldn't get it back? Once she'd lost her family's love, it was gone forever.

God, he hated himself sometimes. He hated that he had to be the one to take the light of excitement and exploration out of her eyes.

But what the hell was he going to do if something happened to her? Who was he to protect her? He'd never saved anyone. Hell, he couldn't even save himself.

She'd be safer at home, safer under her parents' watchful eyes. Well, he couldn't exactly say they were watchful as she'd been sneaking out of her house and coming to his every night for almost two weeks now. So perhaps he would have to make them watchful.

With a smile, Stephen reached for the door to the assembly room.

He spotted Josephine Hale immediately. Tall with that flame of red hair, she was easy to spot.

Stephen took a breath. She was going to kill him. He forced one foot forward, then the other, and he was halfway across the ballroom before she looked away from her conversation with her cousins and saw him coming. Her eyes were windows to her thoughts.

Do not do it! she screamed at him silently. *Do not come over here.*

He marched on, and the heads of the *ton* began to turn. The whispers rose to a hiss, and the fans fluttered like hummingbirds' wings.

Josephine turned her back to him and tried to urge her cousins to walk with her. They gave her perplexed looks, and it wasn't until Lady Madeleine saw him coming and guessed his intent, that her mouth dropped open. "Oh, no," he heard her say.

With a smile he dropped a bow and held out his hand. "Miss Hale," he said loudly, so that everyone now watching them—and that was a good portion of those not dancing—could not help but hear or read his lips. "May I have this dance?"

Chapter 14

❧

"**D**o you see why I hate him?" Josie said, hours later, as she sat crushed together with her cousins on one side of the Valentine town coach.

"I thought your mother was going to faint," Maddie said from her right.

"I thought she was going to cry," Ashley said from the left.

"You are sadly mistaken," Josie informed her. "That's how she looks when she's contemplating murder."

"You were only dancing," Lord Valentine said oh-so-reasonably from the other side of the carriage, where he was seated beside his wife, Catie.

"Dancing with *Lord Westman*," Josie shot back.

"Do you know what that means?" She was practically screaming, and Valentine shrank back slightly.

"Apparently not."

"I am doomed. As soon as I step foot in the town house, I will be subjected to tortures none of you can imagine."

"Lord, Josie! Must you be so dramatic?" Catie asked. "And if you were already in so much trouble, why did you sneak away and come with us? Your mother has probably sent men out to search for you by now."

"Probably. And it's all Westman's fault. The dratted man!"

A Hale and a Doubleday dancing. It was a tale to rival Romeo and Juliet.

Josie had been fuming, even as she'd accepted Westman's hand. What else could she do?

And so Josie had danced with him, and she had told herself that she detested every second in his presence, every touch, every lingering glance. But the truth was that he set her on fire. Even boiling mad at him, she wanted to grab him and kiss him.

What was wrong with her? She should hate him. He'd promised to be her partner and then deserted her. He knew how important the treasure was to her, and yet he virtually insured she would not be able to go after it. He'd lied to her, betrayed her.

Oh, very well. Catie was right. Josie was being a bit dramatic. She was sure he was doing everything for her own good and all that rot.

But that didn't mean she had to like it.

Much.

Or at all. What did she care if Westman worried about her safety and whether or not she was protected? What did she care if he climbed walls to shield her or stood guard over her in Seven Dials? Of course, it made her feel warm and secure and cared for. But what use did she have for those feelings?

Josie was no wilting violet.

The problem was she still wanted him. She should have stayed away from overbearing men—they had a feral charm that proved hard to resist.

Valentine's town coach slowed near Lord Castleigh's house and Ashley and Maddie climbed out. Maddie looked back at Josie. "Are you coming in? Ashley's staying over."

Josie sighed. "No." She glanced at Catie and Valentine. "I actually have another destination in mind."

With a shrug, Maddie turned away, and as soon as the footman closed the door, Josie grabbed Catie's hand. "You needed my help once," she began, "and I swore to do everything I could. And had you not married Lord Valentine, you know I would have kept my promise."

Catie squeezed her hand. "I never doubted you, Josie. You've always been there for me."

Josie nodded. She hated asking Catie for this favor. She glanced at Valentine. He was not going to like this. "Now I need to ask something of you. I need to borrow your carriage."

"Where do you need to go?" Valentine asked. "I'll take you, of course."

"No." Josie shook her head. "I must go alone. And I must go now. This very moment, in fact."

"Young lady," Valentine began. "You're in enough trouble as it is. I don't think—"

Josie ignored him and stared at Catie. The two girls were still holding hands, and Catie squeezed hers. Josie did not want to be the source of an argument between her cousin and her new husband, but she couldn't see any other way. She needed transportation, and she had none of her own.

"When your mother finally finds you, she—"

"Quint," Catie said quietly, still looking at Josie. "Give her the carriage."

One of Britain's greatest orators closed his mouth then opened it again, gaping at his wife. "I beg your pardon."

"You heard me." Finally, Catie turned to him. "I do not ask very much of you, but I am asking you to grant me this one favor. Give my cousin the carriage."

"But that's not a good idea. Let's consider the matter logically, and perhaps together—"

"Quint," Catie said, and Josie was impressed by the authority in her voice. She'd never heard Catie speak so forcefully before. "We know it's not a good idea, and we know it's not logical. It's an adventure. It's a crusade." She winked at Josie. "It's something my cousin must do. Now, are you going to give her the carriage or do I have to get out now and help her steal one?"

Valentine looked from his wife to her cousin. "You are serious?"

Josie nodded.

Valentine shook his head and blew out a long breath. "Very well. The carriage and my coachman are yours."

"Oh, thank you!" Josie leaned over and gave both him and Catie a kiss on the cheek. Then she leaned back, smiled, and said, "Now, would you please get out?"

Stephen came awake slowly. He was careful to maintain his deep, steady breathing and to keep his facial muscles lax. Even he was not entirely certain whether he was still awake or asleep until he heard the scuff of a boot on the floor. Fury jumped in his veins, and he had to struggle not to attack the intruder before the interloper assaulted him.

But years of training with the Punjabi trackers in India had honed Stephen's instincts. He ignored the impulse to attack and instead played dead. Mind racing, Stephen catalogued the facts as they were.

One: He was in an inn on the road to Cornwall. Two: He had not been asleep more than three or four hours. Three: Someone was pilfering his room, going through his belongings.

The map.

He had hidden it beneath his pillow, and without

moving his hand to check, he was not certain it was still there. Stephen didn't know how long the trespasser had been searching, but it wouldn't take anyone long to realize the map was close to Stephen. He didn't relish the result when the prowler narrowed the search.

Stephen prepared to strike. Mentally, he inventoried the possible weapons in the room: candlestick near the bed, pistol in the sack at the foot of the bed, knife in his boot . . .

And then the prowler moved closer. So close that Stephen could smell him. But there was no expected scent of sweat or horse manure. Instead, what floated over him was the heady mix of vanilla and lavender.

Josephine.

His eyes popped open at once to the sight of a rounded derriere. She was bent over, searching through his valise. With a roar of anger and frustration, Stephen reached out and caught her about the waist, hauling her against him on the bed.

She didn't cry out, and she didn't acquiesce. She fought him, elbowing him in the throat and then turning and raking her nails across his cheek. He pulled back quickly, and she didn't draw blood, but Stephen was angry enough to catch her arm and twist it until she cried out.

She lunged at him again, this time with teeth bared, but Stephen avoided the thrust by cutting to the side and, in the same motion, pushing her hard on the bed. She went down in a tangle of soft feminine flesh and wild red curls.

"What the hell do you think you're doing?" He grasped the hand she raised to hit him and pinned it to the mattress with its twin. He was on top of her now—naked—straddling her hips, his eyes locked with hers.

"Good morning to you too, my lord." Her tone was acerbic, her face a mask of calm. She could pretend to be unmoved by her position all she wanted, but he could feel her tremble, and he'd seen the fright in her eyes when he'd first grabbed her.

"Don't play games with me, Miss Hale. How did you get here?"

"The same way you did. By horse and carriage." She tried to wriggle one wrist free and scowled at him when he held it fast. "You're hurting me," she said.

"I don't care." But he loosened his hold a fraction. "How did you find me?"

She gave an exaggerated sigh and looked away, turning her head to the side. "You really don't have very much faith in me, do you Lord Westman? Surely you realize anyone with half a brain could follow a nobleman traveling in his own coach."

"Goddamn it!" he said. Of course he knew that, but why was she following him to begin with? Why wasn't the little hellion at home? Why hadn't her mother grabbed her after the ball and locked her away for the next decade?

"Blaspheming isn't going to change anything," she said, and he glanced back to see those bright green eyes staring at him, hard as emeralds. "I'm not going home, and if you try and get rid of me, I'll only show up where you least expect it. I will find that treasure."

And she meant it, too. She'd do exactly as she said, and what could he do to stop her?

Tie her up and leave her? She'd find a way out.

Take her home? She'd proven too many times she could escape.

The sad truth was that if she weren't with him, she would probably be roaming the countryside by herself.

For once in his life, a woman was safer with him than away from him. He wanted to put his head in his hands and laugh at the irony.

She must have felt his capitulation because her next words were spoken more gently. "I'll make you glad I'm with you." Her voice was husky and low, and Stephen felt his body react instantly. Without intending to, he'd put himself in the worst position imaginable—in bed with Josephine Hale. She was too close, too available, too beautiful.

"I'm regretting it already," he whispered, refusing to meet her gaze, knowing he'd see the same desire he felt reflected in those green depths.

"This might be our last chance," she said, and Stephen had to meet her eyes then.

Did she mean what he thought she did?

One quick glance at her face told him she did. Arms shaking with the enormity of restraint he was exercising, Stephen released her wrists and pushed away from her.

He was naked, and the proof of his arousal was evident. She didn't look away, like a lady should. But, hell, she didn't do anything a lady should.

Stephen began searching the room desperately for his trousers. Had he left them on the floor or . . .

There on the chair.

Like a man fleeing an angry mob, Stephen flung himself from the bed and toward the chair. Snatching up the trousers, he leaned over to pull them on.

"You're wasting your time," Josephine said from the bed behind him. "They'll only come off again."

Stephen turned to look at her. She gave him a cat smile, then reached up to unfasten the buttons of the man's shirt she was wearing and tugged it out of the waistband of her trousers. Stephen swung back around, but as if to punctuate her statement, her shirt fluttered like a white flag onto the floor before him.

Oh, God. Oh, no.

This was too much temptation. This, no mortal man could resist.

He closed his eyes to shut out the picture of Josephine, bare-breasted on the bed behind him. But the action only served to enhance the mental image.

He had to get out of here. He had to escape, now, while he still could.

He fastened his trousers and looked about for his shirt. "I'm going to go check on the coach and horses," Stephen managed to sputter out. Where the hell was his damn shirt? "I'll return in a few moments. In the meantime, I suggest you dress yourself."

"I don't think so," she murmured, still behind him. And he could have sworn he felt the tip of her fingers on the back of his leg. He jumped forward.

"In fact, I don't think you're going to make it out the door."

Stephen tried to remember what he'd been doing. He had to get out of here before he forgot all his good intentions and succumbed to her charms.

Her many, many charms.

"Look, Miss Hale, I don't know what you're doing—"

"Don't you?" she purred, and he heard the rustle of more fabric behind him.

His breath hitched. "—but I'm going to leave now."

Her buff-colored trousers landed at his feet.

"Go ahead. Leave me."

But he didn't move. He couldn't stop remembering the way she'd tasted, the way her mouth moved against his, the way she reacted to his touch.

But if he took her, if he surrendered to her now, what did that say about him? That he truly was a rake. That all those promises he'd made to himself would be dust. Could he ever forgive himself if he ruined Josephine? Could she forgive him?

But if he didn't have her . . . If he let this opportunity pass, then what would he be?

His life had been so lonely, so empty until Josephine Hale had climbed through his library window. He'd had nothing but his memories and his regrets, and then she'd stumbled in and changed everything.

She'd given him hope, given him a purpose, given him her friendship.

And now she wanted to give him her body.

She was a virgin. An impetuous eighteen-year-old, she didn't know what she wanted.

"I don't see you walking away, Stephen." Her voice washed over him like warm, heavy cream. "And here I am, naked and cold without you. I want you."

Stephen swallowed and clenched his fists.

"I can't stop thinking about the way your body feels pressed against mine, the way your hands feel on my breasts, and the pleasure your tongue gives me on my—"

Stephen swung around now, unable to stop himself. So perhaps she did know what she wanted. And she was making him so hot and hard that he could hardly deny what he wanted anymore either.

He looked down at her, drunk in the sight of her on the bed, lounging like the goddess Venus in his favorite Titian painting. Stephen's breath caught, and he reached for her. His hand slid through her cropped curls, freeing them from their pins and fanning them over her cheek. Her eyes, hard emeralds, darkened and when he slid two fingers over her cheek and down to her chin, her lips opened in silent pleasure.

"Yes," she murmured. "This is what I want."

He wanted it, too. He'd wanted her for too long, dreamed about this moment, imagined it in excruciating detail.

Still cupping her jaw, he resisted one last time. "You're a dangerous woman, Miss Hale. You're an enchantress."

She circled his wrist with one hand and rubbed her palm up his bare arm. Heat shot through him. Heat and desire in endless waves.

"I don't want you," he lied. "I don't want this."

She glanced down at the hard bulge that belied his words. "Then walk away," she murmured, her hand brushing against his inner arm and touching his chest. Stephen took in a quick breath, and Josephine rose to her knees, slowly, like a graceful tigress on the hunt. She placed both hands on his chest. "You're warm," she whispered. "So warm."

Her hands traced a path up and down, up and down, then down and down until they rested at his waistband.

Bloody hell, how he wanted her to continue. He couldn't seem to resist her. She was kneeling before him, naked, not even long hair to hide the dips and curves of her slender body. The dawn light filtered through the drapes, and even more temptation was revealed to him. Her white breasts iced with pink aureoles, the sprinkling of freckles above her left hip, the dash of red curls at the juncture of her thighs.

Her hands made their maddening journey back up his chest and circled his neck. With a gentle tug, she pulled him close. "Make me warm," she whispered. "Kiss me . . . everywhere."

Stephen was drowning in the scent of her hair, the smoothness of her cheek. He made one last attempt to pull away, but her lips were so close and so ripe, he had to taste them.

Once his mouth was on hers, he knew the battle was ended. She'd defeated him, and to the victor went the spoils, and so he gave her a kiss of sweet surrender, long and hot and calculated to dizzy her brain as much as his own.

With a low moan, she pressed against him, her small, slim body sending skittering shocks of pleasure through his as flesh met flesh. *Pleasure,* was Stephen's last coherent thought. He wanted to give it, and yes, God, he wanted to receive.

She was eager. All the energy pent up within her seemed to push against him, wanting to get out, wanting to infuse itself within him. He tried to slow her down, kissing her languidly, tasting her fully, running his hands all over her, learning her body.

But she would not be slowed. Each kiss he bestowed, she trumped with one deeper and more passionate. Each caress was matched with one more daring, more risky. Each attempt to hold her off, to hold her at bay, failed when she refused to play along.

Her hands slid up and down his back, pulling him harder against her breasts and into her warmth, and then her palms dipped lower, stroking his buttocks through his trousers. Desire shot through him, sharp as a knife, and he groaned out the need.

"You like that, don't you?" she whispered, working her hands over him, dipping them between his legs, and cupping his balls through the trousers.

"Oh, God," he moaned and resisted the urge to snatch her by the hair, flip her over, and plunge into her like an animal. "We must slow down." He managed to get the words out somehow. "I don't want to hurt you."

"I'm not afraid." Her hands had now worked their way around his waistband and were dangerously close to his erection. "I want you to hurt me. I want you to pleasure me. I want to feel it all."

And then the fall of his trousers was loose and her warm hands were on him. "Oh!" she said, leaning back to look at his cock. "It's like velvet. Sleek and smooth and—"

"You're driving me mad," he growled, pushing his trousers to his knees and then down to his ankles. "You're—"

He watched, bereft of speech as her hands glided along his cock, up and down, around. And then, coyly, she leaned forward and touched the tip to one of her hard, budding nipples.

He almost came then. Stephen took a sharp breath and clenched his hands. He wanted to be inside her, he wanted to take her slowly, but if she kept up like this, he would be fortunate to last more than three seconds.

He had to take over. Much as he was enjoying her explorations, he had to get this under control or lose control all together. With regret, he took her hands in his and stepped backward. Her face fell immediately. "Was that wrong?" she asked. "I thought you liked it."

He gave a rueful laugh and cupped her cheeks. "I do like it. I like it too much."

Her eyes were still full of skepticism, so he added, "You can't do anything wrong with me. Nothing you do will be wrong."

She smiled again, and he shook his head at the mixture of strength and vulnerability in her. One moment, she was ready to try anything, to conquer the world. The next she was tentative and unsure. He loved both sides of her, and he loved that he would be the one to take her on this new adventure.

Kneeling on the bed beside her, he pulled her close for a long embrace, then cupped her cheek again and kissed her slowly. As usual, her excitement bubbled forth, and she tried to speed his kisses to fever pitch, but this time he wouldn't allow it.

He was going to take his time with her no matter how much it depleted his self-control. And so he kept his kiss deep and passionate and slow, and after a moment, she responded in kind. But the experience of kissing Josephine Hale this deeply, this intimately, was more than he'd anticipated. He felt drugged on her mouth, the feel of her body, the sound of her ragged breathing.

As though entering a dream, he reached forward and caressed one breast. She moaned, arching for him, giving herself so completely that Stephen was taken aback. A moment of responsibility he'd never before felt stole over him.

He had to do this well; he had to do this right. She trusted him. Completely. It was in the arch of her nude body, the whispers from her mouth, urging him on, the way she followed wherever he led. She had no doubts, no reservations. Had anyone ever trusted him so completely before? Had he ever wanted anyone to?

Rewarding her trust and openness, he continued to stroke her, memorizing the feel of her, noting each small gasp, each loud moan, each quick intake of breath until her body was like an instrument to him. He was the virtuoso, playing her exquisitely.

And now it was time for the final score. He reached between her legs and cupped her. She was warm, shockingly so. Waves of heat emanated from her, the fire burning hotter as his hand rested there. And now she was all but purring in his ear and pushing against him.

He couldn't remember ever feeling as though a woman wanted him so much. And he knew he'd never wanted to be inside a woman as much as he wanted her.

Slowly, so slowly, he inched his fingers apart until he formed a V at her most sensitive spot. Then he squeezed. Gently, almost imperceptibly. Her body went rigid, and then she gasped with pleasure. He squeezed again, and this time she moaned aloud. "More. More."

He intended to oblige her, but he changed positions, extending one finger and teasing her tiny hard nub with it. She writhed against him, and he could feel her limbs go weak and limp. He wrapped one arm around her, supporting her as the finger played her lightly, bringing her to new heights he could well imagine.

And then, when he'd measured her breathing, measured her moans, and knew she was at the point of climax, he inserted the finger inside her. She screamed, her body so taut she felt as though she would break. Sliding the wet finger out, he ran it lightly across that hard nub once more, then slid it back inside, and this time he felt the first spasms of her orgasm.

"Oh, don't stop," she moaned in his ear, her breath coming quick and making him want her even more. "Don't—"

Her next words were lost as he slid the finger out and in and then felt her come against him.

It was a full body climax. She shuddered,

convulsed violently, clinging to him, screaming out her pleasure, until finally she slumped, exhausted, against him.

But Stephen was not through. He wanted to give her more. He wanted to drown her in pleasure. Gently, he lowered her to the bed, bent over her and began to kiss her back to awareness. Her neck was long and slim, and her hair must have been washed in the lavender scent he had smelled earlier.

When he felt her arms go around him, he moved to kiss her collarbone and the slope of her pretty white shoulders. Of course, her small, high breasts were waiting for him next. There he suckled and nipped, teased and taunted, until she was all but offering herself to him.

He was kneeling between her legs, and she had opened to him so that the tip of his erection rested at the juncture of her thighs. The temptation there was enormous. He could smell her on his fingers, and he had felt the heat inside her a moment before. Now he wanted to be surrounded by that heat, to envelop himself in her.

But not yet. Not until she was so drunk on pleasure she would never feel the pain of his entry.

And so he bent to kiss her belly. Her flesh rippled, and she giggled. "That tickles," she said, her voice husky from the pleasure he'd given her.

"Not for long," he murmured, moving lower. The curls at the V between her legs were red as the hair on her head, and he reached to part them, so that he had a tantalizing view of the temptation that waited for him.

She didn't try and protest or offer false modesty. She opened for him, once again trusting him with this intimate act. He parted her folds, revealing the pink, tender flesh, now sleek and wet. Leaning closer, he breathed warm air on her and watched her hands close convulsively on the sheets beneath her. He opened her wider, breathed again, and then tasted her with the tip of his tongue.

She moaned and arched, and he tasted again, this time probing deeper. She was so sweet, and he pulled back to tell her. But by now her eyes were dark with arousal, and she only shook her head.

He dipped to taste her again, and then spreading her folds so that he could see the tiny reddish nub buried there, he tapped his tongue on it.

She jumped and cried out. He tapped again, so lightly he was not even certain he was touching her. But he must have been because he could see her coming apart. He tapped again, and her hips came off the bed. She offered herself to him, and he took, bringing her to orgasm again.

But this time he did not intend to allow her to come down. Just as he saw her go over the edge, he rose up on his knees and inserted the head of his cock into her. Her eyes opened and she blinked at him.

"I can still stop," he croaked. God, he didn't want to, but he could still cease if she asked.

In answer, she rose again, took more of him inside her, and Stephen had to grip her hips to keep from plunging his full length into her.

"More," she pleaded, attempting to arch again. "More."

He moved again, felt the barrier of her maidenhead, and paused. A fraction of an inch and she would be his.

He looked at her—at her tousled curls, her bright green eyes, her parted pink lips. She was watching him too, begging him to continue. Closing his eyes, he plunged deeper. Plunged into heaven.

God, she was so hot and so wet. He was ready to spill his seed in her after the first thrust. But he also knew he had hurt her. He felt her tense, and he opened his eyes.

Tears ran down her cheeks, and he leaned down to kiss them away. "I'm sorry," he murmured. "I didn't want to hurt you."

"I know," she answered. "Don't stop."

"We should wait. Are you—?"

"Don't stop," she demanded, and rose to tempt him further.

Stephen needed little encouragement to plunge into her again. He thrust deeper and felt his own need heighten. Faster and harder, she urged him until he was so senseless with pleasure that he was clinging to her. He hadn't even climaxed, and already he was crying out.

"I can't—"

He had intended to pull out of her, to spill his

seed outside of her womb so as not to impregnate her, but he found he could do little but drive into her more deeply.

"Josephine—" he began again. She didn't answer, just tightened her legs around him, pulling him over the edge and plunging him into an explosion of light and sound and exquisite feeling.

Chapter 15

Josie lay in Westman's arms, listening to the slow rise and fall of his breathing. After their lovemaking, he'd pulled her against his chest and cradled her in the envelope of his arms. She'd never felt so safe or so cared for.

She sighed with contentment. She was tired and sore and wonderfully satiated. She had known it would be like this with him. She had wanted him, and she'd had him, and she didn't regret it. Lying here in his arms, the zing of the pleasure he'd given her still coursing through her limbs—how could she regret this?

She only hoped he felt the same.

He'd said he didn't want her, and she'd known it was a lie; but now that her mind was clearer, she revisited those words. He didn't have to mean that he didn't want her physically—she had known he wanted her that way almost from the beginning—but he could mean that he didn't want any more from her. He wanted her body and the pleasure she gave him, but that was all.

And Josie never expected anything more. She'd wanted a man who would treat her as an equal. What would be more equal than taking the pleasure she gave and offering nothing more? That was as much as she offered, after all.

Then why did she feel like she was missing something? She had everything she wanted. She was on an adventure to find her grandfather's treasure, and she'd finally found a lover. What more was there?

To prove her grandfather innocent of the murder of James Doubleday. She still had that before her, of course.

But that wasn't what caused the hole in her heart.

She thought about Catie, about the way she looked at Valentine, and the way he looked at her, too. It was obvious to anyone who saw them that they were in love. It was patently clear that they completed one another. That together, they were so much more than alone.

But Josie didn't want a husband. She wanted to be free, to be independent. And she certainly didn't want a husband like Westman. He could please her in bed, but would he ever please her anywhere else?

She'd grown up under the autocratic rule of men

like her father. She didn't need to bind herself to another in hopes of filling up some imaginary hole in her heart.

She was not thinking straight. She must be tired, after traveling all day and much of the night, having slept only in the small snatches she could catch in Valentine's jouncing coach. She was exhausted and keyed up about her adventure. That was all this pondering and musing was. She would feel better after she had rested.

A few hours' sleep would be the end of musings about a hole in her heart. There was no hole. Everything was perfect, and if she were smart, she would get some rest before Westman awoke and they started for Cornwall. She had a big adventure ahead of her.

But Josie couldn't sleep.

Beside her Westman slept heavily and soundly. His arm pinned her to the bed, and it took a good five minutes to extricate her body. It was full morning now. She could hear the noise of horses in the stable yard, smell the scents of baked bread and frying ham, and feel the rising sun chase away the cold from the room. She sat on the edge of the bed and contemplated her clothing.

The boy's shirt, trousers, and cap were comfortable, but they garnered her strange looks when people realized she was not actually a boy. The innkeeper here had tried to run her off last night before Valentine's man had stepped in and vouched for her.

Josie almost wished she had a dress, though it wouldn't serve her very well while she explored shorelines and secret caves. Still, it would be another full day and then some of travel, and a dress would make her life easier in the interim. She was about to lift her trousers and shirt from the floor, when something beneath the pillow where she'd been lying caught her eye.

So this was where Westman had hidden the map. She glanced at him, still sleeping with a lock of brown hair over his forehead. He looked young in his sleep, young and deceptively innocent.

She opened the map, paired the pieces, and studied the landmarks given. How were they ever going to find the treasure with such scanty information? They might have to search for years to find three islands or rocks or whatever those landmarks on the map were. And what if rocks that had been off the shore in 1760 had eroded beneath the waves by 1811? Did erosion work that quickly?

"Not planning to abscond with the map and leave me without a partner, are you?" Westman asked.

She turned at his voice and couldn't help smiling at him when she saw him watching her sleepily. A shaft of sunlight ran along his hair, highlighting the strands of auburn woven with the chestnut.

"Leave you? Never." She leaned forward and kissed him. She'd meant it to be a light kiss, a friendly good morning, but Westman changed the tone as soon as her lips were on his.

The back of his hand cupped her neck and he held her tightly and kissed her with a passion that took her breath away. Apparently, he did not regret the events of a few hours before.

When he released her, she didn't pull back right away. Instead she memorized the dark flecks in his amazing blue eyes, traced a finger over the fine lines in his forehead, and tapped his nose lightly with hers.

Had she ever imagined that she would be with a man as handsome or skilled as he? That she would feel so happy to have a man wake in the morning and want to kiss her? That she would feel content just to look in his eyes?

Finally, she pulled away. She needed distance before she became too attached. But Westman didn't allow her to go far. He grabbed her hand when she stood to dress and pulled her back down on the bed.

"I like you far too well in what you're wearing right now to allow you a change of clothing."

She snorted. "I'm not wearing anything."

"Let's keep it that way a bit longer." He pulled her in for another kiss, and Josie was just beginning to enjoy it when she noticed the heat of the sun on her back.

"Westman," she whispered against his cheek. "It's getting late. Perhaps we should be off?"

"Treasure, treasure, treasure," he murmured, caressing one of her legs with his fingers. "Is that all you can think about?"

"I don't always think about treasure," she protested. "Only for the last twelve years."

He chuckled and pulled her close again. "I'll get your mind off treasure."

And she believed he could. He had done things to her last night, made her feel things, she had not known she could feel. And yet, she did feel the pressure to be on their way. Her parents were undoubtedly worried about her right now, and Catie was a very bad liar. She'd promised Josie to pen a note to Mavis Hale, saying that Josie would be staying with Lord and Lady Valentine for a few days. But Josie was under no illusions that her mother would approve the arrangement, and if her mother's requests that Josie return home were not complied with, she just might take it upon herself to search Catie's town house herself.

Not that she'd have to. Catie would probably tell all as soon as her aunt Mavis knocked on the door.

Josie knew her time could be running out this very minute. And yet, it was so hard to pull away from Westman. She could have stayed in his arms all day.

Reluctantly, she drew back. "Westman, we really should be going."

"My man was instructed to wake me at eight. It's early yet—"

There was a tap at the door, and a low voice called, " 'Tis eight o' the clock, milord."

Westman scowled, and Josie grinned. "It's not meant to be," she said and rose to dress.

"Wait." Westman caught her arm and looked up at her with an intensity that almost made her squirm.

"What's wrong?" she asked. "Is there something—?"

"No, no." He shook his head. "It's only . . . I have something . . . oh, bloody hell. There's no good way or time to do this."

And then to her horror, he slid off the bed and sunk down on one knee.

"Miss Hale, will you do me the honor of becoming my wife?"

"Oh, good Lord! *No!*"

Stephen knelt on the cold, hard floor and stared up at Josephine Hale. Had she just refused his offer of marriage? "I beg your pardon," he said, his voice growing hard.

She shook her head at him. "I said no."

"I see." He rose, looked about for his trousers, and located them in a heap on the floor. Thankfully, she was doing the same, and when he faced her again, she was dressed. "Might I ask why you refuse my offer? Why, after I kneel on the bloody hard floor and make you a respectable offer, you refuse it?"

She looked up from tucking her shirttails into her boy's trousers. "Because I do not want to marry you." She began to turn away from him, searching for her boots, but he grabbed her elbow and turned her back to face him.

"And you think I want to marry you?" he asked with a laugh. "But there's no choice now. What's done is done."

"Yes, and it was a very pleasant romp. So thank you, but no thank you."

Stephen stared at her. He'd never met a woman so unmoved by an experience like what they'd shared last night. Well, he'd never before felt an experience like that, so perhaps that was part of it. Not that an enjoyable few hours in bed were usually grounds for him to propose marriage, but this time was different.

"Miss Hale," Stephen said, "I understand your reservations, but I must ask you to think logically."

She shot him a glare.

"You are compromised. I don't know what, if any, arrangements were made to cover up this excursion of yours, but let me assure you that people will find out. Servants talk. Travelers talk. Word will get back to Town that we were together here. Your reputation will be in tatters. We must marry, not only to save it, but because I do not relish the thought of your father jamming a pistol in my temple and demanding we marry."

Josephine smiled indulgently. "Daddy would never do that. He might send one of my brothers, but they're young, and you can certainly outmaneuver them."

Stephen ran a hand through his hair, frustrated, as usual. "Yes, I probably can outmaneuver your brothers, but you miss my point."

"No, I didn't. You're worried about my reputation, and I find that very sweet."

"Sweet? *Sweet?* Miss Hale, I am a lot of things, but I am not sweet."

She rolled her eyes. "Very well, I find it thoughtful, but you needn't worry. Once we find the treasure, no one will care about the rest. And if they do, we'll tell them all to go to the devil. I'll be an independent woman then. It won't matter what Society says."

Stephen could see that, like most females, Josephine Hale was sadly lacking in logic. He was going to get nowhere unless he made the issue patently clear. "And what about the child?" he said, crossing his arms. "How do you intend to deal with that small matter?"

She frowned at him, opened her mouth, then closed it again.

Stephen raised a brow. He had her now.

"W-What are you talking about?" she finally stammered. "What child?"

Stephen indicated her flat belly. "My child. The one you may very well be carrying in your womb at this moment. You see, Miss Hale"—he leaned forward, closing the gap between them—"in your haste to seduce me early this morning, there is one issue you did not take into consideration. That of protection."

"Protection?"

"Surely you know where babies come from?"

She nodded. "Yes, but I thought—" She blushed

and Stephen's brows rose higher. Now this was new. He did not think he could recall seeing her blush before.

"Yes? You thought?" he prodded.

"I thought there were ways to prevent that. I was under the impression rakes—er, men like you—knew these things."

Stephen smiled indulgently. "And you are not incorrect. I do know how to prevent pregnancy, and had I been expecting your visit I might have prepared by procuring a packet of French letters. You know what those are, Miss Hale?"

She nodded. "A sheath that you put—" She blushed again.

"Right," he said, saving her. Though it was tempting to allow her to stumble and blush through the conversation, he was not that much of an ass. "But I did not have any French letters with me, which left me only one other option for protecting you."

She frowned. "Which is?"

"Withdrawal. I could have withdrawn at the moment of climax, and I assure you, Miss Hale, that I fully intended to, but here is where I must make a confession."

He took another step nearer, and she would have backed away, but he took her arm and kept her close.

"Making love to you was an amazing experience. I thoroughly enjoyed it, so much so that I lost my head." Her eyes grew wide, and he stroked her cheek with one finger. "I couldn't have pulled out even had I wanted to, and let me assure you that, by the end, pulling away from you was the last thing on my mind. And so I have put you at risk, and I rather fear that a child would inhibit your plan of complete independence, not to mention the difficulties one would pose for me and my family were my heir born a bastard."

He waited for a response, but as she only stared at him, he continued, "I am not a friend of marriage. In the past, I have avoided it with alacrity, but I am willing to take responsibilities for my actions. I expect you to do the same."

Again, he paused, waited, and still she did not speak. He could see her pondering the problem. He could almost hear the cogs turning in her brain. She sighed, looked down, and paced to the window, then stared out of it for a good five minutes.

Stephen considered himself a patient man, but the longer she pondered, the harder it was not to feel annoyed. Was his proposal so odious that she had to think this hard? Was he such poor husband material that she wavered this much? He felt he should be insulted, but he couldn't quite put his finger on why.

After all, it wasn't as though he wanted to marry her either. It was something he was obligated to do. Forced to do. He had learned from his past sins, and he would do the penance.

Why the hell was she having such a hard time seeing that for herself?

"Miss Hale," he began.

At the window, she held up a finger. One moment.

Stephen stared. Who the devil did this woman think she was? He wasn't going to be put off any longer.

"Don't you bloody well hold your finger up to me, Miss Hale," he said, crossing the room in three strides and took the offending digit by the root. Her eyes flashed fire, and she yanked it away again. "I'm not one of your servants or another of your fawning suitors. I'm the Earl of Westman, and I won't be shooed away or treated like an inconvenience."

"Oh, you have made your position clear from the start, my lord," she spat at him. "It has always been I who was the inconvenience. From the moment I mentioned the treasure, all I have been was in your way of getting to it. And now it seems I am likely to be in your way for the rest of my life."

"I wouldn't put it like that—"

"I would!" She poked him, and he backed up. "You call me a mistake, an impulse, a responsibility. You call me a distraction and a temptation and a partner, but you never call me by my name! You never call me Josie. You never call me sweetheart. You never call me anything but Miss Hale or once—it might have been twice, I've been known to make mistakes—you called me Josephine. And now you ask me to marry you? Even if I could tolerate a sterile, loveless marriage with an overbearing, arrogant cretin, do you think I would bring a child into it? Better I raise a baby alone."

"Sterile?" Stephen roared, trying not to reach out and shake her. "You call what happened between us this morning sterile?"

"And what would you call it? With nothing but lust behind it, do you not think it will become a sterile act? You don't love me, Lord Westman. You don't even love yourself, and deep down you can hardly blame me for refusing your offer not once now, but three times. Do us both a favor, my lord, and take the hint."

Chapter 16

After four hours with nothing to do but stare at her fingers, Josie decided they were too wrinkled. She'd turned them this way and that, held them up to the light and then back under the carriage shadows, and now she was just plain sick of them.

She glanced over at Westman, still brooding on his side of the Doubleday family coach. He'd been sitting like that, arms crossed over his chest, hat pulled low, eyes focused resolutely out the window, since they'd taken their places this morning. She'd squirmed and shifted, trying to get comfortable during this long trek to Cornwall, but he had not moved.

Not once.

It was actually rather unnerving after a while, and she'd taken to staring at him under her lashes to be certain he still breathed. When she had once again established that he was still alive, she'd turn back to her fingers and her own musings.

She wished she had a book to read. She wished one of her cousins were here to talk to. She wished Westman wasn't such a typical man.

She had known he would be angry when she refused his offer. She could have anticipated his response exactly, right down to the way he pouted now—not that he would think of it as pouting. He probably thought he was punishing her with silence. He'd retreated into that man cave as Josie had seen her father and brothers do so often, and she didn't know when or if he'd ever emerge.

And she didn't care.

Despite all of Westman's reasons for marriage, Josie couldn't get past all the reasons they shouldn't. He didn't love her. Sometimes she wondered if he even liked her. And she knew he didn't like himself much at present. He blamed himself for his family's misfortunes and . . .

There was something else. Something he needed to atone for.

A past scandal? On that point Westman was right: There would be scandal when they returned from Cornwall. Catie was always telling Josie that just because she wanted something didn't make it true. Josie was afraid that this was one of those times. She could not wish the scandal away, even the treasure might not be enough to buy her forgiveness.

But she could fight scandal. She would stand up to the criticism, the ostracism, and the censure. And if there was a baby—she gulped hard at that thought—then she would do her best to protect the child from Society's slings and arrows as well.

What she would not do was marry a man like Westman—a man who, under the guise of protection, took away all her freedoms.

Because, make no mistake, Westman *was* an arrogant, pigheaded man. He was the kind of man who took what he wanted without asking. He was the kind of man who expected women to do what he said. He was the kind of man Josie knew she should never love.

In the carriage, she shifted again, and bit her bottom lip hard.

Love. Back to that again. She drew her gaze to Westman's face

Did he love her? Could he love her?

"Is there something wrong with my face or have your eyes just gotten stuck?" Westman growled suddenly, and Josie quickly looked away. She hadn't meant to be caught staring at him, but he so resembled a statue that she'd quite forgotten he was actually awake and alert.

"I was just wondering whether you were still alive, my lord."

"Why? Because I can sit still for more than three seconds at a time?" His blue eyes flicked to her, and she almost drew back at the sneer in them. "Some of us were taught not to fidget."

"Some of us were taught to be polite."

He snorted. "Why bother, when those you are with do not appreciate it?"

Oh, now this was too much. He was insulting her? "Look, Westman, I know I hurt your feelings this morning—"

"Hurt my feelings?" He laughed. "Miss Hale, I was simply trying to do you a favor this morning. The only person you've hurt is yourself."

Josie rolled her eyes and went back to her view of green fields patterned by shadows of clouds. And she thought *she'd* been defensive.

The rest of the journey loomed long and arduous before her. But then she should have expected it to be fraught with conflict. The treasure obviously deserved its reputation for causing bad luck.

A few more miles rolled by and the driver inquired if they would like to stop and stretch their legs at the next inn. Westman agreed, and Josie was soon being helped out of the carriage by the footman. She'd sent Valentine's coach back to London with a note to Catie not to worry. Now she wished she had kept the conveyance. Anything to be away from Westman for a bit.

With that in mind, she decided to forgo the inn and walk the stiffness out of her legs. She started off at a brisk pace, heading toward a pretty paddock where several of the inn's posting horses were grazing. It was a sunny spring day with a nip in the air, but the flowers were already beginning to bloom. She brushed past pale lemon daffodils and sun-kissed primroses, stopping to admire them, and then trekking on.

The pip, pip, pip of a blackbird echoed across the afternoon, and she measured her step to its rhythm.

The farther from the coach and Westman, the better she felt. Why, she could almost smell the sea air of Cornwall and feel the gentle ocean breeze. And on that breeze she swore she could hear the tinkle of gold doubloons tumbling over one another.

Soon, she thought, trying to keep her excitement from bubbling over. It was too much to contain now that they were so close, and she did a little hop-skip. The blackbird suddenly abandoned its treetop post with a sharp, staccato warning call. She looked up and heard a crack and felt something hot and hard whiz past her cheek.

She held a hand to it, touched her cheek gingerly, surprised when the hand she pulled away had a scarlet trickle of blood on the finger. Her body rigid with alarm, her eyes snapped quick images of the field and narrowed when she spotted two men several yards away.

As soon as she caught sight of them, they ducked back into the copse of trees, but not before she saw the glint of the pistol. She was on her belly in the next instant, and this time when she heard the crack, she didn't mistake it. She hid in the tall grass, her heart pounding and sweat breaking out all over her body. She tried to think how far it was back to the inn.

Too far for the patrons to have heard the shot? Too far for her to run?

"Did ye hit 'er?" she heard one of the men say in a lower class accent.

"Don't know. Let's go see."

Oh, God. Josie dared not move, but she couldn't lie in the grass either, waiting for them to find that she wasn't dead and finish the job.

She slid along her belly to put some distance between where they had seen her fall and where she now lay, and then poked her head up and stared at the inn.

Oh, God. It was so far away.

The back door was propped open and a comforting plume of smoke rose from the chimney, but all the activity was in the front. Only the horses in the paddock near the stable seemed aware anything was amiss. She could see them prancing with agitated movements.

Her head was aloft for only an instant before she ducked back down, resting her racing mind on the hard ground.

It shook beneath her, and without even looking, she knew the men were closing in. She could hear the crunch of their feet on the brittle grass. Time was running out. If she did not act now, that very grass in front of her face would part, showing the scuffed black of their boots.

Quickly and carefully, she squatted. Her fear made her knees weak, but she'd rather die running than lying in the dirt, paralyzed with fear.

The sound of men moving came closer, and with a cry of terror, Josie launched herself from her hiding place and began to run. She moved in a zigzag pattern, hoping to make the shot more difficult. But behind her, she heard the men's startled voices and knew it would not be long before she felt the hot sting of the bullet.

"Josie!"

She'd been running with her head down, but now it popped up. A man stood ahead of her and to the left. He was dressed in a voluminous greatcoat that swirled about him as he rushed forward.

Westman.

His hand scrambled beneath the coat, fumbled, and pulled out a pistol of his own.

Josie could have cried with relief.

"Get down, you fool!" he ordered, and she dove just as the pistol behind her exploded.

The acrid smell of gunpowder fouled the sweetness of the field and the spring breeze. Then there was another blast from Westman, and her assailants were retreating.

They went quickly and without grace, and when Josie popped her head up again, they had a good start. A moment later, Westman reached her and hauled her up and into his arms. His hands roved over her shoulders, arms, torso, and legs. "Are you all right?" he cupped her cheek. "You're bleeding," he pointed out.

"A scratch." She shook him off. "I'm fine. But they're getting away!" She turned to follow the men, but she'd taken only a step before Westman hauled her back.

"What the devil are you doing?"

Again, she tried to shake him off, but this time he held on. With a frustrated push she freed herself, only to look again and find her quarry had completely disappeared.

"They're gone!" she said, rounding on him.

"Good." He took her wrist and began pulling her back toward the inn. "I suggest we follow their example."

"But—"

"I'm not going to stand in the middle of a field and discuss the matter." He was walking briskly, pulling her along, and Josie stumbled then trotted to keep up. "I don't like being a target."

"Neither do I!"

He snorted and kept pulling until they rounded the corner of the inn and came in sight of the servants in the yard. Westman's men jumped to attention. He addressed the coachman. "Get us a room. Now."

The man nodded and ran for the inn. Westman pulled her against the coach and stood in front of her, shielding her, she supposed, with his body.

The hard, cold coach against her back, Josie looked up at him. "What was that about?"

"I'm trying to protect you."

She shook her aching arm. "By pulling my arm out of the socket and throwing me against the carriage?"

"Ungrateful little wretch," he said, turning back to check on his coachman's progress. The inn's door opened, and the coachman waved them inside. "Come on."

And then the dratted man grabbed her again and yanked her after him through the inn, up the stairs, and into a room where the innkeeper held a door open. Josie felt like a child's doll, only not so well pampered.

It was a small, plain room with only a bed, a small table, and a rickety chair. Westman finally released her and then proceeded to prowl the room, checking every corner and eve. She sank down on the chair, prepared for a long stay. He looked as though he had every intention of barricading the doors and window when the search was over.

"I think we're safe," she said when he looked under the tiny, low bed for a third time. "No one is here but us."

"Just making sure." He turned the bed's sheets and peered under them. "There might be more of them."

"More of them? I'm sure there are criminals and vagabonds all over the countryside. We were just unlucky enough to interrupt two of them today. And since we didn't go after them, they're free to hurt someone else tomorrow."

He straightened from his search and looked at her. "Is that what you thought those men were? Vagabonds?"

"Horse thieves, perhaps," she said, after a minute of thought. "The horses in the paddock were unattended. Maybe they thought to steal them."

"Or maybe they thought to blow your head off so they wouldn't have to share the treasure with you."

Josie gaped at him. "Treasure? What does this have to do with the treasure?"

"Everything. Since I left London—hell, even before that—I had the feeling we were being watched. Followed."

"You never said anything."

He pulled a handkerchief from his coat and handed it to her. When she looked at it blankly, he dabbed her cheek with it. She winced at the sting and then allowed his touch.

"I was being paranoid enough without making you suspicious, too," he said quietly, his breath on her cheek. "And those men. I know you didn't get a good look at them, but one of them looked familiar. I can't place it. Something about his face."

"Westman, really, I don't think—"

And then something struck her. When the men had shot the first time, and she'd fallen to the grass, one had asked the other, "Did ye hit her?"

Her.

She was still wearing her boy's clothing and with

her hair tucked up in a hat, which she had lost in the scuffle with Westman but which she had been wearing when she first emerged from the carriage, she looked like a young boy. From that distance, the men could not have possibly guessed she was a girl.

Unless they knew who she was

Unless they were searching for her and Westman.

"What is it?" he asked, watching her closely.

Her head snapped up. "We have to go after them. We can't let them get to the treasure before we do."

She was up and on her way to the door, but Westman was faster. He stepped in front of it, blocking her way. "Slow down, Miss Impatient. They went through the woods, and they're armed. Even if we both had pistols and could shoot, I'd want a dozen men before I went off tracking two men who have a hundred places in which to hide, take aim, and fire."

"But the treasure—"

"Is safe. We have the map. That's what they're after. It has to be. Shoot us and steal it, and they're on their way."

Josie shook her head. "But no one knows about the treasure. No one knows we found the map."

Westman stepped back, paced across the floor, and considered. Josie slid away from the door and sat on the bed, watching him pace. "We should make a list of everyone who knows about the treasure and our search," she said.

"Exactly." He paused at the edge of the table. "There's your cousin Miss Brittany and Lord and Lady Valentine. I assume you told them in order to procure their carriage."

"Yes, but they wouldn't ever—"

"We're not blaming anyone. Then your cousin, Lady Madeleine. Does she know?"

Josie nodded. "And my mother and father and brothers. They know about the treasure, though they have no idea I've been searching for the other half of the map. But they know the treasure existed. Whether or not they believe it still exists is another question."

"Very well, if we're listing everyone who knows about the treasure, then we add my mother and grandmother. My sister as well, though, truly none of them believe in it. Perhaps my grandmother. She did have the last journals." He was silent, apparently thinking for a moment. "Who else?"

"I can't think of anyone without thinking of everyone."

Westman began pacing again.

"Everyone in the *ton* has heard rumors of the treasure," she continued, "but that wouldn't cause any of them to go after us now. It must be someone who is aware of our search."

Westman stopped before her. "That leaves us with your cousins. How much have you told them?"

Josie shook her head. "Snippets. Nothing, really, but can you truly suspect them?"

"No," he agreed. "It's not reasonable. We have to think harder. Someone is trying to kill us, and I'm not leaving until I know who it is."

Chapter 17

An hour passed, maybe more, and Stephen called for wine, then bread and cheese, then a fire. He and Josephine were safe in their nest and getting nowhere.

They'd added the warehouse owner in Seven Dials to their list of people who might know of their search for the treasure, and that had sparked off a bit of conjecture. Had the owner suspected their true purpose in coming to the warehouse, and, if so, whom had he told?

"What does it matter?" Josephine had asked. She was lying on the bed, and Stephen thought she might be a bit tipsy. She'd drunk a good many glasses of wine, and her speech was slurred. One arm was slung over her head, and she waved the other around expansively when talking.

Yes, she was definitely tipsy.

Stephen was glad. He didn't want any more trouble from her tonight. The fool girl had actually wanted to go after the men who'd shot at her. He'd had to hold her back.

The little idiot! She didn't even carry a knife, much less a pistol. Was she going to argue her way into apprehending them?

He chuckled to himself. She probably could, too. She'd argued her way into his life. She was good at getting what she wanted.

But so was he.

Damn, why hadn't the little chit just stayed in London where she would have been safe? Correction: Had she stayed in London, they both would have been safe—she from gunmen and bullets and he from her ample charms.

He glanced at her on the bed, where a few of those ample charms were in evidence. Her shirt collar was unbuttoned so he could see the long lines of her throat, and she'd removed her boots, so that her small ankles were on display. He thought about wrapping a hand around that ankle, kissing her there, and then allowing his lips to travel up her calf, to her thigh . . .

He wanted her again.

He knew he couldn't have her, but as he watched her lie on the bed, watched the subtle rise and fall of her breasts beneath the boy's shirt, all he could think about was stripping that shirt off and glorying in the treasures beneath. She was a beautiful woman, and she would be a fascinating lover.

She was a bit unschooled, as one might expect, but she'd pleased him immensely—more than he could ever have anticipated.

One night with Josephine Hale, and he was captivated. But it wasn't just one night. He'd been charmed slowly and over days and days spent in her company, and Westman knew he was a drowning man. He'd known since the first night they'd met; only he hadn't wanted to admit it.

But he was drowning, all right. Floundering like a fool. What else could he call behavior whereby he knelt naked on the floor and begged a woman to marry him? Especially when he had known what the answer would be.

She didn't want him. Maybe he should let her face the consequences of her foolishness. Let her be sorry.

He thought of this afternoon, and his gut clenched. Damn it. Was he supposed to stand back and allow the little idiot to get herself killed?

He couldn't chance another attack. He had to figure out who those men were or face them later, closer to the treasure. Face them tomorrow, quite possibly.

Stephen scoured his brain, thought back on the images he'd stored from the afternoon. One of the men was a complete stranger. He knew he'd never seen that one before. But the other . . .

He put his head in his hands and pulled his fingers through his thick, tangled hair.

"What's wrong?" Josie asked. She leaned on one elbow and peered over at him.

"I knew that man today."

"You've said that a dozen times." She lay back on the pillow and looked back up at the ceiling. "Not the man who shot at me. The other one. There was something familiar about him to you."

Stephen nodded. "If I can just figure out where I last saw him—"

"Seven Dials?"

"No."

"Are you sure? He could have been leaning against the wall of a warehouse or selling something in the street."

"No, that's not it." Though the suggestion did spark something.

"Well, whoever he was, we won't find him tonight." She yawned. "Can you order something for dinner? I'm starving."

Stephen glanced at the bread and cheese plate she had all but devoured.

"I'll send a man down for dinner."

"Good. And tomorrow morning I want—"

"Stop giving me orders."

"Fine, but wouldn't it be wonderful if, by tomorrow evening, we were in possession of the treasure?"

Stephen watched her green eyes light up. Josie and the treasure. Truly, she was obsessed with it. He went to the door and ordered one of the grooms he'd stationed outside to fetch them stew and bread and closed the door again. Then he sat at the table and rubbed the bridge of his nose, willing his mind to conjure up the memory of the man who'd tried to kill Josie today.

"Are you still thinking about that man?" she asked, rising wobbly to sit on the edge of the bed. "We wouldn't have to speculate if we'd gone after him today. We'd have him here and could question him."

Stephen scowled at her. "No, we'd be dead right now if we'd done that. You and I were in no position to chase after two armed men."

"Well, I think—"

"Miss Hale, I know what I'm talking about. I worked with the army in India, and I trained specifically with the Punjabi trackers. I do know something of what I speak."

"I heard you were in India," she said, sitting straighter. "I've always wanted to go there."

He laughed. "Why? It's hot and rank and full of disease."

"But it's also full of—"

"Adventure. I should have guessed. I did not go for the adventure. My father sent me, and I went because I had no other choice." He let out a bitter laugh. "Because if I hadn't gone of my own free will, he threatened to have me kidnapped and transported."

She gasped and put a hand to her mouth. It was an overdramatic gesture—the wine's influence—but he still found her shock touching. He found anyone's concern for him touching. He hadn't experienced much tenderness in his life.

"Why would your father do that to you?" she asked, hand still resting on her lips. "Didn't he worry that you'd be hurt or fall ill?"

"I think he would have preferred that. My father didn't like me." It was a harsh truth, and one he'd never before revealed. And he didn't know why he told her now. Perhaps because he didn't think she'd remember or maybe because she seemed to care. Or maybe it was time he told someone.

"My brother was always the favored one." Stephen leaned back in his chair and propped his foot on the edge of the table. "He was the heir and the perfect son. I suppose I had too much of my grandfather in me. I was always getting into trouble."

Josephine nodded. "I was too, but that didn't mean my parents wanted to get rid of me. Well, not most the time."

Josephine was watching him closely now, her expression serious. "You must have been very wicked to be sent so far away."

Stephen felt the bile rise in his throat, but he forced himself to look her in the face. "I ruined a girl," he said baldly, unwilling to soften the facts.

"She was no older that you. Innocent. Naive. She thought she loved me. I bedded her and thought no more about it."

Josie didn't blink, but her hands were clenched in her lap.

"It was the girl's first Season. Her family had scraped together the funds to sponsor her, and all their hopes were pinned on her marrying well. When I wouldn't see her anymore"—he clenched his jaw and forced himself to say it, to relive it— "when I had tired of her, she grew increasingly upset. She confronted me at the theater, and I made a public spectacle of her. She was disgraced, and her family's hopes shattered."

"What happened to her?" Josie whispered.

Westman took a long breath. "She killed herself. Her mother found her hanging from a rope tied to a beam in the attic."

"Oh, Stephen." Josephine's eyes were shiny with moisture.

He held his hand up. "Don't pity me, Miss Hale. My suffering was nothing to what I'd caused."

Josie stared at her white knuckles, then looked up at him, green eyes dry now and hard as emeralds. "I'm not that girl, you know. You haven't ruined me. I'd never allow that to happen."

"You're so young. You think you're invincible."

She smiled. "I will be when we find the treasure."

"The goddamn treasure again—"

A knock sounded on the door, and Stephen rose

to answer it. Taking the food from the servant girl, he placed it on the table then gave her a half-shilling. When he turned from closing the door, Josephine had already dragged the table closer to the bed and was breaking off a piece of bread.

"I don't want to argue," she said.

He didn't protest. Anything to forget his sins.

"What was India like?" she asked.

"Hot. I was always so hot. Even when I was naked"—he grinned at her—"forgive me for mentioning that indelicacy—"

"Oh, no! I'm enjoying the image. Go on."

Cheeky girl. He liked that. "Even when I was naked, I was still uncomfortably warm. I used to dream about the cold winters in England. I fantasized about snow and ice."

"You dreamed about it?" She dipped her bread in her stew, and he lifted his own spoon for a taste. "Nothing romantic about red noses and shivering."

"I'll take the cold weather over the hot any day. Ask any Englishman who's been to India, and he'll tell you the same."

She ate another bite of bread then reached for the wine. She bumped the bottle and almost toppled it. When she finally had it steadied, she fumbled with the cork and knocked her spoon on the floor. Before she could spill the entire bottle all over herself, Stephen took it from her and filled her glass halfway. "I'm thirsty," she said, eyeing the glass with displeasure.

He corked the bottle.

With a shrug, she sipped her wine. "So what else do you remember of India?"

He thought back and tried to decide how to arrange all the colors and smells and tastes that had been his life for all those years into something comprehensible to her. "It's far more civilized than the reports will lead you to believe. The people there have their own customs and traditions. They have their own religion, older than ours, and just as developed. They have their own classes of Society, very much like ours, and—"

"Yes, but what about the adventures?" she asked eagerly, holding out her glass for more wine.

With reservation, he poured another sip into her glass. Already her face was flushed, and her eyes were too bright.

"Religion and class are all very interesting, but did you go on adventures?"

"You are incredibly single-minded." He broke off a piece of the warm bread and took a bite. "Has anyone ever told you that?"

"You," she answered. "Especially when you don't want to talk about something."

He inclined his head. "There were adventures, but none like what you imagine. I was there to protect His Majesty's trading interests, not to seek my own fame and fortune. Mostly I sat behind a desk and wrote reports."

"Oh." Her face fell so quickly it was comic.

"I went to India, and I did my duty," Stephen

explained. He pushed away from his plate. "I had a lot of time to think when I was there. A lot of time to feel sorry for myself and wish I'd done things differently. And a lot of time to repent for all my sins."

"With the girl?"

"That wasn't all. I gambled, lost a vast amount of our family fortune."

"So that's true." She set her glass down. "I didn't want to believe—"

"I tried to warn you," he said. "I told you to stay away from me. And in the end, I did exactly what I always have—I took advantage of our relationship."

"You treated me with nothing but respect," she countered. "*I* seduced *you*."

"I knew what I was doing. I could have resisted—"

She put a hand on his arm, leaning closer. The temptation to kiss her made it difficult for him to concentrate.

"You could have done a lot of things, and yet everything you did for me was well-intentioned." She waved her arms exuberantly, and he caught the wine bottle and set it on the floor before she sent it flying.

"I didn't like it when you tried to drag me away from Seven Dials, or when you yelled at me for climbing out of the window, but you were worried and acted out of kindness. I didn't like it when you took my map or left on this trip without me, but I understand your reasons."

"You do?" he said skeptically.

"I don't like them, but I know how you men are."

"We men? I see."

"Face it, Stephen Doubleday, you are not a bad man. You are not the reprobate your Society has made you out to be."

Much to her displeasure, he was sure. He'd never met a lady so desperate to get involved with a rogue. And he'd never been unable to oblige.

But she was wrong. Underneath all the good intentions, he was exactly the man his Society made him out to be. And it would take mere seconds to show her that.

He stood and looked down at her, already imagining her beneath him on the bed. He was watching her lips move and imagining all the wicked ways he could put them to good use.

"Don't paint me too pretty, Miss Hale. I'm not the angel you seem to think."

"Oh, please. I've never met a better-behaved scoundrel. I really had expected so much worse from you."

A challenge? He couldn't believe this. Did she realize the treacherous ground she was treading on? He shouldn't touch her tonight. He shouldn't ever touch her again. And yet she goaded him. Called him an angel. If she could just see into his mind, she'd see how far from the truth that moniker was.

"Are you saying I've disappointed .you?" he said quietly, stepping closer to her until he stood over her.

"No, not disappointed—well, the first time I kissed you I was disappointed, but—"

He moved the table away from the bed, giving himself clear access to her, and then he took hold of her and dragged her to her feet.

Her eyes widened even as she fell into his embrace. "You're not thinking to . . . now, are you? I mean—"

"You've had too much to drink, Miss Hale. That is an interesting position. A compromising position."

"And you're going to take advantage of me?" she breathed, excitement making her words husky. "Ooh, I like that."

"Do you?" He yanked her shirttails out of her boy's trousers and pulled the shirt over her head. She'd bound her breasts with a strip of linen, and he smiled when he saw it. So that was why he hadn't been able to see the shape of her breasts all night. With slow, deliberate movements, he loosened the knot holding the material in place and began to unwrap her.

"I'm going to strip you bare, Josephine," he said, turning her until she laughed. She stumbled, but his hands were on her warm torso, holding her steady.

"I want to see those perfect breasts of yours, squeeze them in my hands, suck on your nipples. Would you like that?"

"Oh, yes," she said, and he executed the last turn. Her back was to him, and he reached around her cupping her in his hands, kneading her flesh.

"I love the way you feel, do you know that?" he whispered in her ear. She shivered.

"I love the way you feel." She pushed her bottom against his hard cock. "I want to feel you everywhere."

He dipped his hands lower, running them along her abdomen until they reached her belly. Slipping them inside the waistband, he loosened the flap and pushed the trousers over her hips.

She wore nothing underneath, and his hands were soon filled with her warm flesh. He cupped her bottom, wedged his thigh between her legs, and spread them slightly. "I want to bend you over and plunge inside you," he growled in her ear. "I want to take you right now. Like this."

In illustration, he bent her at the waist, but instead of loosening his own trousers, he knelt behind her, spread her thighs, and dipped his tongue into her. She was as sweet as he remembered, all the more so because he had her the way he wanted. He pulled back, admiring her pink flesh, then adjusted slightly and ran his tongue along her small, hard nub. Her legs tensed, and she moaned with pleasure.

She was at an awkward angle, and he knew her

balance was already sketchy, so he kept one arm around her waist, holding her to his mouth as he suckled and licked. She was so tense, so ready, that it was a matter of seconds before she came. And then it was fast and hard, her bucking against him like a horse.

And didn't that just give him a dozen more wicked ideas.

Chapter 18

Josie's head was spinning, partly from the wine and partly from Westman's skilled lips and fingers. She had barely got her breath back, when he pulled her up and turned her around.

To her surprise, he tugged her into a gentle embrace, holding her carefully, almost as though she were a porcelain doll. It was nice. She'd never been treated like a fragile thing before. And she was not under the illusion that any man would have acted the same. He was an exceptional lover. Even inexperienced as she was, she knew that there was something remarkable between them.

Had she ever imagined that a man could give her so much pleasure? Had she ever understood how consuming being held by a man like Westman could be? Why, he could make her forget all about treasure and clearing her grandfather's name with one kiss. And tonight she wanted to forget.

Tonight she wanted to give him as much pleasure as he had given her. An idea sprang to mind, and she lifted her lashes to peer at him surreptitiously. She caught a brief glimpse of his cheek.

Surely she shouldn't consider doing something so wicked. What would he think of her? What would she think of herself? Could she sit across from him in the carriage all day tomorrow after . . .

Oh, drat the consequences. It was one more new adventure. Who knew when or if she would ever again find a lover like this? And tomorrow Westman might start all the marriage proposing again. This might be her only opportunity to experience it all.

She slid her hands from around his waist, allowed them a brief excursion to the hard muscles of his back, then dragged them and herself away.

"I think we have a problem, Lord Westman," she said, stepping back.

She was naked and quite aware of that fact, but be it the wine or the recent pleasure, she didn't really care right now. She sat on the bed, loving the way his eyes flowed over her body hungrily. It made all the heat coil in her belly again. It made her thighs moist and her nipples harden.

"A problem, Miss Hale? I would think you might feel relatively worry free at the moment."

"Oh, I'm far from satisfied, my lord, especially when you are still wearing so many clothes."

He looked down at his shirt, coat, and trousers, then back up at her. "I see the problem. How would you like to resolve it?"

"Strip for me." She waved her arm as in a command. "Take it all off. And do it slowly."

She didn't know what demon had possessed her, what wild spirit had given her this brash courage. Even Westman looked surprised at her suggestion. Surprised but not offended.

She eyed the bulge in his pants. No, not offended at all.

With infinite grace, he lifted a hand to his cravat, loosened the cloth, and stripped it off. Next came his coat. It was tight and molded to his figure, and she had watched one of his men help him struggle into it this morning, but now it fell off him like water.

Next were his boots. He sat in the lone chair to wrench those free, then set them neatly on the floor and pulled off his stockings as well.

Barefoot and coatless, he looked quite vulnerable. She liked it. She wanted him just as naked and just as aroused as she was.

"Take it all off, my lord," she ordered. "Start with the shirt."

He complied with a nod. There were three buttons at the top, and he loosened them, then began to drag the shirt over his head.

"Slowly, my lord," she reminded him. "Slowly."

He paused, glanced at her, then inclined his head. His next movement was slow and languorous as a cat's. She was treated to a revelation of one delicious inch after another of the bronzed, toned skin of his abdomen. And then the material moved over his chest proper, revealing that light smattering of chestnut hair. Josie felt her breath quicken.

He pulled the garment off, tossed it at her feet, and she stared at his corded shoulders, his chiseled biceps. She admired the way his muscles bunched when he flexed his hands.

"Would you like me to turn around?" he asked, his tone sarcastic.

She would have. Anything to see more of him. She could have stared at him for days, studied him for years. His body was so beautiful. It had been honed and refined by hard work in India, tanned there as well, and she felt like a pale milksop beside him.

"Your trousers, my lord," Josie said, pointing to the offending garment. "Turn around and take them off." She could imagine the dips and planes of his back, glowing quietly bronze in the candlelight. She could imagine the whisper of wool against skin, and then the black material sliding over his round, tight bottom.

He stepped closer to her. "Haven't you had enough of games, Miss Hale?"

"Not yet," she murmured. "In fact, there is something I'd like to try, if you will allow it." *Here it goes,* she thought. If he thought her the most wanton woman he'd ever met after this, she couldn't blame him.

She glanced up at him. As she expected, he looked intrigued. "I'll keep an open mind."

She lifted her hand, ran it up his thigh muscles, then rested it on his hard erection.

"So far, I'm in agreement." His voice was strained, and she noticed when she pressed against him harder, he had to gasp in a breath.

Oh, dear, but she was truly wanton because she loved this. She loved pleasing him, having this effect on him, driving him as mad with desire as he had driven her. Buoyed by her success thus far, she fumbled with the fall of his trousers, loosened it, then pushed the black material over his slim hips and down to his knees.

He didn't move away, his expression still one of casual interest, but given another moment, she intended to change that expression to something more like passion. She scooted back on the bed, swung her knees around, and knelt before him. His erection, thick and hard, rose magnificently before her, and even though she wanted to draw out the anticipation, she couldn't stop her hand from cupping the tip.

"I like that," he said, reaching for her. "Let me show you—"

"No." She held a hand up, and he blinked at her in surprise.

"I want to kiss you."

He moved close again. "And I want to kiss you."

She reached out, cupped the tip of him again. "I want to kiss you here."

"Oh, God." He shook his head, his expression one of agonized restraint. "Jos—Miss Hale—I don't think—"

"Good. I don't want you to." And then she bent and kissed the tip of him softly.

He was velvet against her lips, warm and so smooth, and she took a chance and darted her tongue out to tease him. His breath hitched in and his whole body swayed for a moment.

She darted her tongue out again, and when his response pleased her, she bent lower and swirled her tongue around the circumference of him.

"Oh, God," he moaned, and she felt his hand on her shoulder as he attempted to steady himself.

She swirled again, this time holding him steady by wrapping a hand along the root. At the same time, she opened her mouth and took the head inside. The hand on her shoulder tightened, and she knew she was expected to do more, but she paused, uncertain.

"Take more of me inside your mouth," he whispered, his voice full of gravel. "Make me hot and wet."

She did so, watching the way his leg muscles

tensed and his back arched. At one point, she even slid her hands around to his buttocks and gripped the tense muscles there.

She kissed and licked, drew away, repeated, and she knew each tiny movement of her mouth brought him closer to ecstasy. His grip on her shoulder was almost painful, and he was all but rocking with her, when he suddenly pulled back.

She looked up, her mouth open in surprise.

"I don't want to end it this way," he said, gesturing to her. "I love what you're doing." He was panting, gasping for breath. "But I want to be inside you."

Josie wanted the same thing. She loved touching him, but she missed the feel of his hands on her. In silent acquiescence, she scooted back on the bed and began to lie down.

"Oh, no," he said, shaking his head. "Not this time. This time I lie down."

She felt her cheeks heat at his suggestion. She knew what he wanted—well, she'd heard whispers that hinted at it—but she had no idea how it really worked. "But I—I don't know what to do."

Lord, this was mortifying.

"I'll show you," he said, kneeling on the bed beside her. "I'll enjoy showing you." He took her in his arms, held her against his chest, and she would have burrowed in if she could. He was so warm and he smelled so good. His arms were strong and his breathing steady, though she could feel the hardness of his erection pushing insistently against her belly.

With gradual movements, he pulled her down on the bed until she was half spread over him. She leaned up on one elbow and looked into his deep blue eyes. "Your eyes are huge," she murmured. "So dark. So blue."

"Desire for you." He stroked her cheek. "Disbelief that I'm actually here, lying next to you. You're so beautiful."

She shook her head. "Ashley is beautiful. Maddie is striking. I'm the fun one."

"You're that too, and you're beautiful to me."

She didn't know why, but her heart seemed to expand in her chest when he spoke those words. She'd heard them before, knew they were lies men told women to be polite or to get what they wanted, but Westman looked so sincere. His eyes did not lie. Josie leaned down and kissed his soft, full lips and felt his hand on her back tighten.

As always, he kissed her deeply, with passion and desire, but there was something else there as well. Why hadn't she noticed it before? Had it been there before?

He deepened the kiss, his tongue thrusting into her as she imagined he wanted to do with his body, and then he was pulling her on top of him.

She rose, using his chest as a lever, and he smiled up at her. "You look like a goddess on your throne."

She positioned herself above him, felt his hard erection graze her aching core. "Are you prepared to worship me?"

"I'm prepared to offer myself up for your pleasure."

She took the tip of him inside her, just the tip, and he groaned. His hands settled on her hips, holding her tightly, and yet she was still in control.

"More," he breathed. "Please, please, more."

She slid a fraction lower, and he closed his eyes, his expression mirroring pain. "Are you hurt?" she asked.

"You're torturing me. Put me out of my misery."

And with one last movement, she took him fully inside her. His hard length stretched her and filled her with swirls of pleasure that danced and multiplied. And then she moved, and the coils danced faster, spinning inside her and driving her onward.

"You feel so good," he ground out, matching her rhythm. "So tight. So beautiful."

And when she looked down at him, the heat of his gaze made her body tighten.

"So beautiful," he repeated, and then she arched back and the pleasure inside her reached a crescendo. She bucked against him, unable to slow her movements. Her body wanted fast, fast, fast. Inside her, she could feel him swell and thicken, and she bit her lip to stifle the cry. But it was too late and the orgasm too strong. With a final thrust, she flew over the edge, crying with the joy of it, falling against him, only to be caught by his warm, strong arms.

Stephen held her as she slept. He'd told her about his past, and she still hadn't understood her fate. She still thought the treasure could save her.

And maybe it could. If one had enough money, Society could forgive anything. But Stephen was not going to rely on fool's gold. Treasure or no, Josie would be his. And if their families disapproved, damn them all. He'd rather go to hell than watch Josie suffer for his mistakes.

He looked at Josie again. Even now, lying in his arms, he knew she wasn't dreaming of him. She was dreaming of treasure. The challenge of the treasure.

She wanted a challenge, an adventure? He'd give her one.

Morning came quickly and Stephen and Josie were on their way before dawn had fully broken. Stephen had been studying the treasure map and had decided the most likely place to begin their search of the Cornish coast was Polperro. A sheltered village of fishermen with quaint cottages and Saxon and Roman bridges, Polperro was known for its smuggling. Wagonloads of contraband left the city, traveling across the Bodmin Moor to London.

The place had been mentioned more than once in James Doubleday's journals. He and Nathan Hale had owned several houses with cellars where they could hide and dodge the customs men. Stephen had told Josie of his plan, and she had agreed, then promptly fell back asleep on the other side of the carriage.

He couldn't blame her. He'd awakened her two more times in the night and made love to her. He couldn't get enough of her, and for once, maybe that had been to his advantage. It was better if she slept now. She'd need her strength for treasure hunting.

She slept most of the morning, and by two or three in the afternoon, they'd arrived in Polperro. Stephen woke her, then instructed the driver to take them on a brisk ride along the coastline. He and Josie watched for terrain that matched the map, but after an hour, they gave up and decided to stop at an inn.

Stephen would have eaten and stayed in for the night, preferring to start their search fresh in the morning, but Josie had slept all day and was more than eager to begin. She argued that waiting would give the men who had attacked them at the inn time to track and follow them. Now was the safest time to search.

She all but dragged him out of the inn, and as the sun sank lower behind the pretty color-washed houses of the village, they headed down to the beach.

It had been a sunny day that had heated up the shore enough so that by afternoon it was still pleasant to walk. The last rays of sun filtered through the clouds when Josie and Stephen stepped onto the beach. There were not many other people out at this time. A few fishermen pulled boats in, hauling their catch toward the town; and a family played in the surf and sand, the children dancing in the cold water.

"This is nice," Josie said, turning to him and giving him that smile that melted his heart every time.

"A bit domestic for me," he lied, and she nodded as though that was exactly what she'd expected him to say.

"Well, we're far from domestic. Grandchildren of pirates and treasure hunters that we are." She took his hand, and as always, Stephen had the urge to pull her into his arms and kiss her senseless. Instead, he squeezed her hand, and after a moment, released it.

"You're dressed like a young boy," he said, when she gave him an inquisitive glance. "I don't want to elicit comment."

They continued down the beach, by unspoken consent heading for the more remote, craggy areas. "I thought perhaps you'd tired of me," she finally said, her voice barely audible in the breeze.

"Hardly." His tone was world-weary, urbane. "I give you at least another week. Perhaps two."

She made a sound like a small cry, and when he looked at her, he saw the quick flash of pain. And then she caught him looking, and her demeanor changed. He saw the veil descend, saw the icy expression settle into place.

He hid a smile. Soon, she'd be asking—no, begging—him to marry her.

"Let's climb up a bit," she suggested after another quarter mile. She pointed to a crop of granite rocks rising out of the shoreline a few yards away. "It's going to be dark in a few minutes. Let's use the last of the light to climb up and decide where to search tomorrow."

The rocks were worn smooth by wind and water, but that did not make the climb any easier. Josie had good balance and a lithe step, but he still had to assist her at some of the more treacherous spots. Finally, they reached the top and, panting, looked out over the violet water.

The first stars sprinkled the sky, and the sun was an orange paper lantern. "It's beautiful," Josie said. "Just beautiful."

Westman was looking at her, her skin bathed in the vibrant light, and thinking the same thing.

And then he heard a crack, and there was a flash of pain in his calf.

He stared down, saw the trickle of blood seeping through his ripped trousers, and his gaze met Josie's wide-eyed green eyes.

"Get down!"

They fell in a tangle of arms and legs. But even flat on the ground, there was nowhere to hide. They were on the highest point for miles, and around them was nothing but hard, unyielding granite. The sea was on one side and the perilous climb down on the other. No trees, no bushes, just rocks and sparse grass.

They were the perfect targets.

Chapter 19

❦

Josie landed on a rock and her shoulder exploded with pain. But she wasn't shot. That was the most important thing.

"Stephen," she croaked when she could force a bit of air back into her lungs. "Are you badly hurt? You're bleeding."

"A nick, that's all," he answered. He was practically on top of her, shielding her with his body. He was always trying to protect her—an annoying habit until right now, when she really needed it.

She heard another crash from the area of the beach where they had come from, and a shot whizzed over their heads. "That was close!" she screamed, and Stephen pulled her against him.

"We have to get down from here. We're sitting targets."

Of course they were, she thought. She knew this treasure was bad luck. Being shot at was probably only one of the trials they'd endure.

Josie glanced around. All about them was smooth granite and soft grass. Then she spotted the opening. "There." She pointed to the fissure in the rock. "We can climb down there."

"And if they climb up after us?" Westman shot back, but he was already moving toward the slice in the rock.

"One problem at a time," Josie told him. "I solved this one. You take the next."

"So nice of you to share."

His body disappeared over the wall of rock. Another shot whizzed by, this one closer. "Josie, get down here!"

She pulled herself along the ground until she was at the edge of the rock, and then she looked down.

Her head swam and spun so violently she thought she would be ill. The drop was twenty feet or more, straight down into the churning water and jagged rocks below.

Oh, no. She was not going that way. Anything but that. She'd face pistols before that.

She began to inch back, feeling the imaginary bite of the bullet in the small of her back. It would be a piercing pain, she knew, and then she'd lie here, her blood draining away until the men found her and finished her off.

A hand reached out and caught her wrist. "Get down here," Stephen ordered, his head poking over the lip of the cliff.

She shook her head and tried to escape, but his hand was like a vise. "I can't." She reared back violently, her hair falling into her eyes. "I'm afraid of heights, of falling."

Once the admission was out, she couldn't take it back. She glanced up at him, sure his eyes would reflect disgust at her weakness, but Westman's blue eyes met hers with unwavering solidity. "Yes, you can, Josephine. You can do it. Climb over. I'll catch you."

The bullets had stopped, but Josie heard another sound far more distressing. The men were climbing up the rocks. She could hear their boots scraping on the granite and the muffled curses that followed.

"They're coming," she squeaked. Her limbs were shaking, but she forced herself back to the edge of the cliff, back to Westman and his steadfast faith in her. She would scoot over the edge and join him. He had done it, so why couldn't she? And he would be there to catch her. She wouldn't fall.

But when she looked down again, when she saw that drop, her body rebelled. "I can't do it," she said, pulling away again. Lord, but she was a coward. Her grandfather would have been so disappointed.

Westman didn't let go of her, and his grip on her

wrist was punishing. She could hear the men coming closer, knew time was running out.

"You can do it," Westman said. "Look at me, only me, and you can do it."

His gaze met hers and held, and she forced herself to ignore the approaching voices and the sheer drop and stare into his blue eyes. She had once thought she could stare at them for days. Now she would test their power, and her own courage.

She inched closer to the lip, closer to Westman, felt the ground open into empty space beneath her shoulders, and wanted desperately to look down.

"Look right here," Westman demanded. "Right here."

She had hated his protectiveness, had never thought that she needed that kind of care. Now she knew she'd been wrong. She needed him, needed at this moment to be taken care of, and there was no shame in that. It didn't make her weak or unequal. It made her human.

She stared into those blue eyes, darker than the sky on a clear day but lighter than the deep of the ocean. His strong hands grasped her under her arms, supporting her.

"I have you," he promised her. "Come to me."

She stared into those eyes, as blue as a placid lake or a tiny speckled bird's egg. Her eyes locked on his, she allowed him to lift her and pull her over the edge. For a moment, it seemed his balance, and thus hers, teetered. For an instant, she feared they would crash over the cliff into the hungry waves below.

And then he had her, and she was burrowed into his coat, safe and warm and surrounded by the smells of horse and earth and man.

Like a baby, she clutched his coat and held on. She could feel the tears stinging behind her eyelids, fighting to be free, but Josie didn't cry. She hadn't cried when she was eight and broke her arm after a fall from a tree, and she wouldn't cry now. But she thanked God he had been there to save her—that he would be there to save her.

"Josie," Westman whispered. She felt his finger under her chin and grudgingly allowed him to lift her face from its safe cocoon. She was once again staring into those calm, sure eyes. "We can't stay here. They'll find us. We have to move down."

Josie chanced to look down and the feeling of falling overwhelmed her. She clutched Westman as her body was shocked into rigid fear.

"Josie," his voice was low and calm. Listening to him speak, she would have thought they were alone in bed, making slow, leisurely love, with all the time in the world. And yet above her, she could hear the men climbing the final few feet.

"I have you. I won't let you fall. We must climb down. There, see that ledge?"

She closed her eyes and shook her head. "I can't look down," she whispered, fighting the nausea that churned her stomach at the very thought.

"Then just listen." His voice soothed and placated. "There's a wide ledge, perhaps three feet, just a short climb down. I'm going to lower you onto the ledge and then come down after. I'm betting there's a space underneath the ledge, a place we can hide."

"You're betting?" she said, trying to keep her voice from jittering. "I don't think this is something I want you to wager on."

"Oh, come on." His voice had turned teasing. "I thought you liked adventure. Let's take a risk."

She opened her eyes. "You know what? I don't think I like risks anymore. I would much prefer to be home practicing my embroidery. Yes, I think that's what I want to do."

He grinned at her. They were hanging on to the lip of a cliff, a deadly drop beneath them, and he was smiling. "Too late. I'm going to lower you now."

He took her hands in his, and she clamped her teeth together, trying to force some of the famous Hale courage into her blood. Where had it all gone now that she needed it? What had the *Morning Post* called her? The Unflappable Josephine Hale. Lord, she felt distinctly flappable right now.

Westman wedged himself closer to the rock at their backs, then hands clamped securely on her, he lifted her.

She let out a small squeak—just one—and dropped. She tried very hard to watch her feet and only her feet. The dark water churning below her was nothing. It didn't matter. The ledge Westman had told her about was inching closer. Her dangling feet almost touched it. Another inch. There.

"Okay?" Westman asked above her. "I'm letting go. Brace yourself."

He released one hand, and she clutched at a rock outcropping before he released the next. With tiny steps, she pushed herself to the far end of the ledge, giving Westman as much room as possible. She dared not look up, but she could hear him above her, see tiny showers of dust and rock cascade past her and into the abyss below.

And even over the roar of the surf and the howl of the wind, she could hear the men's voices. They were at the top of the outcrop now, and they were searching for them. It wouldn't be long until they looked over the edge. When they shot, would she be dead before she fell? Or would the bullet hit her, pushing her off the cliff, and into a slow falling arc that gave her three impossibly long seconds to contemplate her violent death?

"I'm here," Westman said, and then she felt his large solid body beside her. The ledge was too small for the both of them, and she teetered for a moment before regaining her hold.

"They're here," Josie said in the direction of Westman's ear.

He looked up and nodded. "Then it's time I test my theory. I'm betting five pounds there's a space to hide beneath this ledge. You?"

She stared at him. "Am I supposed to bet against you?"

He winked at her. "No, you're supposed to give me a kiss for luck."

"Luck? If you go over that ledge and there's nowhere to hide . . ."

"Just kiss me, Josie. I'll come for you in a moment."

She did as she was told, kissing him quickly but with feeling. After all, if they were going to die, she wanted one last good kiss.

And then Westman was gone. He knelt down, positioned his hands on the rock, and, holding on, dropped his body off the ledge.

One after the other, his hands released the rock, and he disappeared. She listened for the sound of his body thumping against the rock. She listened for the splash as he hit the water below.

"There she is!" a voice boomed from above. "Shoot her."

Josie's head snapped back, and she stared up. That was far worse than looking down. The sense of falling hit her harder than ever, and she grappled with the tiny handholds that were her lifelines.

Above her, the darkening sky surrounding them, were the two men from the inn yesterday. They'd followed. Either that or known where to go. In the dusky light, she saw one of them lift something that glinted silver and point it.

She hugged the rock tighter, squeezing her eyes shut, and then her feet were out from under her, and she was on her knees. The bullet hit six inches from where she now knelt, sending a spray of rock into her face. She fell on her belly, holding on to the ledge with both hands as she'd watched Westman do. The air flew out of her lungs at the strength of her impact on the rock that had been beneath her.

Her feet dangled in the void, nothing below but rock and water. Nothing waiting above but another bullet, which she knew might come any time. She slipped lower, her hands too weak to hold the rock for long. She slipped over the edge, held on for one moment, and then let herself fall.

Stephen caught her, almost falling himself, and pulled her back into the safety of the small alcove. It had not been directly under the ledge, as he'd hoped, but a bit to the left, which made it a stretch to reach. And it was tiny, so tiny that Stephen doubted it could be called an alcove. Dent was a better description.

But there was room for both of them, barely, and only if they pressed tightly together. Josie was all but on top of him at the moment, and clutching his neck so tightly, he could hardly breathe.

"You're all right," he said in her ear, trying to be heard against the wind and the crash of the waves below. "I told you I wouldn't let you fall."

"You're crazy." Her voice shook with fear and something else. Emotion? He pulled away and looked into her face.

"Are you crying?"

"No." She wiped away a stray tear. "It's the wind.

It stings my eyes." Her breath hitched. "I—I thought you'd fallen."

"I was right here waiting for you."

She was sobbing now, quite loudly, and he cupped the back of her head with one hand and shushed her.

"It's fine now."

"Fine? There are men shooting at us from above and there's a hundred-foot drop below."

"It's closer to twenty feet."

"It's a long drop! What are we going to do?"

That was actually a good question. What were they going to do? They couldn't climb back up. The ledge obscured them from their assailants' view, but it also obstructed their sight. They'd have no way of knowing when or if the men left. Even if they had been certain the men were gone, the climb was barely possible going down. They'd never climb back up safely, not in the dark, which was rapidly closing in.

Stephen stared out at the violet sky and the indigo water. Josie was right. It was a long way down, but they could manage it. He'd done a bit of climbing while in India. The drop looked steeper than it was. All the way down, there were handholds and outcroppings. Once they reached the bottom, the granite boulders that lay there could act as stepping-stones back to shore.

The darkness was the problem. They couldn't climb down in the dark. "The moon," Stephen said suddenly.

Josie pulled away from his chest and looked over his shoulder. "What moon?"

"Is there one tonight? Do you know?"

"I didn't look outside last night," she admitted. "I don't know where we are in the cycle."

"I don't either, but if we get a bit of light from the moon, it should be enough to show us the way down."

"Down?" Josie sounded like she'd choked on the word. "We're not going *down*."

"It's the only way out of here. Besides, there's lots of hand and footholds."

"Westman," she protested. "It's a sheer drop."

"You're scared. It's all right. I'll get us down safely." With that, he settled back into the dented rock and tried to get comfortable. He liked holding Josie in his arms, but he would have preferred a bit more space. Added to his discomfort, his calf burned where the bullet had scraped the skin. He was fortunate the bullet hadn't done more damage. Still, it hurt like hell.

Bending his legs to alleviate some of the pressure, he pushed his back against the wall and positioned his body so that most of his weight was there. He pulled Josie between his legs, offering her one knee to sit on. When that grew tired, he would switch her to the other one.

Night's veil, which had seemed to drop so quickly earlier, now descended slowly, and he watched the sky with impatience for the appearance of more sparkling stars.

"Do you think we'll ever find the treasure?" Josie asked, her breath on his neck.

"No doubt," he said. "We have to find it now. We can't go home with nothing. At least I can't. This is my last hope. This or I pack up my mother and leave for the Continent."

"Perhaps your mother would enjoy France."

"Would yours?"

She laughed. "No. And you know I can't go back without the treasure either."

"No, then you just might be forced to marry me."

"And then we could both go live in France."

He smiled. He had to give her credit. She'd been shaken up after the drop and the shots fired at her. He'd been shaken up too, worried out of his mind that she'd been hit. But now that she'd had her crying jag, she'd recovered. She was no fragile flower.

There was a moment of silence, and he listened hard for the men above them. Only the sound of the wind and waves penetrated their solitude.

"Actually, just about anywhere is better than here," Josie said. "Did you see the men shooting at us?"

"No. You?"

"Yes."

"The same ones we met yesterday at the inn?"

"They must have followed us."

"Or known where we would go."

"That's what I was thinking, too." She sighed.

"And we're right back where we left off last night."

"But of all the people we've named, of all the people who knew or might have guessed what we were up to, who would know where to look for us? We didn't even know where to start until we found the other half of the map." His leg was falling asleep, and he lifted her, transferring her to his other knee.

"That's true," she said, settling on his thigh. "And as far as we know, your half of the map had been hidden in a bank vault for fifty years. No one could have had access to that map. Could they?"

"No." But his heart had stuttered.

"What is it?" she asked. "I can tell you've just thought of something."

"The bank," he murmured. "We didn't have the clerk on our first list."

"That's true," Josie said, and her voice sounded excited. "But remember that we didn't even open the haversack at the bank. He couldn't have known what was inside or what we were searching for."

"True, but if he knew who we were and who originally purchased the box, he might have deduced that we were searching for the treasure."

She shook her head. "A corrupt bank clerk? I suppose it's feasible, but he's surrounded by wealth. Why waste time with a fabled treasure? If he wanted to steal from bank patrons, why not concentrate on some of the real treasures already in the bank? Surely most of those deposit boxes are filled with more than sextants and yellowed treasure maps."

She was right, as usual. But it was an angle they hadn't considered, and something about it rang true for him. Something about the bank, the vault, poked at him. He was forgetting something there . . .

"Westman," Josie said.

He looked up at her, smiled at the wild disarray of her hair.

"I can see you," she said with a grimace.

He felt his own face break into a huge grin. "That's my girl." Looking past her, he saw the moon rising above them, bright and white and almost full. God, it was gorgeous.

Josie looked at it with somewhat less warmth. "I still don't want to climb down."

"Trade places with me. I want to take a look up there. See if our friends are still waiting around."

"Be careful."

She shoved her body into the dent, and he maneuvered carefully around her, then angled so that he was as far out as possible. He grabbed the ledge, held on, and peered out and up. Then, as the trackers in India had taught him, he stood still, listening, watching for any movement from above.

There was nothing.

The men could be waiting for them to make a move so that they had a clear shot. Or they might have gone back down to the beach. After all, one false step and he and Josie were dead.

They'd been lucky to make it this far. He climbed back down and studied the path to the churning ocean below.

Time to see if their luck would last.

Chapter 20

Josie's boots were wet, her hands were scraped, and every single pore inside her vibrated with terror. But she couldn't remember a time when she'd been happier. She could have kissed the rocks beneath her feet, if it didn't mean bending closer to the water sloshing at her feet.

She didn't know how they'd done it, but they'd climbed down. Just as Westman had promised, there'd been places for her hands and feet when she most needed them. The way had been tricky, but not nearly as steep as it had looked from above.

And now they were safe, more or less. They still had to go back to the beach and the inn, but at least they would do it from the ground.

Lord, if she ever arrived home safely, she

promised she would never climb out of a window again.

She promised she would stay on the ground, avoid adventure, avoid heights altogether. Why, she'd even avoid the box seats at the theater.

"Keep moving," Westman called from ahead of her, and Josie reluctantly plodded on. They weren't headed back toward the beach the way they'd come. Westman worried that their fellow treasure hunters might be waiting for them there, and so he had proposed going around the outcropping. At first it seemed like a good idea, but the rock fixture was bigger than it looked. Now that night had truly descended, it was bitterly cold. Her wet toes were numb and her fingers chilled to the bone.

Finally, they reached a small bar of sand, and they both paused to set their boots on solid ground. Maneuvering on the rocks had been difficult, especially when her legs were wobbly from having climbed down the cliff.

Josie looked around her. Behind her was a wall of granite, this one really too steep to climb, in front of her was the sea, cold and deep and seemingly limitless. On either side were rocks and small patches of beach. She couldn't see past the rocks, so it was impossible to tell how far they went on.

"Perhaps we should turn back," Josie said. Her teeth were chattering, and she let Westman hear it. He'd already given her his coat, so it was not as though he could do more to warm her. But it was easier to blame him for her discomfort than her own single-minded search for the treasure. If she'd only been willing to wait until morning . . .

Westman ran a hand through his hair, holding some of the longer strands that the wind whipped out of his face. "You may be right. Even if the rocks taper off up ahead, we still have to circle back to Polperro. It'll take most of the night."

Most of the night. The words fell heavy as stones on the sand. She was tired and hungry and cold, and she just wanted to be back at the inn. Why had she ever thought she wanted adventure? Her pampered life in London had obviously not prepared her for it.

Now, Westman was another story. She had to admit that he'd impressed her. He wasn't some spoiled English nobleman. He was cunning and brave and athletic. The climb down the rocks had left her panting for breath. Westman hadn't even been winded, despite the fact that his leg was injured.

"Look," Westman said finally, "let's go a bit farther, past that formation there, to see what's on the other side."

Josie studied the black rocks and frowned. "And if it looks like all this just goes on and on, then we turn back."

"Then we turn back."

She sighed. "All right."

He grinned at her and took her hand. "You wanted excitement, Miss Hale. You wanted to be a treasure hunter. Welcome to it."

"I'm beginning to have a lot more respect for my grandfather," she said, matching Westman stride for stride as they headed for the rocks ahead. "Do you think he and your grandfather walked along this same beach?"

Westman shrugged. "Parts of it, maybe. If we've read the map correctly."

"And I'm sure they came under cover of darkness. But they didn't have a warm inn to go back to." She shivered, thinking about *The Good Groom*. Had it been a comfortable ship? "If our grandfathers had been caught, they would have been hanged."

"Piracy was illegal."

"And yet everyone knew they were pirates."

"There was no proof."

No proof, Josie repeated in her mind. If only it worked that way for other scandals. But the *ton* wouldn't need proof that she'd slept with Westman to condemn her. Even the mere hint of impropriety could ruin a girl.

Josie figured that by the time they returned to London, there would be more than hints. The thought forced her to push on, jogging a little so Westman would not drag her.

She had to find this treasure. Westman needed the money, and now so did she. What had started out as an adventure, an attempt to prove her grandfather innocent of the murder of Stephen's grandfather, had become her last chance at freedom.

If she returned to London, penniless, she was

doomed. With her reputation in tatters, her parents would foist her on the first man they could find who would have her. She'd be a bride so quickly, her head would spin. And they wouldn't marry her to a young, handsome man like Westman. She'd get an old man with ten kids, desperate for a nanny/bed warmer.

She shivered at the thought.

Of course, she could marry Westman. If they didn't find the treasure, it would be the easiest thing to do, the expected thing. The *ton* would already be scandalized by their star-crossed love affair. Why not marry?

She glanced sideways at Westman. He had asked her.

And she had said no. And she had meant no. But what if she had no choice? Would he still have her now that she'd refused him once?

She didn't think so. The more she thought about things and observed him over the last day, the more she realized that he had really only asked her to marry him out of a feeling of obligation. Why, he'd even told her this afternoon that he thought he would tire of her in a week or two.

That had hurt. Josie knew she had a liberal dose of pride, but Westman had cut it to the quick. Of course, he would tire of her. What did one expect from a rake? But no woman wanted to be reminded that she was not infinitely alluring.

Especially when she felt no sign of tiring of him. Especially when every moment in his company made her like him more, respect him more, want him more. Lord, she could hardly wait to get back to the inn, not just so she could have something warm to drink and curl up near a fire, but so that she could curl up next to Westman. She wanted his arms around her, his lips close to her ear, whispering . . . whispering what?

That he loved her? The thought made her feel like laughing. Those were words she'd never hear from Stephen Doubleday. Those were words she didn't need to hear from him or any man.

Stephen looked back at her, and she swallowed quickly, afraid her face would betray her thoughts. "We're almost there. Are you going to make it? Do you need to rest for a moment?"

Drat! She was huffing and puffing again. He must think her a complete weakling. "I'm fine," she called over the wind and waves. "Keep going."

She just had to keep that warm inn fire and Westman's hot body in mind. That would keep her moving.

Westman took her hand again and helped her forward, and though she would never have said so aloud, Josie was grateful. She, who had resented it when men offered to help poor little her, resented it when men offered protection, resented it when men treated her as anything less than an equal, was once again glad to have a man here to take care of her.

Not just any man. Westman. She was glad it was he. She could trust him, did trust him. She wanted to laugh again. She, Josephine Hale, trusted a man. Amazing.

The strip of sand they'd been walking on ended, and Stephen had to release her hand as they went, single-file, around a jutting rock. Westman went first, keeping his hand on hers for as long as possible, and when his feet were out of sight, Josie followed.

Her boots sloshed in the freezing water, and the toes she had thought were numb, screamed in protest. But she slogged through, keeping her scraped fingers on the rock below her shoulder. The jut of rock was about five feet in length, about three times that in height, and about a quarter of the way across it, the wind began to die down, so that when Josie stepped back onto sandy beach, there was barely any wind at all.

Looking around, she saw that they had stepped into what appeared to be a bowl in the rock. It was deep enough to fit a small cottage and large enough to accommodate sixty men or more.

Best of all, inside there was a respite from the wind and waves. Here the water only lapped at the extended beach, and the light breeze didn't bite and chill.

With an exhausted sigh, Josie went to Westman, who had moved toward the center of the bowl, and put her hand on his shoulder. "What now? There's no way out of here, and we can't see—"

But Westman shook his head, silencing her. She frowned then noticed he was staring intently at the sea. She followed his gaze, and then her hand tightened. About a quarter of a mile offshore, slightly to their right, were three huge rocks protruding from the water. They stood like sentinels guarding the small cove, and the ocean waves crashed mightily against them, so that they took the brunt of the force and the cove was left in relative peace.

Westman held out a hand. "Do you have the map?"

Josie shook her head. "I thought you—"

"It's in my coat pocket."

"Oh." She fumbled through his coat, her fingers so cold that she could hardly control them, and then she grasped the paper and pulled it out.

She held it out to Westman, careful not to let go until he had a firm grip on it. Even in the cove, there was still a stiff breeze, and Westman held the map tightly. He pieced the two sections together, and Josie watched as all the landmarks fell into place. She studied the three rocks at the end of the cove and then their representation on the map. Directly across from the rocks was a large X.

As one, Josie and Westman turned and looked behind them. Her eyes scanned the towering granite rocks, looking for any sign of a hiding place. But she saw nothing but rocks. No caves, no openings of any sort.

"Do you think they buried the treasure?" Josie asked, digging the heel of her boot into the soft sand.

"It's a possibility," Westman acknowledged. "It's also a possibility that we're missing something. It's too dark in here to see properly."

He was right. The clouds had come in, and only intermittent light shone from the moon.

"Should we wait until morning?" she asked, excited by the prospect of seeing the place in the light, and yet hoping Westman would not agree to the scheme. The inn was calling to her, and not even treasure seemed to matter as much as a fire and a hot cup of tea.

To her relief, Westman shook his head. "We still don't know where our friends from London are. Let's go back and plan a strategy. Then we can decide when to return and with what supplies."

Josie sighed. "So back the way we came?" She was so tired that even her hair felt exhausted.

"You know the way, madam."

She did, and, unfortunately, it was a long, long way.

Stephen made Josie wait until dusk before they returned to the cove. He'd gone out in the afternoon, purchased lanterns, shovels, rope, and two pistols. If their friends returned, he'd be ready.

The trek back to the cove had been easier in the late afternoon light, but by the time they'd reached the hidden spot, the sun was once again abed. They lit the lanterns and used the dying rays of day to search. Stephen looked out at the water frequently, comparing the location of the rocks to his position.

He tried to imagine the best place to anchor a ship offshore. Where would his grandfather have stood on deck? What would he have seen? What memories would he have taken back with him, relied on as he drew the map months later?

Josie had begun her search at the far end of the cove. This morning, she had stared at the map for hours. Her theory was that the treasure was buried, and the strokes of pen on the map indicated the number of footsteps she should take to reach the spot. Personally, Stephen thought she was sleep-deprived and had read one too many novels, but he kept his mouth shut.

What did he know? Besides, she was out of his way.

He'd decided to investigate the rock surrounding the cove, to search for hidden entrances to caves or passageways. He'd done his own extensive staring at the map, and he didn't think the X indicated the beach. There were a thousand beaches. Why choose this one to bury treasure? The real appeal of this spot was the granite cliffs.

They'd been searching for perhaps an hour, Josie walking and counting, confusing her numbers, and starting over. Westman watching her, while running his hands along the rock, climbing up partway and then back down again in disappointment. Each of them carried a lantern, several more lit the small cove, and the shovels and picks were waiting to be used.

And still they'd found nothing.

Stephen's calf was throbbing again, his head hurt; he was tired of the goddamn treasure. Leaning back against the rock, he sank down, placing the pistols, wrapped in cloth, beside him. This search might take days or weeks. He opened his eyes and watched Josie pace off another section of sand.

What was he going to do with her? She couldn't stay here with him. It was far too dangerous. He hadn't wasted his time this afternoon trying to convince her to stay at the inn while he returned to the cove. He knew she would demand to go where he went.

The best he could do was to keep her inside while he bought supplies, and even that had been a fight. He knew being shot at last night had scared her, but it still wasn't enough to dissuade her from continuing their search. And the longer they searched, the longer they stayed in Polperro, the more dangerous it would be for them.

The more dangerous it would be for her. He didn't care what happened to him. If he didn't find the treasure, he would make his fortune another way. But he could not allow her to be harmed. He'd sworn to protect her, even if it was a promise made to himself, and he would see it through.

The problem was how to convince Josie to see things his way.

Impossible, he knew. Closing his eyes again, he leaned his head back. He wished he had a drink. He wished he had a bed. He wished . . .

The sand beneath his right buttock was sinking, and Stephen put his hand down to keep from falling sideways.

His hand sunk, too.

He opened his eyes and pulled his hand away to study the ground. There was a dip beside him, a place where the sand sank away.

Lifting his lantern, he studied the rock beside him. He didn't see anything unusual at first, but then . . . wait . . .

Stephen rose and ran to one of the shovels. Shovel in hand, he began to tear at the sand where he'd been sitting. The sand cleared easily away, and then Stephen saw the gap in the rock. It was a large gap, big enough for him to stick a hand through.

He put his hand between the shelf of rock that had obviously been placed over the cave's entrance and the rock of the cliff. Between the spaces, the air was cool, damp.

His throat closed, and he looked at Josie. She was standing, watching him, her eyes huge and expectant. He couldn't speak, but his face must have spoken volumes because she rushed toward him, carrying her own lantern and grabbing another on the way.

"You've found it," she said for him.

He nodded. She watched as he inserted his hand into the gap again.

"Oh, my God." Pushing him aside, she did the same. "There's a cave here." He could see her hand move and knew she was wriggling her fingers behind the rock. "They put a rock over it to conceal it, and over time the sand has deposited against it. Do you think we can dig the rock out? Open the cave?"

"Get a shovel," Stephen commanded. He was already bent and digging. A moment later, Josie was beside him, flinging sand over her shoulder. It was soft and loose, and they cleared the edges of the rock within a quarter of an hour.

"How are we going to move it?" Josie asked, defining one edge of the boulder by scraping more sand away. "It's wedged in well. They may have had twenty men lift it and put it in place."

Stephen shook his head. "They would have kept the number of men who knew about the hiding place to a minimum. Our grandfathers and one or two others at most. More than likely, it was only our grandfathers. Let's give it a try."

They finished defining the edges first, scraping as much sand away as possible, and then Stephen rocked one side back and forth to loosen it. When it gave, Josie wedged her slim shoulder in the growing gap between rock and cave and pushed, while he pulled from the outside. Slowly, the rock came away.

"I can fit inside!" Josie exclaimed, her voice punctuated with pants. "Just a bit more, and we can both make it through."

Stephen summoned the last of his strength and heaved at the rock. It moved with a groan; his or the rock's, he couldn't be sure. With an excited yip, Josie disappeared inside the cave, and he lifted his lantern then followed.

The entrance was low, and he had to bend to fit his shoulders inside. Even then, the top of his head scraped the ceiling. It was pitch-black inside and silent, a drastic change from the noise of the breeze and the waves outside. In front of him, Josie blocked what little he could see of the cave's interior.

"See anything?" he whispered. For some reason, whispering seemed appropriate.

"No, but there's a bend. Let's see if it widens there." Stepping carefully, she wended her way through the narrow opening and deeper into the cave. Stephen followed, stooping the farther in they went. Just when the cave began to close in, the walls pressing against him, and he was about to balk at taking another step, Josie moved forward and spread her arms wide. "This is so much better," she whispered, turning to face him. The smile on her face was contagious.

He stepped into the new room and lifted his lantern. Over her shoulder, in the dribble of light from the lantern, he saw the glint of gold.

"Josie," he whispered. "Josie, turn around."

She spun around, holding her lantern aloft. In the soft glow, a spill of gold glistened. Stephen stepped closer, illuminating three huge black chests, and the gold that glittered was centered on the floor beneath one whose lock was broken. Even from this distance, Stephen could see the skull and crossbones etched on the locks—an etching that matched the key they'd found in his grandfather's box.

With halting steps, Josie moved forward, slipped her fingers under the lid of the damaged chest, and flipped it open. The shock of golden light from within caused her to inhale sharply and step back, plowing into him.

She stood there, and he could feel the warmth and tension radiating from her.

"We've found it," she whispered. "We've found it."

He put his arms around her, rested his chin on the back of her head. Together, they stared at the treasure. "This is it." His voice sounded so normal, so calm. How could that be when inside he was shaking like a rabbit? "This is it," he said louder, listening to his voice echo through the cave. He squeezed Josie tight. "We're rich!"

"Correction," a voice said from behind him. "*We're* rich."

Chapter 21

Josie jumped, rapping her head hard on Westman's chin. He spun her around, and she was staring directly into the face of a one-eyed man.

He was old, his partner far younger and holding a pistol pointed at her heart. Westman immediately took her by the waist and pushed her behind him.

"Good evening, Lord Westman. Miss 'ale," the one-eyed man said. "Thought we might find ye 'ere."

"Thought we might see you two again," Westman said, angling his body to shield her. Josie took the opportunity to back up, closer to the treasure. If she could just close the lid of the trunk she'd opened, maybe the men wouldn't see . . .

"Miss 'ale," the one-eyed man said. "I wouldn't go touching that if I were you. It's not yourn."

She paused, hand hovering above the trunk. Slowly, she turned back to the men. "It is mine. I've been searching for this treasure since I was six years old."

"Josephine," Westman warned, but she ignored him, pushing past him when he tried to hold her back with an out-flung arm.

"This was my grandfather's treasure, and I don't care if you have a gun." She flicked her wrist in the direction of the younger man. He was probably her age but shorter, skinny, too. He looked like he hadn't eaten in a week. She could have taken him— except, of course, he had that pistol. "You can't have it."

"Aye, lass, we can," the one-eyed man said, stepping forward. "Because it was mine long afore it was yourn."

"Is that so?"

"*Josephine,*" Westman said again. He grabbed her elbow, but she pulled away.

She put her hands on her hips and stared into the one-eyed man's good eye. This close she could see that a shriveled eyelid covered the other. "Who are you?" she hissed.

He doffed his old cap and offered her a low bow. "Me name's Jack. You might know me as One-Eyed Jack."

"Oh, Jesus," Westman said from behind her.

"You were on *The Good Groom,*" Josie said.

"We read about you in James Doubleday's journals."

"And 'ere I am in the flesh, wanting me piece of the treasure. Yer grandfathers weren't none too fond of sharing. Family trait, I see."

"Too much jabbering," the man with the pistol said, waving his weapon, at Josie, then Westman. "I say we take 'em out and shoot 'em. Now that they found the treasure for us, we don't need 'em."

"First we get 'em to 'elp us load the treasure."

"We're not helping you with anything," Josie spat. "We're not—"

Westman hauled her up against him and put a hand over her mouth. "We'll help," he said, then murmured in her ear, "Are you *trying* to get us killed?"

"Lift them trunks and carry 'em outside," One-Eyed Jack ordered. "And don't do anything foolish. My sight ain't what it was, but I can still use a cutlass good as any man."

Westman pushed Josie back toward the treasure chests, and, together, they lifted the first one. It was heavy, and she stumbled under the weight. One-Eyed Jack led them through the narrow passage back toward the beach, and the man with the pistol followed.

"*Why* are we helping them steal our treasure?" Josie hissed at Westman.

"Because some things are more important than treasure. I value your life, Josephine Hale."

They emerged into the night and had to struggle

to wedge the chest through the small opening between the rock and the cave. When they got it through, Josie dropped it immediately. Her hands were dented and red.

"O'er there, lass." One-Eyed Jack pointed to a small rowboat bobbing in the waves at the edge of the beach. No wonder she and Westman hadn't seen the men following them tonight. They'd never thought to look out at the water.

Josie shook her head. "If you want it in there, you carry it."

His hand shot out with lightning speed and gripped her hair hard. He pulled it, yanking her head back. "Like yourn grandfather, ye are. Too stubborn and too much pride."

"Let her go," Westman said quietly. He cocked a pistol, and the sound punctuated his words.

Josie swerved to see him clearly just as the other man came up behind him. "Stephen, behind you!"

She was too late.

The roar of the gun blast was deafening. It resounded in Josie's ears long after there should have been silence. And then she realized that the sound was her screaming. Wrenching her body away from Jack, she fell on the ground beside Stephen. She pulled him into a sitting position, into her arms. It was too dark to see, but she could feel the spreading moisture on the back of his coat.

Blood.

"Josie," Stephen rasped.

She looked down at him, into his blue eyes.

"Get away. Run—"

"Shh." She put a finger over his lips. "I'm not leaving without you."

"Goddamn it," he choked out, then coughed. "I knew you were going to say that."

She felt something hard and solid press into her palm, looked down and saw the glint of the pistol he'd been holding.

"Get up, Miss 'ale," One-Eyed Jack ordered. "I warned you not to try anything foolish."

She glanced down at Stephen and reluctantly began to pull away. She had one chance to get him to the inn. She prayed she wouldn't ruin it.

She was almost to her feet, when Stephen grabbed her wrist. "Be careful."

She winked at him. "Always."

She stood, her back to Jack and the man who'd shot Stephen. Buying time to steady the pistol in her hands and place her finger on the trigger, she squared her shoulders and turned slowly. Raising the gun, she pointed it at Jack. The other man was looking down, priming his weapon for the next shot.

"Drop it, sir."

The other man looked up at her, saw the gun, then looked at Jack. The old pirate had liberated his sword from the scabbard at his belt, but Josie knew it would be little use against her pistol. Of course, she only had one shot, so if she killed his partner, he might be able to use it after all.

She looked back at the man who shot Stephen. "Drop your weapon, sir."

"Make me, wench," he sneered at her then went back to priming.

Jack smiled. "Can't do it, can ye lass?"

"Just watch me," she ground out. Her hand was shaking, but she raised the pistol and aimed it at One-Eyed Jack. His eyes widened. She squinted then screwed her eyes shut. Finger trembling, she pulled the trigger.

Click.

Josie opened her eyes and stared down at the pistol. She shook it, pointed, pulled the trigger again.

Click.

"Sand, lass," One-Eyed Jack said with a laugh. "It can be a real bitch."

Josie stepped back, and her toe brushed Stephen's leg. Shielding him as best she could, she tried to stand straight. Inside the accusations bowed her.

She'd failed, not her courage but the pistol. She had failed.

Her heart was pounding, and she felt a bead of sweat trickle down her back. Jack's associate gave a triumphant exclamation, raised his primed gun, and pointed it directly at her. At least it was she and not Westman. He would have a chance . . .

She squeezed her eyes shut, said a quick prayer, and then the blast exploded in her head.

Her body jolted and swayed, and she waited to fall.

And waited.

She opened her eyes, then widened them. The

man with the pistol lay in a heap against the entrance to the cave—what had been his head was a mass of blood and tissue.

"No sand in this one," Westman said from behind her. She glanced at him, saw that he was lying on his injured side, the pistol in his good hand. While she watched, he slumped back down, his eyes closed.

No, Stephen. Hold on, she prayed.

Then she turned back to the dead man, swayed, and her chin scraped something sharp and pointed. She looked down and saw Jack's sword directed at her, the tip grazing her face. There was a smile on Jack's old, withered face. Narrowing her eyes, she said, "Put that sword down."

He laughed. "Just like yer grandfather, ye are. Ye got no pistol, no sword, and yet yer issuing orders."

She shrugged. "I've been told I can be a bit headstrong."

"So was yer Nathan 'ale. Pity I was only able to do away with Cap'n Doubleday."

"*You?*" She felt as though a physical blow had slammed into her. "You killed James Doubleday?"

"And now it's your turn."

"Oh, I don't think so."

Hours of playing pirate with her brothers, under her grandfather's coaching, had prepared Josie for just this moment.

One-Eyed Jack lunged, and Josie skirted to the side at the last minute. Jack's sword cut through air, and he stumbled forward. Josie swiveled and lunged, kicking him hard in the gut.

He bent over double, glaring at her with hate. She took a step back and tripped over Westman's leg. Pinwheeling her arms to keep her balance, she went down anyway, falling beside Westman. She hit the sand and Westman clutched her arm.

He pressed warm metal into her hand. In the dim light, the jewels in the dagger glowed with eerie brilliance.

One-Eyed Jack reared up, his sword ready. Josie rose to her knees, took a deep breath, and flung the dagger, just like her grandfather had showed her.

Her aim was true, and Jack fell back, the dagger protruding from his good eye. His body went rigid, his back bowing, and his mouth a rictus of pain. His legs spasmed before Josie turned away.

She sobbed, grabbing at Stephen and pulling him close. The blood had spread, and his entire back felt damp to her touch. "Stephen." His eyes were closing, his head lolling back. "Stephen, hold on."

He opened his eyes and gave her a wary smile. "Always carry an extra weapon," he rasped. "Learned that in India." His eyes closed, his smile faded, and he slipped into unconsciousness. Josie lay him down, placed her head on his chest, and listened to his heartbeat. The thump was sluggish but steady.

She rose to her knees, staring down at him. "Don't die, Westman," she ordered him. He didn't move, and tears spilled down her cheeks. "Please don't die."

She looked at the carnage around her: two dead men, a cave full of treasure, and a man whose life-blood was draining away. How much more bad luck would the treasure bring?

One-Eyed Jack was lying face up, and moonlight glinted off the jewels in the dagger. James Double-day's dagger, the one from the bank vault. She hadn't even known Stephen was carrying it. Had he heard Jack's confession? Did Stephen know he had avenged his grandfather's death?

Now she knew for certain that her own grandfather was not the murderer. Perhaps that was the real treasure, the vindication of her grandfather's name, even if the secret would remain in this remote cove forever.

In her hand, Westman's fingers jerked and then went still. She squeezed him tightly. He'd saved her life. He'd protected her, put her safety ahead of his own. "You're the real treasure," she whispered. "All this time I was searching, and you were right here."

He didn't open his eyes, didn't hear, but his chest rose and fell, and Josie buried her face in her hands. If he died, it was her fault. If he died, it was her greed, her obsession that killed him.

No more. She was through with this treasure. She didn't want it anymore—couldn't stand to look at the shining doubloons without bile rising in her belly.

All the senseless death, all the risk, all the sacrifice. And for what?

She'd rather leave the treasure here to wash away or be found by fishermen than touch it ever again. She glanced at Stephen. His body lay where it had fallen, a dark stain spreading on the sand beneath his shoulder. The price of the treasure was too high.

She had to get him back to Polperro, back to the inn, where a surgeon could see him and treat his wound.

Her eyes lit on the small boat, now dragged sideways by the current. It would be the fastest way back, the only way, as Westman was obviously incapable of making it back on foot. But how was she going to get him in the boat?

She looked at him again, and her breath hitched. He appeared so still, so lifeless. Unable to resist, she embraced him again and held him tightly.

"Stephen," she whispered. "Stephen, I swear, if you make it through this I will never say a cross word to you again. I will never mention treasure or adventure. And I promise never to climb out of another window." She looked into his face, still as death. "Stephen, please don't die. If you make it through this, I'll—I'll—" She took a deep breath. If she was going to make promises, they had better mean something.

"It was me who brought you into this," she whispered. "If you die, it's my fault. If you'll just live, I promise I'll never interfere in your life again.

I'll leave you alone. Forever. Just don't die." She hugged him tighter. "You're all I have."

His body was heavy and limp, and it was going to hurt him more to drag him down to the edge of the beach, but she had no choice. She glanced at the two dead men, grateful they'd come by boat. If she hadn't had the boat then . . . well, she didn't want to think what she would have had to do.

And so with as much care as she could manage and as much tenderness, she got hold of her lover and began dragging his lifeless body away from the treasure.

Stephen woke with a dull ache in his head and a screaming pain in his shoulder.

"Lie still," a woman's voice said. He opened his eyes and saw Josie at his bedside. Sitting there, lit only by a fire, she looked small and thin and pale. She leaned over him, her fingers roaming his aching body as though she couldn't believe he was really there.

"Are you well?" he asked, reaching for her hand with the arm that didn't howl in misery.

"Am I well?" She made a sound somewhere between a laugh and a sob. "You were shot, lost half the blood in your body, had a surgeon slice you open, and you ask how I am?" Tears welled in her eyes, and he pulled her down to cradle her to his chest. "I've been sitting here for two days, praying you would wake," she mumbled against his chest.

"I'm awake now," he whispered. "You don't have to worry anymore."

She wrapped her arms around him and continued to sob. He shushed her and kissed her hair. When she had finally ceased crying and lay spent in his arms, he looked around the room. She'd said he'd been asleep for two days. And somehow in that time she'd gotten him back to the inn and into the bed they'd shared. How had she gotten him back here?

And, more importantly, where the hell was the treasure?

He remembered a little of the night they'd found it. The cave, the glitter of gold, the men with guns.

"I know where I saw that man now."

Josie sat up, sniffled, and wiped her nose. "What man? One-Eyed Jack?"

"He was at the bank. He was one of the guards in the vault."

She sniffled again. "That makes sense. The crew didn't know where our grandfathers hid the treasure."

Stephen tried to sit up, but she put a hand on his chest, holding him down.

"They may have been given a portion," he said, resigned to lying still. His damn shoulder hurt too much otherwise. "But Jack must have known that his measure was paltry compared to the true bounty."

"And so he went to our grandfathers, or your

grandfather, at least, confronted him, demanded to know the treasure's location."

A shiver ran down Stephen's back, and something from a dream echoed in his mind. "And when he wouldn't tell, Jack killed him."

"You heard his confession, then," Josie whispered. "I was afraid I was the only one."

"I don't know what I heard, but as soon as I realized I recognized Jack from the bank, I put the pieces together. He must have known there was a clue to the treasure in the deposit box. Maybe my grandfather taunted him with the knowledge. Maybe he followed him, saw him go in with the haversack and come out with nothing."

Josie took a long breath. "And all these years, Jack stood in that vault, day after day, plotting a way to get inside that box."

"Or waiting for someone like us to open it for him."

She took his hand again, squeezed it, and the way she looked at him made his heart ache with longing. "How sad to die so close to getting what you've always wanted."

She looked down, new tears in her eyes.

"What's wrong?" Stephen asked as she released his hand.

"I have to go." She wouldn't meet his eyes. "You're all right. You're going to make it. I have to leave."

"Leave? What are you talking about?" His gaze darted about the room again. "Where's the treasure now?" he asked. "How did you get it out? How did you get *me* out? I vaguely remember a rowboat."

"It was One-Eyed Jack's. He'd planned his escape better than us, and I used it to get you back to Polperro."

Concern tightened its grip on Stephen's gut. Josie would not have left that treasure out of her sight. But he could hardly imagine how she'd managed to drag him to the rowboat, much less three heavy treasure chests. "Where's the treasure?" he asked again.

She shrugged. "I don't care. Probably still sitting on the sand outside the cave."

"You left it?" He ignored the pain in his shoulder and the spurt of lightheadedness and shot straight up. "You just left it?"

"You were dying, Stephen. I could take you or the treasure. I chose you."

Something in her tone made him look more closely. She looked tired, but there was something else in her face—a vulnerability that hadn't been there before. For a second Stephen dared to hope that she meant the words as he'd taken them: *You mean more to me than the treasure, more to me than anything.*

And then Stephen pushed the ludicrous thought away. This was Josephine Hale—the unflappable, audacious, fearless Josephine Hale. She wasn't falling in love with him.

"I can imagine how hard that decision was for you."

"I understand why you think that of me—why you think I'd choose money and riches over your life."

He wanted to say no, to erase the hurt from her eyes. Instead, he waited. Without the treasure, she had to see how much she needed him. She was his now. She couldn't go back home unmarried.

She met his eyes. "I think that about says it all, then." Lifting her boy's cap from the chair, she put it over her curls. She strode for the door, head held high, hands clenched at her sides. "Good-bye, Stephen."

"Good-bye?" What the hell was this? She was supposed to beg him to marry her. He was supposed to save her.

She opened the door and walked out without looking back.

He hadn't gone after her right away. Why the hell should he? And by the time he'd pushed his pride aside and was thinking clearly, she was gone.

He could have murdered her when he found out she'd taken his carriage. He could have murdered his coachman too, except that the man had driven Josie away.

If Josie had any coin—and Westman couldn't believe she hadn't pocketed at least a handful of the doubloons—Westman knew his "loyal" servants would have forsaken him in no time.

And so here he was, with no money, no carriage, and no Josie.

But this time he wasn't going to take it. He'd never fought back, not when his mother told him he was worthless compared to his brother, not when his father shipped him off to India, not when he'd come home and been told it was his responsibility to save the family.

This time he was going to fight back. He couldn't fight his father and brother, but he could still save his family. And he would have Josie. She did need him. She just hadn't realized it yet.

She was his, no man's but his.

He would claim her.

No matter what it took.

Chapter 22

It took Josie three days to return to London. It took three minutes for her mother to haul her into the Hale town house, push her up the stairs, and lock her in her room.

It took her cousins three hours to show up and sneak Josie out of the house.

The Hale-Doubleday scandal, as the papers called it, was raging through the city, and Josie knew her cousins took a risk coming to see her.

Even so, she'd refused to climb out of the window. After the cliffs of Polperro, she was done with heights, but her cousins scooted her out the back door when her mother was out.

It had been hard for Josie to look at Westman's

house, so close to hers, and know he wasn't there. He was lying penniless and injured because of her. It had been humbling to know she was so selfish that she had almost got him killed. At least she had stuck to her promise. He had lived, and she had left him. She'd never again be his problem.

"You were never his problem," Catie said, shaking Josie's shoulders.

"And what happened to Lord Westman isn't your fault," Maddie chimed in.

Ashley came to sit next to her. As usual, the four of them had sneaked over to Maddie's house and were lounging on her huge bed. There was a Fullbright–Hale family meeting going on downstairs, so it was the safest spot for the four of them. Their parents would never expect the girls to stay near a family meeting. Not to mention, Josie was supposed to be locked in her room at the Hale house all the way across Mayfair.

But her cousins had come for her, and she'd sneaked out at their urging—well, their mild suggestion, anyway—all the while her parents were meeting with Maddie's father to consult with the Earl of Castleigh as to what should be done about Josie.

Or, as her mother was now calling her, the Black Spot on the Hale Family Name.

"It is my fault. If I weren't so concerned about the treasure—"

"*You* concerned?" Ashley said, her light green eyes wide. "In the end, *he* was the one blaming you for saving his life over taking the treasure. *He's* the selfish one."

Josie shook her head. "You don't understand. He's not selfish at all. He saved me from getting killed. Twice. More than twice, probably half a dozen times over the last few days. And everything he put up with from me. The man is practically a saint."

Ashley snorted, and Josie gave in.

"Well, he's not that patient, but I did give him trouble. And he took it all in stride. He's the most giving, bravest, most loving, most—"

"Oh, stop or I'm going to wretch," Ashley moaned. "He's a man, not a god."

Josie crossed her arms, rounding on Ashley with an angry retort ready, but Catie, lovely Catie with her soft voice and her hazel eyes, put a hand on her arm.

"She's in love with him, Ashley. She's entitled to wax a bit poetic."

Josie's mouth dropped open. "What? I am not in love with that—that *caveman*. I told you already. I hate him. He's arrogant, ungrateful, overprotective—"

Catie was smiling at her, which made Josie all the angrier.

"Stop smiling! I'm not in love with him. In fact, when he asked me to marry him, I said no."

"You said what?" Maddie cried.

"*He* said what?" Ashley exclaimed.

Josie took a deep breath. Drat that Catie! If she hadn't goaded so much . . .

Josie sighed. Who was she fooling? She would have told them anyway.

"He asked me to marry him."

Maddie clasped her hands together, pressing them over her heart. With her glossy brown hair, her blue eyes, and her stylish clothes, Maddie looked the picture of propriety—and usually was.

"It wasn't like that, Maddie," Josie said, shaking her head. Why did Maddie have to make everything so romantic? "He only did it out of obligation. It was the morning after I"—she swallowed—"um, seduced him."

"You did what?" Maddie's love-struck look was gone, and her eyes were wide with shock.

"I seduced him." Josie looked down at her hands. "My mother is right. I *am* the Black Spot of the Hale Family, or whatever she's calling me these days. I'm a wanton. A loose woman. I took advantage of him, and I'm not even sorry."

"Was it good?" Ashley wanted to know.

"It was only once, right?" Maddie pleaded.

"Girls!" Catie cut in. "That's not important right now." She winked at them. "We can get the details later. But right now we need to set something straight, Josie. No man is seduced who doesn't want to be. If you and Westman made love, it was because he wanted it as much as you."

"That doesn't change the fact that he only asked me to marry him out of obligation."

"And that doesn't mean you two shouldn't marry or that it couldn't end up being a love match."

"Catie, just because you and Lord Valentine fell in love after an obligatory union, doesn't mean everyone will," Josie told her. "Westman does not love me."

"Are you sure?" Catie asked. "Because if you refused his offer of marriage, you can't expect him to profess his undying devotion later."

"Undying devotion?" Josie gave a harsh laugh. "How about no devotion? He as much as told me he knew he'd tire of me in a week or two."

"Was that before or after you refused him?"

"After, but—"

Catie was smiling again.

"That doesn't matter," Josie said in exasperation. "You don't know him like I do. He doesn't love me. He just felt obligated to marry me after we—well, you know. And as for devotion, I'm the one who has none. I made him all these promises when he was lying half dead on the beach—"

"Promises?" Maddie asked.

"Yes, like that I would never say a cross word to him again."

Ashley laughed, and Josie ignored her.

"And I'd never again mention treasure and never

climb out of another window—I kept that one, so far. But there was another—that if he lived, I would leave him alone."

Maddie rolled her eyes. "As though your promising that would save him. Your quick thinking saved him. Who got him back to the inn? Who called for the surgeon?"

"Who ran away?" Catie said. "Josie, why did you promise that on the beach?" She turned her hazel gaze directly on Josie. "Did you really think that would save him, or did you just want a way out?"

"What does it matter? I'm glad I left," Josie said defiantly. "He accused me of caring more about the treasure than him."

"Have you ever given him reason to believe otherwise?" Catie asked.

Josie opened her mouth to say that of course she had, that he should have known she cared about him very much. She'd made that clear.

Hadn't she?

"You know why I think you ran away?" Catie said. "I think you were scared. I think you started to feel something for Westman on that beach, and you knew when he woke up, you might have to face the possibility that he might not feel the same. You were scared of needing someone who might not need you."

The three girls blinked at her.

"When did you become so wise?" Ashley said finally.

"She's not," Josie broke in. "That's not it at all. I wasn't scared and I didn't feel—oh, who am I talking to?" She buried her face in her hands, trying to compose her thoughts. They were jumping about her head like mad grasshoppers, and every single one of them seemed to corroborate Catie's outrageous statements.

"This can't be," she whined, keeping her face in her hands. "I can't be in love with Westman. I just can't."

She felt Maddie sit beside her, elbowing Ashley out of the way. "Why can't it be possible? I think it's romantic."

"Of course, you do. It's not you," Josie moaned. "You aren't going to go around the rest of your life pining for some asinine man who will never love you. Drat!" She stood, balled her hands together, and paced the room. "I swore this would never happen. Never with a man like Westman."

Catie caught her hand as she passed by. "So did I, Josie, and as you can see, everything turned out well."

"But Valentine is not like Westman."

Catie arched a brow.

"Well, all right, he is a lot like Westman. But Valentine isn't a rake."

"And what rakish things has Westman done lately?" Ashley asked. "Well, besides the obvious running off with you, anyway. Everyone knows that before you came along, he was trying to reform. Why, the few times I saw the man, I couldn't even get him to flirt with me. He kept talking about you."

"Really?" Josie sank back on the bed, aware that she probably had a sappy smile on her face. But she couldn't help it. Her cousins thought Westman cared for her? It couldn't be true. But what if it were—

"Oh, I don't know." She fell back on the bed, stretching out. "He's said so many things, and I have, too. I don't know what to think anymore."

"What matters now is what you feel," Catie told her. "Do you care for Westman? Do you think you could be happy married to him?"

Josie threw up her hands. "I don't know. Not if he doesn't love me."

"We can work on that," Ashley said. Josie gave her a narrow look, and she added, "Work on getting him to admit it, anyway."

"But the larger problem is what's happening downstairs," Catie told her.

"My father and your mother are trying to 'handle the crisis'," Maddie interjected. She said the last in a deep voice that was a pretty good imitation of her father.

"Which means," Ashley added, "they will decide to marry you off. My guess? Top of the list is old Lord Crutchkins."

Josie sprang up. "Eew! Never!"

"You know your mother, Josie."

Oh, Lord, she did, too. "But—but she can't do that! I have to agree, and I won't! I won't."

"How can you not?" Maddie said quietly. "You have no money, nowhere to go. And the scandal—"

Josie flopped back down and rolled into a ball. "This is all just horrible. I've ruined everything. Drat! I should have left Westman and taken the treasure, then I'd be rich and independent."

"Maybe you could go back for it," Ashley suggested.

Josie saw Catie throw her a scowl and a don't-give-her-ideas look.

"She'd still be ostracized," Maddie added quickly.

"Maybe not," Josie argued. "The *ton* can forgive anything if one has enough blunt."

"Josie, don't be so naive. You think because you want something, you can make it true. You've been compromised. The only way to salvage your relationship is to marry."

Josie rolled her eyes.

"So, what if we could convince the family to marry you to Westman?"

At the thought, Josie's heart sped up, despite the fact that she didn't want it to. She didn't want to feel this way for Stephen, especially when she knew he didn't feel anything but obligation for her. She did know that, didn't she?

"That would never work," Maddie said, puncturing Josie's little bubble. "The Hales and the

Doubledays are enemies. Aunt Mavis would rather kill Josie and bury her in an unmarked grave than marry her to Westman."

"Lovely analogy," Ashley said. "Unfortunately, it's accurate."

Slowly Josie began to uncoil. "But what if we weren't enemies? What if I could prove that my grandfather didn't kill Westman's?"

"You've been trying to do that for years," Ashley said. "Do you have proof now?"

"Not proof exactly," Josie said, "but I know who did do it."

"And it wasn't your grandfather?" Catie asked. "You know for certain."

Josie nodded.

Maddie shook her head. "I don't know if that will matter if you can't prove it."

"Well, we can't allow them to marry her to some old man with only two teeth in his mouth. We have to do something to help her and Westman," Catie, the eldest and always the planner, said.

"We'll stall the wedding preparations to Crutchkins," Ashley said. "And in the meantime, we'll pray Westman returns."

"I can try and hinder the plans," Catie offered.

"And we can keep a watch on Westman's town house," Ashley said, indicating Maddie and Josie.

Josie just shook her head. "This is never going to work. Even if Westman comes back, how can I prove our families are no longer enemies?"

"We'll work that out later." Catie took her hands

and pulled her off the bed. "Right now, we'd better get you back to your room."

"Wonderful." Josie gathered up her gloves. "What am I supposed to do in there for hours and hours and hours?"

Catie smiled. "Plan your wedding?"

Chapter 23

It was late when Stephen strode out of Thomas Coutts & Company. His business had taken longer than he'd anticipated, and he was tired and far from finished with his plans for the evening. Raising his hand, he summoned a hack and directed the jarvey to drive to the Doubleday town house in Mayfair.

But he wasn't going home. Not yet. Not until he had the promises he craved from a certain feisty redhead. He'd already heard word she was home. Her irate parents had put her under lock and key, and Stephen was glad of it.

It meant she would be there when he came to fetch her.

He patted his pocket, where the special license

felt thick and heavy. He would have been through here earlier, if he hadn't had to see the Archbishop of Canterbury first.

Stephen continued patting his pocket and stared out the window, his heart thumping hard against his rib cage when the cab turned down his street.

The windows at the Hale household were full of light. He would have no reprieve.

He straightened his cravat as the coach slowed.

They were home. She was home. Good. He wanted to get this over with. He wanted to have done with it, and the sooner the better.

The coach stopped, and Westman climbed out, tossing the jarvey the fare. The coach drove off, and Westman stood in front of his own house and stared at his next-door neighbor's home.

He took a deep breath and tried to make his leaden feet move.

Now or never, he reminded himself.

Of course, *now* was a relative term. What was one more hour within which to think things over, plan which words to say? Maybe he would have a drink first, change clothes . . .

And put the whole damn thing off.

No. Stephen forced his feet to move, marched himself up the front walk of the Hale house.

He wasn't waiting. He didn't care if the words were right. Josie was his, and he wasn't waiting another second to claim her.

He reached the door and pounded hard three

times. "Open up!" he ordered. "This is Stephen Doubleday, Earl of Westman. I demand entrance."

A meek butler opened the door a moment later, and Stephen took a step back. Perhaps he had been a bit too enthusiastic.

"My lord," the old man said. "May I help you?"

"I must see Miss Hale at once."

The butler raised an eyebrow. "She is not at home, sir."

"Then Mr. Hale."

"Not at home."

Stephen's eyes narrowed. "Mrs. Hale."

"Not at—"

"Bloody hell. I'm coming in."

The butler protested, but Stephen pushed right past him. "Josephine. Josie!"

"Good Lord!" A tall woman with dark hair and Josie's green eyes swept into the foyer, her dark skirts swirling after her. "Are you mad? Barton, call for a footman to escort Lord Westman out."

Ignoring the cold reception, Stephen bowed. "Mrs. Hale, a pleasure."

"I wish I could say the same. Now, get out of my house, you useless philanderer."

Well, he supposed he deserved that one.

"Speaking of your daughter," he said. "Is she home?"

"As though I would allow you to speak to her."

"God's breath, what is going on?" Joseph Hale hobbled down the stairs, his walk stiff and jerky.

Westman made another sweep. "I have come for your daughter's hand."

Both parents frowned at him, and he added, "In marriage."

"Too late!" Josie's mother said, waving her arms. "Too late."

Stephen swore his heart stopped for a moment, and he felt all the blood drain from his heart to pool at his feet. "What do you mean, 'too late'?" He said the words slowly, carefully. But inside it was a fight to keep calm, to stop himself from sprinting up the stairs and tearing the house apart searching for her.

"She's already engaged."

Stephen breathed again. Not much, but a tiny bubble of oxygen forced its way into his paralyzed lungs.

Engaged. Not married.

She was still his.

"To Lord Crutchkins," her father declared. "His lordship has made her an offer, and my daughter has accepted."

Stephen laughed. He couldn't help it. Josie with that old codger. Josie with that elderly, weasel-faced peer, who couldn't even walk without the help of a cane? A day with Josie and the man would expire from heart palpitations.

Mrs. Hale snapped her fingers at him. "You

laugh, sir?" She snapped again. "Pray, what do you find so amusing? After all, were it not for you, my daughter would not be in this humiliating position."

"Then allow me to do all I can to get her out of it," Stephen said. "I am here to claim your daughter's hand in marriage."

"Ridiculous," Mrs. Hale spat. "You cannot marry her. You're a rake, a libertine."

Stephen felt the blow, but allowed it to glance off him.

"Your family is penniless, a step away from debtor's prison."

He shook his head. "Madam," he warned.

"Added to that, everyone knows the Doubledays are liars."

Stephen clenched his fists and held back his temper.

"There is nothing you can say that will persuade me to allow you—the enemy of my own good, decent family—to marry my daughter."

Stephen forced a thin smile. "Am I to assume, then, that you would prefer it if I did not call you *mother*?"

"Oh!" She threw her hands up. "Get out! Get out of this house! Get—"

But Stephen wasn't listening to her anymore. A shimmer of pale ivory had caught his eye, and he looked up the stairs to see a slim figure in a long white gown standing at the top.

"You came for me," Josie said. "I can't believe you came for me." She glided down the stairs, and Stephen saw the tears shimmer in her eyes.

"I couldn't stay away." He began to move closer, but a footman stepped between him.

"Lord Westman, I demand that you leave this house at once," Josie's mother ordered. "At once."

But Josie kept moving forward, and Westman couldn't take his eyes off her. "God," he breathed. "You are so beautiful."

She shook her head. "Pretty words, and I don't deserve them. I am so sorry. I should never have run away. I was a coward. I was afraid."

"You? Afraid?"

"Yes, I—"

Her mother caught her by the arm as she reached the bottom of the stairs. "Get back upstairs this instant, young lady. You are not to speak to this man ever again. You are not—"

"Oh, for God's sake, Mavis," Mr. Hale said, pulling his wife aside. "You never know when to quit."

Stephen didn't think Mavis Hale was used to her husband—to anyone—contradicting her, and her mouth dropped open in shock. "But, Mr. Hale. Lord Crutchkins."

"Can go to an early grave, for all I care." Josie's father began to pull her away, motioning the footman between Stephen and Josie away as well. "We're not going to win this one, Mrs. Hale. Your daughter has always made up her own mind. It looks like she's set it on Lord Westman."

Mrs. Hale looked from her daughter to her husband. "But he's the enemy. Your father and his grandfather"—she shook her head—"Lord Westman is not welcome here. He is—"

"Our new son-in-law."

Josie's father had his wife almost all the way through the door of the dining room before he turned back to Stephen. "You are our new son-in-law, aren't you, sir?"

Stephen pulled out the special license. "Give me an hour, sir."

The dining room door closed, and Josie and Stephen were left alone. She was staring at the paper. "You procured a special license."

He put it back in his pocket. "I couldn't bear to wait. I had to have you. I wanted you to be mine. In every way."

She stared at him. "If you're saying this out of obligation again, then you can walk back out the door. I'm not the girl you ruined all those years ago. You don't have to save me."

"I know that now. Hell, Josie, you might have to save me. I'm about to make a fool of myself. I've never said this before."

He reached forward, took her hand, and knelt before her. "I love you. I have loved you for weeks, but I've been too much of a coward to tell you." He shook his head when she tried to interrupt. "No, you see, *I* am the coward. Not you. I know you don't love me. I know I'm not the man you want or imagined yourself with, but, Josie, I'm the man you should be with."

"Oh, Stephen." The tears were falling in large drops down her cheeks and onto her light, muslin dress as she knelt beside him, clutching his hand.

"I can make you love me, Josie, and I'll try to be the man you want. I won't be arrogant or overprotective."

She reached forward and put a hand on his lips. "Shh. You sound like me."

He frowned, confusion sweeping through him.

"While you were unconscious on the beach, I made all these promises to you. That I would never say a cross word to you, that I would never talk about treasure or adventure or climb out another window."

He laughed.

She nodded and smiled. "I know. All these promises that we'll change, when really I don't want you to change at all." She leaned close to whisper. "I like that you protect me. I like that you worry about me. Stephen, I love you exactly as you are."

His heart stopped. It sputtered and died, and he didn't even mind. He'd never imagined a few words from a woman could make him so happy, but Josie's words had sunk into his heart and warmed his soul. This was all he needed. He could die a happy man now.

He swept her into his arms and stared into her dark green eyes. "I love you too, Josie." He pulled her flush against him. "God, I love you."

Her arms went about him, hard and unyielding. "I knew you did. Somehow I knew, but I was so scared that I was wrong about what I'd felt"—she pulled back—"when we were together. At other times you said—but then I said—"

Now it was his turn to put a finger over her lips. "This is what I say now: I love you Josephine Hale. I want you to be my wife."

She grinned. "Are you asking me to marry you?"

He raised a brow. "I don't know. Your last response left something to be desired. This time I'm thinking about just throwing you over my shoulder and carrying you to the priest."

She shook her head. "Ask me again."

Reluctantly, he reached into his pocket and pulled out the small wooden box. Josie stood again and offered her hand. "Josie—Josephine Hale, will you marry me?"

She leaned down and kissed him. "Yes, Stephen Doubleday, I will."

His hands were trembling, his whole body was shaking, and so he fumbled the first attempt to open the box. He succeeded on the second, and had the satisfaction of seeing her eyes widen to the size of saucers. "Stephen?" She gave him a wondering look, and he had to take the ring out and place it on her finger.

It was huge, far too big for her small, delicate

hand, but he'd known it would be and didn't care.

She'd wanted treasure. Now she had it.

"It's a diamond." He indicated the large pink heart-shaped stone in the center. "I had someone look at it today. It's rare, but it's definitely a diamond."

She stared at the gold ring, its large pink diamond in the center with the two smaller white diamonds flanking it. "It's beautiful. Where did you—how did you—?"

With a smile, he pulled a pouch out of his pocket. "Hold out your hand."

She did so, and he poured two dozen doubloons over her fingers.

"The treasure!" she screamed, catching doubloons before they could fall. "The ring, too?"

He nodded. "Do you think I would leave it? We almost fell off a cliff. I was shot in the shoulder." He rotated his still sore arm. "I wasn't going to leave it."

"But it's bad luck. It's brought us nothing but misfortune."

He shook his head. "It brought me you. And it belongs with us. With you."

"I don't want it," she said.

"But it's yours." He pulled out the key to the new, somewhat larger, deposit box in the vault at Coutts's bank. "You never lost hope or faith, and you never gave in. It belongs to you."

She took the key and looked up at him. "But your family, your debt—"

He closed her hand over the key. "I don't need the treasure to restore my family. Never did."

She leaned up and kissed him, then held up a doubloon. "I'm finally a pirate. My grandfather would have been so proud."

"He loved you. And so do I."

Chapter 24

It was not a romantic wedding. Stephen had carried her outside, summoned a hack, and knocked on church officials' doors until he found one willing to marry them right then.

They'd been married in the first house where the vicar had opened the door. The vicar had been sleepy-eyed and his wife, in her nightgown, their only witness.

And then Stephen had taken Josie home.

To his home, to his bed.

He'd thought of everything, and there were rose petals strewn on the coverlet, candles flickering throughout the room, and wine on the bedside table. She'd wanted to appreciate the small touches he'd made, but it was difficult when all she could think was how much she wanted to tear off his shirt.

As soon as he closed the bedroom door, she did just that. His skin was warm to her touch, and her mouth went dry as she watched the candlelight play light and shadow over his bare chest. "I like you naked," she murmured, touching her tongue to the hollow at the base of his throat. His pulse jumped and she smiled. "I like you hot and naked."

"It's a good thing," he said, "because I intend to be hot and naked with you a lot. Come here."

And then he kissed her, cutting off all thought and all awareness—everything but the touch of his tongue, the sleek stroking of his hands, and her own growing arousal.

He took his time with her. She protested at first, wanting him to hurry, wanting him inside her as quickly as possible. But much as she thought she wanted him to go fast, she liked his slow caresses and teasing kisses. She liked the way he undressed her as though she were made of china. He undid each button, each lace slowly, then kissed the patch of flesh he revealed.

When she was down to her chemise and stockings, he slowed even more. "So beautiful," he murmured, flicking the strap of her chemise off her shoulder. The tips of his fingers danced over her flesh, touching her so lightly that he sent shivers up her spine. And then his fingers made a slow, tantalizing trail, across her collarbone, to her other shoulder. He played at dislodging that strap as well, then traveled back to her bare shoulder, where he bent and kissed her sensitive flesh.

He stepped back, his eyes mimicking what his fingers had done; he devoured her, touching her, arousing her with his gaze.

She was standing before the fire and knew he could see through her light shift. She loved the way he looked at her, like she was the most beautiful woman on earth, instead of a thin, gangly girl with an impish face.

He made her feel lush and ripe and sensual.

Reaching up, she slipped a finger under the strap of her chemise, ran the finger along the material as his blue eyes darkened. Slowly, she allowed the strap to dangle and fall. The undergarment's material slithered with the strap until the swell of one breast was bared.

She traced it with two fingers, her eyes inviting him to do the same, inviting him to take her as he wished. She was his now.

Her eyes roved over his body—the bronze skin of his chest that was the color of beach sand, the square mountains of his shoulders, the V of hair forming a trail from his navel down.

Her eyes met his, and when she saw how large his pupils were and how dark blue his irises, her breathing increased, and she felt her nipples harden in anticipation.

He wet his lips and smiled. "So beautiful," he murmured again. Reaching for her, he wrapped a hand around her waist and pulled her into his warm embrace.

He took her where she wanted to be, where she'd always known she belonged, where she felt at home.

Leaning down, he kissed her neck, her shoulder, her breast. "I love the way you taste."

He tugged the neck of the chemise down farther, his hands floating over her skin, heating it, arousing it, sensitizing it to his touch. His alone. She was bare to the waist, arching for him while his hands cupped her, stroked her, stoked the flame in her until it burned white-hot. She moaned, and he captured the small mew with his mouth. "I love the way you sound."

Sweeping her off her feet and into his arms, he lifted her, carried her to the rose-strewn bed, and lay her down. "I want to hear you cry with pleasure. I want to hear you moan."

His hands, instruments of exquisite torture, rode up her thighs, taking the hem of her shift with them. The light material tickled and teased as his hands on her flesh did, and she could not stop her breath from catching in her throat or the small pants escaping her lungs.

"Josie."

Oh, God, but how she loved the way he said her name. It was so much more than a word when he said it. It was desire and passion and love in five letters. It told her everything, meant everything.

No other words were necessary, but she knew he would give them to her anyway—small gifts, tokens of his affection that he presented her one syllable at a time.

Stephen was bending now, kissing the inside of her thigh. "Your smell, your taste," he said, his lips whisper light on her jumping flesh. "I can't get enough of you, Josie. I won't ever get enough of you."

"I want you, too." Her voice was low and husky, and it trembled with need even as his fingers continued their northward trek, teasing and playing, until they parted her and eased inside.

She moaned loudly then and shuddered.

"I want to hear you say my name." His voice was far away and at the same time inside her head. "I want to hear you call my name when you climax."

"Stephen," she breathed as his fingers played her.

"Shh." He rose up, rose over her. "Not yet."

His fingers went to his trousers, and she could see the strain of his erection, the way the material bulged as he pushed to be free. And then he was free, and she uttered a small "oh" at the sight of his desire. Her heart pounded, and her belly trembled. How lovely to be wanted so much. How arousing to be the cause of his hard, straining erection.

She reached for him, took his warm length in her hands. "I want you, Stephen." She looked into his eyes, bent and kissed him intimately. His quick intake of breath made her smile. "Take me, Stephen," she purred.

He pushed her back and slid over her, covering her body with his. His hands were everywhere, and his mouth soon followed. His breath tickled her ear. "Do you want me to take you, Josie?"

She kissed him, the shock of her lips meeting his like the first time—well, the first good time—all over again. "Take me," she pleaded. "Ravish me. Fast and hard."

The color of his blue eyes was so dark now that they were almost black. "Your wish," he growled.

His hands slid under her, flipping her onto her belly. His knee parted her legs, and she could feel his hard length pressing against her intimately. His mouth was on her neck, and his hands on her hips. He lifted her off the bed, arching her and fitting her body to his. He entered her, the tip of his manhood penetrated her, sending ripples of pleasure through every limb and into every pore. Her hair tingled, her fingers felt numb, her throat went dry.

She moved against him, tying to accustom herself to the new position, trying to take more of him inside her. But he thwarted her, continued to tease her by offering her only a mere taste of him. "Take me," she ordered. "I want you."

"Josie." His mouth was behind her ear, his lips on the soft sensitive spot just behind her lobe. She shivered with pleasure and then bucked with it when he plunged inside her.

He was hot and hard and full, and the sensation was so different and yet so pleasurable that she cried out. He readjusted her body, arching her more so that when he drove into her the feeling was heightened and even more exquisite. His hands caressed the curve of her hip then meandered to her breasts. He cupped them, fingering the nipples until they were hard, and when his hands clutched her hips again, those sensitive nipples ached as they rubbed on the soft coverlet. Back and forth. Back and forth.

The pressure in her built, tightened, rose with his every thrust. "Faster," she begged. "Stephen, faster."

He obliged her, his hand dipping between her legs to stroke her. And that was all she needed to send her over the edge. She spiraled up and up, her body singing, her mind full of nothing but Stephen.

When she came down, he was beside her on the bed, propped on one elbow, looking down at her. He kissed her nose, her eyelids, her swollen lips.

Josie reached out to him, pulled him into her embrace, opened so that he could slip back inside her. He looked down at her, and his eyes were so beautiful, so full of love.

For her.

She reached up and joined her hands to his, their fingers interlocking even as their bodies did, even as their gazes united and held.

He moved inside her, and she could feel him swell, feel his manhood expand and engorge, and her own pleasure swelled with it. He rocked again, and she felt him dive over the precipice. "Stephen," she whispered, lifting her lips to him.

With a kiss, he brought her with him.

Stephen was content to forget about the outside world, and for three weeks, he and Josie did just that. They created their own inner world, exploring each other's bodies and spirits, uniting their hearts and minds.

He could not have imagined a life more perfect. Every time he looked at his new wife, his heart clenched with happiness. He could hardly believe his good fortune. He could hardly believe she was his.

They had love, they had the treasure, they had heaven.

And then her cousins knocked on his door.

He supposed he should be grateful there were only three, but somehow the three seemed more like thirty. There was Lady Valentine—Catie—as Josie called her. She was tall and curvy, her dark hair glossy and thick. She had honey hazel eyes and a reluctance to look at him directly. And yet, despite her modesty, she was willful and stubborn. Stephen came to think of her as formidable.

Then there was Lady Madeleine, Lord Castleigh's daughter. She was beautiful, short with ample breasts and hips, huge blue eyes and glossy hair like her cousin. She was kind, polite, sophisticated. And determined to have her way.

The third was Miss Brittany. Josie called her

Ashley, and she was the most classically beautiful. Her wheat-gold hair seemed to shimmer about her face and shoulders. Her skin was porcelain, and her sea green eyes were so large that a man might imagine himself drowning in them. Stephen imagined many men had. She was always laughing, always talking, and inevitably said what was on her mind.

Lastly, there was his Josie. She was something of a mixture of the best traits of all her cousins. She had Catie's height, Ashley's green eyes—though her color was darker and more intense—and Maddie's graceful deportment. And of course, she had her own mischievous smile and crop of auburn curls. She fascinated him, bewitched him.

Frustrated him.

"So, you see, darling," Josie told him. "We must have a breakfast." They were in the dining room, he having come down for the morning meal, expecting a cup of tea and toast and having found, instead, Josie and her three cousins. He would have retreated, forgone breakfast altogether, but her cousins were too quick. They surrounded him, closing in, and trapping him.

"Sorry, old chap," Lord Valentine said. Stephen hadn't seen the man at first, being as he was huddled at the far end of the room, probably out of the women's way. Tall with dark hair and dark eyes, he looked every bit the part of the nation's next prime minister. "I tried to sneak you a message," he was saying. "Warn you of the ambush so you could get out while escape was possible."

Lady Valentine turned a scowl on him. "My lord, please. Must you be so dramatic? This is not an ambush. We simply want to talk to Lord Westman."

Valentine threw him a look full of sympathy.

Stephen glanced back at Josie. "What were you saying? A breakfast?"

She nodded, poured him a cup of tea. Lady Madeleine handed him a plate with a scone, and Lady Valentine offered him cream and sugar. These women definitely wanted something.

"With both of our families. It would be a way to mend some of the broken fences between us."

"We could bring the two families together again," Lady Valentine said. "Just like it was in the time of your grandfathers."

Westman raised a brow, took the tea, and set it down. "A breakfast with both our families?"

"We never had one, darling," Josie added. "It will be our wedding breakfast."

He poked at the teacup, wondering what the women had put in the brew. "We didn't have one for good reason," he said. "Our families hate each other. If we put them together in the same room, they'll tear each other to pieces."

"That's exactly why we need this breakfast," Miss Brittany told him.

"So our families can kill each other?" Stephen asked, incredulous.

"No, so our families can find common ground again," Lady Madeleine said patiently. "So you and Josie can explain that there's no reason for you to be enemies."

"She told us about One-Eyed Jack," Lady Valentine added. "How it was he, not Nathan Hale, that killed your grandfather. We thought that might mend some of the bad feelings."

Stephen looked at Josie. She smiled sweetly, and he wondered just when in the past three weeks she had managed to find time to enlighten her cousins about One-Eyed Jack. It seemed to him, she'd been in his arms, in his bed, night and day.

"You see, my lord," Lady Madeleine said. "The *ton* is talking, gossiping really. Your story has been in all the papers and on the lips of every matron at all the parties."

"I don't care about the gossipmongers," Stephen said. His stomach rumbled, and he took a bite of his scone. "I've lived with gossip all my life."

"And you know I don't care either," Josie told him, "but it makes things hard for our families."

Lady Valentine stepped in. "Just the other night Aunt Mavis and your mother, Lord Westman, were both at the opera, sitting on opposite sides of the theater. Why, the entire evening, everyone was looking from one to the other and whispering about them, watching to see if the ladies would acknowledge each other."

"You might imagine the strain that sort of thing has on their nerves," Josie added.

Stephen narrowed his gaze. "And your mother's delicate nerves concern you?" He remembered her mother coming after him like an attack poodle only a few weeks ago. If she had delicate nerves, they must be deeply buried.

"Oh, let's just be honest," Miss Brittany broke in bluntly. "We don't care about Aunt Mavis or your mother—sorry, but it's true—or Uncle William. That's Maddie's father. What we do care about is Josie, and all of this talk and scandal makes it hard on us."

"My father has forbidden me to see her," Lady Madeleine told him. "He doesn't want any more gossip."

"My parents feel the same," Miss Brittany said.

"And though Lord Valentine would never ask me not to see Josie," Lady Valentine said, "I know the strain gossip puts on his career."

"Catie, I told you I don't care about that," Valentine said. He came up behind her and put his hand on her shoulder.

She smiled up at him. "I do. That's why we need something to mend the gap between your families. End the tension so that we can all be friends again."

Stephen thought about his mother, her acid tongue and lashing temper. He wanted her as far from Josie as possible. Why, the woman hadn't even so much as sent him a note of thanks when he'd written to tell her that all their debts were erased and they had more money than they could ever spend. He'd saved the family, just as he'd promised to do. She'd been silent and ungrateful, giving him none of the approval he'd always desired from her.

But now that he had Josie, he'd told himself that didn't matter. He didn't need anyone's approval but hers, didn't need to prove himself at all anymore.

He would have been more than happy never to see his mother again, but here was Josie asking him to contact his mother, his entire family, and celebrate this marriage with them. He wanted to refuse. He wanted to tell her that Society and Lord Castleigh and his mother could all go to hell. Then he looked at the four women. The friendship they'd formed was obviously special. Who was he to stand between them?

"Very well," he finally agreed, lifting his teacup to sip the warm brew. "When is it?"

Josie smiled. "Tomorrow."

Stephen almost choked.

Chapter 25

T he breakfast was not going well. Josie could see that. Her family was on one side of her drawing room, and Westman's family had camped on the other.

A vast expanse of polished marble floor separated them, and the invisible barrier was as solid as any made of brick and mortar.

They'd made introductions, welcomed everyone, encouraged mingling, and no one was cooperating. Only her cousins made an effort to cross the great divide—and, Josie saw—got nothing for their efforts. They were ignored by Westman's side and chided by her side.

Finally, after trying everything she knew, Josie gave Maddie a pleading look, and Maddie pantomimed lifting her glass and toasting. Good idea.

Josie turned to Stephen, who was standing beside her at the head of the room, looking as troubled as she. "I think you should make a toast." She elbowed him in the side. "Everyone has champagne."

He gave her a doubtful look. "And just what am I supposed to toast? Familial love? Togetherness? This is a disaster."

Josie bit her lip. "How about forgiveness? Forgiveness and love." She took his hand in hers. "Our love."

His gaze softened, and the hard set of his mouth relaxed into a smile. "If that's what you want."

"Just try it. No matter what, it's time I told everyone the truth about One-Eyed Jack. Even if they don't believe it, I will have tried."

Reluctantly, he raised his glass and motioned for silence. Josie held her breath as he began. "Ladies and gentlemen, thank you for coming here this morning. Thank you for supporting Lady Westman and I in our union. We had hoped that our marriage might unite more than simply the two of us. We hoped that it might unite our families as well. Unite them and reconcile them after too many years of senseless fighting."

He took a breath and glanced at her. She nodded encouragement, though their guests remained stone-faced.

"Today is about forgiveness. Forgiveness of past wrongs or perceived wrongs. We ask you to put all that aside, to embrace each other, even as Lady Westman and I have embraced each other."

He pulled her into his arms and held her at his side to demonstrate. Josie smiled up at him. He was wonderful. No man would ever do so much for her.

"Finally, I ask you to raise your glasses and—"

"I think you've asked quite enough of us already," someone called from the back. Josie wasn't certain, but she thought it might be her mean uncle Edmund, Catie's father.

"That's right," Stephen's mother piped up. "How can you ask us to forgive them? Murderers and thieves, that's all they are."

"Mother," Stephen began.

"Liars and philanderers!" Josie's mother interrupted.

Josie closed her eyes, and her stomach clenched. Oh, why had she ever thought this would work? It was hopeless.

"You slander our good name and teach your sons to defile good young women," Josie's mother yelled. The Hale side moved menacingly closer to the Doubleday side.

"Good? Josephine Hale, good? Ha!" Stephen's mother rose and took her own steps to close the gap between the families. How Josie wished that gap would return.

"She's nothing but another little trollop. She—"

Stephen was in front of his mother before Josie even knew what had happened. He glared down at her. "That's enough, Mother," he growled, sending several of the young women from his side skittering back in fear. "Talk about me how you like, but don't you ever impugn my wife."

Far from contrite, his mother looked ready to fight back. Suddenly, Ashley was beside Josie. "Do something," she whispered. "Distract them!"

Josie slid into the angry mob, forcing a path to her husband. "Wait! No! There's no reason for all this." She looked at her mother's angry face, then Stephen's mother's pinched lips. "There's something none of you know or understand. We are not enemies, and never have been. It's all been a horrible misunderstanding," she said.

Skeptical looks surrounded her. Even her Uncle William, who had always been her supporter, looked doubtful.

"You see," Josie began, "when Stephen and I recovered the treasure, we met up with a man who was on the original *Good Groom*. You might not be familiar with the crew or the story of the treasure, but this man was. He was on the ship when the Spanish treasure was taken. His name was One-Eyed Jack."

She waited for someone to say something or for someone to nod their head in understanding, but she was met with blank looks. She looked at Stephen. His expression was kind and supportive, and he reached out and took her hand.

She found, if she held on to him tightly, she could continue. "One-Eyed Jack was a pirate. He'd been searching all these years for the treasure, and he didn't intend to let Stephen and I take it from him. He tried to kill us."

At that revelation, she heard whispers go through the crowd, and she hurried before talk could break out. "His partner shot Stephen." She touched her husband's shoulder gingerly. "And then One-Eyed Jack tried to kill me with his sword. Stephen saved me, but not before One-Eyed Jack said something all of you should know."

She paused, gave the crowd time to take it all in.

"One-Eyed Jack told me that he killed James Doubleday. He said he 'did away with him' and that by killing me, he'd have his revenge on my grandfather, too. So, you see, it wasn't my grandfather that killed James Doubleday after all. It was One-Eyed Jack."

She smiled, triumphant in her revelation. And she waited, waited for the sighs and the tears. Was it too much to expect the families to clap and cheer?

What she heard instead was silence.

And then Westman's mother sniggered. "See?" she said, turning to look at her relatives. "I told you she was a liar. I told you she couldn't be trusted. One-Eyed Jack? What nonsense is this?"

"Mother, I warned you—" Westman said, stepping forward.

"How dare you," Josie's mother screamed. "How dare you call my daughter a liar?"

Josie swung around to face her mother. "Then

you believe me, Mother? You believe us about One-Eyed Jack?"

Her mother looked uncertain. "Well, I don't know about that. A pirate chased you? Sweetheart, you have always been one for exaggeration."

"Lies, you mean!" Westman's mother yelled, and then the whole room erupted into shouts and curses and hurled threats.

Stephen grabbed Josie and began to propel her out of the mob, pulling her to safety, but they'd only taken two steps when they heard the thumping.

They paused, looked around, heard it again.

Thump. Thump. Thump.

A few others heard it as well, and the screaming began to die down.

Thump. Thump. Thump.

Josie looked around, her gaze falling on the figure of a small, elderly woman with white hair and gnarled hands. She was standing on a chair, banging her long ebony cane on a table.

Thump. Thump. Thump.

"Grandmother," Stephen said aloud.

"That's your grandmother?" Josie asked. "That's Maggie from the journals?"

The room had quieted, and her voice carried. The old woman smiled at her. "Now, that's a name I haven't heard in a long time." Her voice wavered and rasped, but it carried. "That's a woman I haven't been in a long time.

"Margaret," Stephen's mother called. "What are you doing? You should get down at once."

"Oh, stubble it, Beatrice. You talk too much and listen too little."

Stephen's mother dropped her mouth open but remained silent.

"And it's my fault this has gone on so long," Margaret Doubleday said, looking at Josie and Stephen. "I should have spoken up earlier. I should have stepped in and mended this feud. You have my highest regard, Lady Westman, for trying to do so now."

"I only wanted to clear my grandfather's name," Josie said. "I've been trying to do so all my life."

Margaret looked sad. "That's my fault, too. I'm a coward, you see, only speaking up now when I know it's safe."

"Grandmother, what are you talking about?" Stephen asked, going to her, helping her off the chair. "What do you know?"

She looked at Josie. "I knew your grandfather was innocent. That's why, despite the pressure from my family, I never accused him, and I never attempted to have him arrested. At the time that's what I thought I could do. I thought that was enough, but now I see it was not."

She looked at Josie and Stephen, then at the families crowded behind them. "You see, I was in the room when this One-Eyed Jack killed James. I was hiding behind a curtain, concealed, but in a position with a view. I saw what happened. I saw this pirate kill my husband, and Nathan Hale was nowhere near."

Josie blinked, too stunned to speak. Here was a woman who had known the truth all along. A woman who could have spared her and her family so much shame these years.

Stephen spoke her thoughts. "But why didn't you say something before? Why did you allow us to believe the rumors and lies? To go on hating each other for decades."

Margaret looked down at her small feet, and Josie could see the pink of her scalp through thin white hair. "Because I'm a coward. I saw this One-Eyed Jack, and I was afraid if I told, then he would come for me. I was afraid, you see. Some pirate's wife I was. I hid instead of fought. If James could have seen me, he would have turned in his grave."

Josie shook her head. As angry as she was at the elderly woman, she could understand her, too. "You weren't a coward," she said quietly, and she felt all eyes turn to her. "You had a son to raise, a little boy to protect. You had to think of him first, and you did what you could. A man like my grandfather could protect himself from scandal and men like One-Eyed Jack, but you were alone." She looked at Stephen and remembered him lying on the beach, his blood leaking from the wound in his shoulder. "I don't know what it's like to lose someone you love, but I can imagine. I can understand the fear and the panic." She reached out and took Margaret's withered hands in hers. "And you told us now. You spoke up when we needed you. Thank you."

The old woman smiled and squeezed her hands. "I don't think I can ever make this up to you, child. But I will do anything you ask."

Josie raised a brow. "Really? In that case, I'd love for you to tell us of your life on *The Good Groom*. I'd love to hear stories of my grandfather and James Doubleday. I want to hear about their friendship and their adventures."

An hour later, Stephen drew Josie away. Quietly and unobtrusively, he pulled her out of the drawing room and downstairs to his library, the room where they'd first met. "What are you doing?" she demanded when he'd closed the door. "I wanted to hear that story about the battle at Corfu."

He smiled at her, cupped her face. "You're amazing, do you know that?"

"Yes."

He laughed and kissed her. "Do you want to know why I think you're amazing?"

She nodded.

"Did you look back at the room as we walked out? Did you see our families sitting together, listening together? You brought them together, Josie. Just like you climbed into my window and brought us together."

"Oh, I think you had a part in that, too."

"A small one," he admitted. He opened his arms to her, and she went into his inviting embrace, kissed his generous lips, pressed against his welcoming body.

"You're an adventure, Josephine Hale," he whispered. "My adventure. What am I going to do when you tire of me and go in search of more fascinating voyages?"

"I'll never tire of you," she promised, looking into his eyes. "And I have a feeling our adventures are far from over."

There was a knock on the door, and before they could separate, Josie's mother burst in. "There you are! Josephine, we've been looking all over. Madeleine and Ashley are missing. No one has seen them for above an hour and a quarter at least. We have to find them."

When Josie and Stephen didn't move, she threw her hands up and ran back out the door. "Madeleine! Ashley!" she cried. The shouts were soon echoed by others.

Josie turned to Westman. "Ready for another adventure?"

He dipped his head to kiss her. "Always."

Avon Romantic Treasures

Unforgettable, enthralling love stories, sparkling with passion and adventure from Romance's bestselling authors

DUKE OF SCANDAL *by Adele Ashworth*
0-06-052841-9/$6.99 US/$9.99 Can

SHE'S NO PRINCESS *by Laura Lee Guhrke*
0-06-077474-6/$6.99 US/$9.99 Can

THE DUKE IN DISGUISE *by Gayle Callen*
0-06-078412-1/$6.99 US/$9.99 Can

TEMPTING THE WOLF *by Lois Greiman*
0-06-078398-2/$6.99 US/$9.99 Can

HIS MISTRESS BY MORNING *by Elizabeth Boyle*
0-06-078402-4/$6.99 US/$9.99 Can

HOW TO SEDUCE A DUKE *by Kathryn Caskie*
0-06-112456-7/$6.99 US/$9.99 Can

A DUKE OF HER OWN *by Lorraine Heath*
0-06-112963-1/$6.99 US/$9.99 Can

AUTUMN IN SCOTLAND *by Karen Ranney*
978-0-06-075745-8/$6.99 US/$9.99 Can

SURRENDER TO A SCOUNDREL *by Julianne MacLean*
978-0-06-081936-7/$6.99 US/$9.99 Can

TWO WEEKS WITH A STRANGER *by Debra Mullins*
978-0-06-079924-3/$6.99 US/$9.99 Can

AVON TRADE *Paperbacks*

978-0-06-052512-5
$13.95 ($17.50 Can.)

978-0-06-078080-7
$13.95 ($17.50 Can.)

978-0-06-089022-3
$13.95 ($17.50 Can.)

0-06-113388-4
$12.95 ($16.95 Can.)

0-06-083691-1
$12.95 ($16.95 Can.)

0-06-081588-4
$12.95 ($16.95 Can.)

Visit www.AuthorTracker.com for exclusive
information on your favorite HarperCollins authors.

Available wherever books are sold, or call 1-800-331-3761 to order.

ATP 0207